PROMISE

Best wishes

PROMISE

DAVID LEVIN

To order additional copies of this book, contact:
Xlibris Corporation
1-888-795-4274
www.Xlibris.com
Orders@Xlibris.com
42494

Part One

Promise

CHAPTER ONE

I was happy listening to my heroes, Promise, play one of their greatest hits. The recorded song played through my earbuds and dried my tears. Grandma touched my hand. I removed the earbuds, and the sad emotions returned. Grandma and I had just laid Mother and Daddy to rest. It made me feel a little bit better to have them next to each other. At least they would be together forever. But to put them in those dark holes made me almost lose it.

Lizzie, as usual, was a pal, like a sister. She kept me going through the funeral. I wished I had a real sister or brother to cry with me. It would have made things better. At least I could have shared my grief with a family member my own age. That could have made this nightmare easier.

Grandma seemed to be in shock, her daughter and son-in-law killed in a car wreck by a drunk driver just a week ago. I was sure she was having a hard time accepting her responsibility of being my mother and father. I hoped we could be some type of family, incomplete as it might be.

I felt numb during the ride back to the funeral home. The black, heavy clouds and rain added to my depression. Everything looked so gray and dead.

We passed Woodway High School, and I noticed several sports cars outside the gym entrance, recalling that today the cheerleaders and jocks were taking pictures for the yearbook. I wiped the haze off the window, rested my head against it, and saw two girls run out of the building, pursued by two boys. The boys caught them, and I could almost hear the girls' giggles and squeals. The rain didn't wash the smiles from their faces or stop their play-fighting.

Soon they were out of sight, and I wondered why the others were having fun when I was hurting so much. I replaced the earbuds and felt Promise's music take away my sadness once more.

CHAPTER TWO

That New Year's Eve, Lizzie and I were at home. We didn't have dates for any party. But the day was still exciting because we were glued to the tube, waiting for Promise's appearance. I turned to her. "This is the most wonderful time of my life! I can't believe they are doing a live concert on television. It's so special because people everywhere want to celebrate the New Year with the greatest musicians on the planet and we're watching too! Isn't it incredible?"

Lizzie patted me on the shoulder. "I know. You've told me, at least a hundred times: Promise's New Year Concert in London in the Millennium Dome, before the largest in-person audience ever to see a live concert. You've given me all the facts, Mary. See. I've memorized them, just like you."

I felt a little embarrassed. "Sorry if I came on too strong. I know I've been going on about it. But doesn't all this make you feel fantastic? Even though we're just watching on television in Houston, it's so incredibly exciting to see the band live. I never thought I would, Lizzie. Honest to goodness. I never did."

She smiled. "You're crazy about them. That's okay. No problem. A lot of people are. It's understandable. Their music is so great. Everyone around the world loves it. Why shouldn't you? If they make you happy, go for it."

I focused on the stage, trying to listen to the warm-up band, and it all seemed dreamlike, as though I weren't really going to see this unbelievable concert at all.

My grandmother came into the room, looked at the television and said, "Goodness, that is a big crowd. I bet you two probably have better seats here though. How long before they sing? Seems like that other band has been performing for a long time."

A smile spread across my face. "Any minute now, I think. You know, Grandma, they are the most popular artists on the planet, with more platinum songs than any other group or individual artist."

She laughed. "I know. You have told me. How many records have they sold? I forgot."

"They don't sell records these days, Grandma. CDs mostly, and some tapes, but more than eight billion of them, more than the entire population of the world. You know, some of the great groups sold from two hundred fifty million to about a billion albums. But Promise has sold more than all of them together! Isn't that unbelievable?"

Grandmother smiled and said, "Unbelievable. I'm glad to see you so happy, Mary. It's been a while since you've laughed like this. If Promise can lift your spirits, then keep listening to their music."

Lizzie squeezed my hand, and I looked at her before responding, "I'm feeling good, almost like a hot chick!"

Grandmother shook her head. "You don't need to be hot. Let's change the subject. Have they ever played in Texas?"

I quickly answered, "No. They perform only in the largest cities in the world, New York, London, Tokyo, and Paris, places like that. All the tickets are gone within a few hours after the announcement of one of their concerts. Most people can't find any to buy, no matter what price they're willing to pay. Oh, there are always rumors that some scalpers have a few tickets for crazy prices, like ten thousand dollars each. But I don't know anybody who actually ever bought a ticket to a Promise concert."

The warm-up band finished its performance, but the overwhelming crowd noise masked what they had played. Then the huge crowd did a very odd thing—it seemed to settle down and become less noisy. I didn't see anyone scurrying along aisles. Maybe the collective thought of actually seeing the most famous musicians in the universe quieted almost everyone there. I expected an announcer to come out on stage, but none came.

Suddenly, the scene went dark and many people screamed. The cameras showed a dark stadium, except for the red exit signs seeming to hang in the air.

Thundering sounds broke through the darkness. My head moved toward the television, and I instinctively squinted against a blinding white light blasting from an opening onto the stage. It was like being at the top of the roller-coaster just before the big fall, and I screamed, "Here they come!"

The crowd roared its approval as four motorcycles rumbled single file through the light, and I could make out each member of the band. Brett rode his bike to the left of the stage and stopped, straddling the gleaming machine with a raised fist; Rion drove to the right, parking on the edge of the stage and jumping on the seat with raised arms; Seth's motorcycle climbed a ramp at the back of the stage, until he reached the elevated drummer's stand where he jumped off the machine and stood triumphantly in front with folded arms. Then, the leader of the band, Tam, roared around the stage. His entrance was the most spectacular as he rode with the front wheel high off the ground and his engine roaring above the cries and yells of the audience. Tam's cycle flew up a low ramp at the front of the stage where he stopped on a raised platform. He jumped off the black bike and did a handstand on the seat, and the crowd screamed and clapped wildly. It made Grandma jump when I clapped and stomped with them.

She looked at me and shook a finger, making no real impression. "Mary, calm down."

I felt electricity in the air. "Gosh, they look just like the pictures I've seen in the magazines. Look at them, Lizzie, human gods in tight black leather pants. What cut upper bodies. They're teasing us, Lizzie, with those black leather vests hanging open to show their incredible abs. I think they are aliens, Liz, I really do."

Lizzie seemed focused on the television. "Yeah, they look better than any jock I ever saw. You think that long blonde hair is real? It sure looks sexy, the way it hangs down to their slim waists. Contrasts against the leather pants. And look at those black cowboy boots. Their legs look long in them. I didn't realize they were so tall."

Grandma also seemed to be excited. "They're all wearing sunglasses. I've never seen large rose-colored lenses like that before. Look how they glisten in the stage lights. I don't know about the streaked black face makeup though. It does make them look ruggedly handsome. But I just don't know if I like it."

"That's the way they look in the pictures, Grandma. It's their stage appearance."

For a moment, it seemed that only the girls were screaming and crying at these magnificent creatures, until I saw some of the boys in a close-up shot and realized they were screaming too.

I squeezed Lizzie's hand. "Everyone, be quiet. They're going to start."

Brett sat down at an electronic piano, and Rion picked up his large base guitar, while Seth sat on a stool behind shiny black drums. Tam held a gleaming gold electric guitar high above his head with a single hand and gazed deliberately across the vast crowd, bringing a sudden hush to the audience.

Without one word or signal, Promise broke into "Fiery Sky," and the entire stage was bathed in red light. Somehow, I didn't hear the lyrics of their new number-one hit, though I knew them well. My mind was totally on Tam as he held the guitar high above his head, strumming its strings, and never missing a note. His head turned slowly from one side of the great audience to the other. He was so beautiful.

Lizzie and I began to sway to the rhythmic beats of the drums, all the while Tam's fingers making the guitar sing in an incredible series of chords and notes, causing the crowd to break into thunderous applause. His strumming made me feel fire, burning brighter and brighter, high note, higher note, higher note still, then rapidly down the scale, and very fast up again. His fingers flew across the strings so fast I couldn't follow them, even when the camera came in tight on his hands.

They followed with hit after hit, "Old Man's Dreams," "With You," "Courage," "Julie's Song," "Clouds," "Roaring Wind," "No Stranger in Darkness," "Cambio Bay," "Morning's Feel," "Far Beyond Forever," "Storm Cove," and "Peaceful Blue."

As they played and sang, I experienced joy, sensed the warmth of a friend, felt strength from somewhere outside of me, cried as a child walked in Heaven, envisioned white puffs crossing a blue sky, enjoyed the virtual power of the wind on the cliffs above the sea, envisioned a peaceful dark night—without anything to fear, swayed in the gentle breezes of a tropical island, felt sunshine on my face, looked with wonder toward the horizon, breathed a sigh of relief at the mental image of a nearby shore, and yearned to see what was in the clear depths of the ocean.

Then, all too soon, Tam announced their final song, and I couldn't believe it was almost over. I wanted this glorious night to last much longer.

Tam stood in front of the band, holding his guitar high, and he began to play and sing their greatest hit, "Wailin' on High,"

Some day in my twilight time,
When stillness shall close my eyes,
And men put me in the ground,
Do not raise your cries,
Or look for me in that place,
Or stay there long to stare.

Look for me in another land,
For I will not be there.
When you feel the thunder
Or see lightnin' pierce the sky,
There is where I'll be,
Wailin' way up high,
Singin' songs and dancin',
With everyone I love,
Rockin' and rollin'
With the Big Guy up above.

The crowd turned unusually quiet, and I listened to the lyrics and began to cry. Tam had so much power to touch people deep inside. I knew I might never ever see him on live television again, and that thought made me cry harder. It would be so incredible to feel these heart-penetrating emotions once more, but I was afraid it wouldn't happen again in my life.

Grandma was looking at me, tears streaming down her wrinkled cheeks.

I cleared my throat and said, "They got to you too. See, they're not just for kids. Promise is for the whole world—everybody, everywhere. Grandma, tell me something."

"What is it?"

"Be honest with me. Didn't you feel their music speak to your heart, at least a little?"

She looked at me and blew her nose. "More than just a little."

CHAPTER THREE

The bus ride to school on Monday was long. To deal with the boredom, I replayed several of Promise's songs in my mind, reliving some of the emotions the band had created in me. It made me feel better. The bus jerked to a stop in front of the school, and, as I waited for the other students to exit, I said under my breath, "Shit, the junior bitches are there, ready to make fun of us bus riders again."

Ben Thomas, one of the school geeks, must have heard me. "Ignore them, Mary," he said. "They're selfish and materialistic. But so what? Just tell them how wonderful they are, or better yet, avoid them, and they'll leave you alone. You need to chill out and stop being so sensitive about what they think."

Without looking at him I said, "Easy for you to say. They don't pick on you, not like they do me."

"They used to, before my psychology class," he responded.

I was puzzled. "What did your psychology class do to help?"

He whispered, as though telling some secret. "I learned not to stimulate them. You know, not give them a reason to turn on me. Avoidance is best, but praise may also work. Try it. You will save yourself a lot of grief. Besides, you know you can't beat them. Look at poor Cheryl Moss. They drove her off the cheerleader squad, to another school. She developed too much anxiety, turned to a psychosis, and then to depression."

"Too much psychology, Ben. I heard she just wanted to go to a private school, some place smaller than Woodway."

His thick glasses glinted in the morning sun. "In her senior year? No way. It was depression. I'm sure the bitches caused it by organizing all their cliquish activities and leaving her out, like some outcast. And their mothers put pressure on the cheerleader sponsor to criticize her for her weight and clothes. I'm telling you, it was all a conspiracy to open up a place on the squad for one of their friends."

Climbing down the bus steps, looking straight ahead, I thought about taking his advice, but I could feel the junior bitches' mocking stares, bringing my blood to a slow boil. Maybe I wanted a fight—to give them back a little of what they dished out. It seemed more than fair.

I made a beeline for the school newspaper room, my regular hangout before school started. Being a reporter for the paper was fun and looked good on my college applications. But it also created that problem Ben Thomas noted—it made me stand out. That could make other kids jealous: the cool kids, the always-smiling cheerleaders, the tough-acting jocks, and those super kids with the pushy parents who made sure everything was perfect for their little jerks. Many of the pretty or athletic or popular kids seemed to get their jollies making fun of the rest of us. I couldn't help it that I was red-haired and chubby. But I supposed clownish looks just weren't cool these days, especially with so many beautiful people on television and in the movies all the time. Gosh, were there really people with such perfect teeth?

The newspaper room seemed peaceful. I breathed deeply and forced my thoughts to change, beginning to think about the concert. Agnes Grunfeld, another nerd friend, walked up, leaned toward me with a cupped hand over her mouth and whispered, "Well, what did you think about it? Were they as good as you really had imagined?" She stopped, raised her eyebrows and said, "I was blown away. You?"

"Me too. Yeah, they were incredible, better than the magazines and papers ever described. And those glossy pictures don't really show their great looks. Gosh, Tam is so beautiful," I responded, paying only slight attention to my chubby soul mate.

She carefully looked over her shoulder. "Oh man. The junior bitches just passed by. They glanced through the door and rolled their eyes. I hate Tiffany and Paige. They make me feel so self-conscious. They're probably not satisfied with just tormenting us. Bet they'd love to scratch our eyes out, if they could get away with it. But they would probably get caught and punished and not be able to cheer at the games, and that would be tragic."

Agnes made a goofy face, which she did particularly well with her drama training, and we laughed quietly. We *co-chubs* often found strength together, a kind of support group for the terminally ordinary.

The bell rang, and I ran to my first class, history, across the school, barely making it before the tardy bell rang. I quickly sat beside Lizzie, just getting settled in.

"Ladies, if you are ready for class, we can continue through the Civil War," Mr. Johnson said, looking directly at us.

Lizzie quickly sat up, and I looked around, only to feel my blood run cold. The most major junior bitch of all, Alexis Poston, was smiling at me.

I felt her smirk, and my mind flashed pictures of Alexis: posing cutely in her head cheerleader's uniform; in a graduation gown holding an award reading, "Number one ranked student in the senior class;" smiling that Miss Perfect smile, as her mother, the meanest, most hateful mother in the world, beamed in the background. Then the mental picture changed to Mrs. Poston happily chatting with the principal, natural for her, since she almost ruled the school, making sure she had a hand in everything Alexis did—cheerleading, pep rallies, grade conferences with teachers, even lunch.

I began to feel sick, knowing that if she thought you were a threat to her precious daughter, she would find a way to hurt you in some way—from leaning on a school sponsor to bar you from an extra curricular activity, or pressuring the principal to punish you, or spreading hateful rumors, or just being nasty to your face. And suddenly I had the feeling that she had made Alexis into her image, a little monster who was just as selfish and hateful as her mother. But then I began to have other mental images: Mrs. Poston's friends in crime, the other overbearing parents, particularly the woman's best friend, Mrs. Hall, mother of the basketball stud everyone was supposed to worship.

After Sherman had taken Atlanta, the bell rang, and Lizzie and I headed for separate classes. I stopped at my locker to exchange books, history for chemistry. Alexis Poston was leaning against her locker, flirting with two boys. They were jocks, starters on the basketball team. Toby Hall, whom everyone expected to get a major college basketball scholarship, seemed to have the edge in her shallow affections, as she giggled and pushed him away. I shouldn't have looked in their direction—bad move, really stupid.

Alexis saw me. "Oh, hi Mary. Any love letters from that little band you hang with, what's its name? I forgot."

Her suitors began to laugh and shake their heads, raising my self-consciousness.

I looked at her over my glasses. "I'm just a fan, like a lot of other people."

"Probably the nuttiest fan on the planet. You seem to know everything about them. And for what? It's not like they know you are alive, or even care, or ever will. What's the point of all that wasted energy? You should focus on yourself more. From your appearance, you could use more effort." Alexis could be so totally hurtful.

Toby began to laugh, before cocking his head and looking at me with an expression that contorted his face. "Say, Mary, got a date to the dance? I heard that Cameron here is looking for a date. Maybe he'll ask you, if one of those Promise guys doesn't ask you first."

Cameron Fields, a tanned, sandy-haired, confident pretty boy, who was likely to be prom king, punched Toby in the arm. "Shut up. That makes me sick. Nobody wants to take her to anything. Besides, you know I'm taking Paige."

Cameron turned to me. "Anyhow, I bet one of those Promise guys really will ask you. I'd go home and wait by the phone if I were you. No telling when it will ring. And you can do a few sit-ups while you wait."

The three laughed loudly, their glee interrupted by the bell for the next class. I ran for chemistry.

Finally, morning classes were over and it was time for lunch. I raced to the cafeteria and sat down at my usual table, waiting for Lizzie to join me. I opened my sack lunch and smiled. Grandma had packed a tuna sandwich, my favorite, some pickles, and an apple. But where were the chips?

I reacted out loud. "What the heck? Where are my potato chips? Heck, Grandma is on that health kick again."

"You shouldn't really have chips. Not good for your condition."

I wheeled around to face the rude person who had made that comment, only to go limp at the sight of Alexis, Paige, and Tiffany.

Alexis held out a hand toward me, flashing her gold and diamond tennis bracelet. "We're only looking out for you, dear. Lord knows you need some help with your appearance. How are you ever going to get a date if you don't take more pride in how you look? Zits, frizzy hair, and fat aren't really in these days. Maybe an appearance consultant would help."

I wanted to crawl in my locker. "I really don't care about getting a date in high school. That's not important to me right now."

The girls laughed and made assorted faces. Tiffany Malloy, a cheerleader and daughter of the owner of a local car dealership, stopped the antics. "Yeah, I'll bet," she mocked, pursing her lips.

They walked off, huddled together in one of their usual conspiracies.

Paige Richelieu, the homecoming queen, girl voted most beautiful the last two years, and daughter of a lawyer, glanced back once to laugh, then turned away and exaggerated the sway of her hips in expensive-looking jeans.

Lizzie came running to the table. "You aren't going to believe this, Mary, but I just heard that the *Houston News* has us ranked third in the state preseason basketball poll. Seems they think Toby and Cameron are going to be great this year. That will give you a lot to write about for the paper, you doing all of the sports articles."

I was still rummaging through my lunch sack, hoping there were chips somewhere. "That's nice," I said, not listening closely.

Lizzie looked squarely at me. "Well, don't you care? I mean, wouldn't it be great to have a winning team for a change?" Then her expression changed. "Maybe we can even get to the finals. You and I could go to Austin for the championship and check out some of those college guys, maybe even get invited to a frat party! Wouldn't that be fun?"

I stopped and turned to her. "Look, Lizzie, that all sounds great, I guess. But right now, I have this potato chip crisis to deal with, and I'm not handling it very well. My head is kind of messed up over it." I turned to the lunch bag again, hoping to find the chips trying to hide from me, and ready to crunch their helpless little bodies.

Lizzie asked, "You mean avoiding them?"

"No, eating the tasty suckers."

Lizzie sat straight up in her chair. "Oh, I see. Can I help?"

"Only if you have fifty cents to loan me."

She shrugged. "Sorry. I'm broke."

I shrugged back. "Shit! I hate being poor."

CHAPTER FOUR

I finished lunch and headed down another hallway to journalism, my favorite class. The journalism students wrote the articles for the school newspaper, and I was proud to say that I had had three articles published in the paper this semester. Oh, they all were about sports, not really my favorite subject, but an area I liked doing as much as some others. Yet, writing about the school sports teams gave me the opportunity to talk about some of the school's lesser lights, like the bench players, assistant coaches, and regular students. That seemed to chap some of the pushy parents, but I loved to shine a little limelight in another direction, away from their little creeps who always seemed to get most of the glory.

I approached our sponsor, a thin, studious man who always lectured the paper's reporters about our articles being factual and written with journalistic quality. "Hello, Mr. Lawless. I have some ideas about another article. The volleyball team . . . ."

Mrs. Poston and Mrs. Hall interrupted my comments when they walked into the room. Mrs. Poston started the conversation. "Mr. Lawless, we would like to see you for a few minutes." She stopped talking and looked at me, before continuing. "In private, please."

He led them to his office and closed the door. I walked quietly to the door and leaned toward it, hoping to hear the conversation, only to hesitate at the thought of the door opening to reveal a glaring Mrs. Poston screaming about my violating some legal right she thought she had. I moved away. After several minutes, I was so curious that I almost mustered the courage to listen at the door again. But before my courage could push me in that direction, the door opened, and the mothers walked out.

Mrs. Poston stopped to address me. "It's Mary, isn't it?"

I swallowed and nodded. "Yes."

"Well, Mary, your clothes are so . . . boyish, the overalls I mean. Take some good advice and get new ones. And do something with your makeup and hair. You do wear makeup, don't you? Alexis is the fashion leader here at the school. You could take lessons from her. She goes shopping for new clothes almost every weekend. And Emilio does her hair and makeup in his salon. He's very good. Would you like his number?"

"I don't think my grandmother has the money for that."

Mrs. Poston looked at me with a slight smile.

"Really? That's too bad," she said, before leaving with Mrs. Hall.

I turned to Mr. Lawless. "Are we in trouble?"

He shook his head. "No. They just want us to write about the starters on the basketball team and the senior cheerleaders. They seem to believe those kids deserve most of the press, for scholarship and district honors purposes. You can do that, can't you?"

I sighed. "I suppose. But it gets so boring always hearing their names around school. It would be refreshing to talk about someone else, help some unknown kid get an honor now and then. Know what I mean?"

He laughed softly and said, "Yeah. But we can't rile those women up or we'll have one of their school board friends on us. Besides, the team is supposed to win the district and the region, maybe even go to the state finals, and Toby and the other starters are the stars. It will be appropriate to write about their success this year, don't you think?"

I nodded. "Right, I guess. Still, I'd sure like to do something else, write in a different vein. Can you imagine how the bench players would feel to see their names in print, and how proud their parents would be?"

Mr. Lawless scratched his chin. "Don't they play their first game tomorrow, against Lincoln? We haven't beaten them in years. Now that would be a story. Why don't you cover the game and have an article ready by Wednesday. That will be a good start to a series on the progress of the team. What do you say about that?"

"The article needs to focus on the stars?" I asked.

He smiled slightly and softly said, "It would be a good idea. Yes, you need to write mostly about the top players, the scorers, the rebounders. You know the drill. Besides, that's factual stuff people like to read about, like I've said before. The newspapers do the same thing. That's commercial journalism."

"I guess. And the cheerleaders too?"

Mr. Lawless rubbed the back of his neck and looked at the floor. "Yes, and the cheerleaders too."

I sat at a table to begin the story, but nothing came to mind. My heart just wasn't in it.

CHAPTER FIVE

Tuesday afternoon finally arrived, and Lizzie drove me to City Arena for the basketball game with Lincoln. The place was filling fast, and the game looked like it would be a sellout. I showed my school newspaper pass to the security guard, and we settled in the stands near the court. Mrs. Poston and Mrs. Hall chatted directly behind our team's bench, surrounded by several teachers and administrators. The cheerleaders were doing tumbling routines along the sideline in front of our fans, receiving loud applause with each pass. Then they did a complicated pyramid, and, as usual, Alexis Poston was the flyer standing on top with her arms raised, smiling with perfectly straight, glistening teeth, obviously the product of a major investment in dental whitening.

Suddenly, the Woodway team took the floor to the cheers, claps, and whistles of their adoring fans. They circled tightly in the center of the floor, placed arms around teammates' shoulders, and swayed side to side to their chants of victory. The Woodway crowd roared its support, and the team started their crisp warm-up drills: dribbling, passing, layups, and shots from the floor. I glanced at Mrs. Poston and Mrs. Hall as they beamed in the direction of their celebrity offspring.

The Lincoln team ran onto the floor to the cheers of their fans on the other side of the court. As usual, they had some athletic-looking players. But their team didn't have the really tall players I had seen in the past, the dominators, the "men-against-boys" guys that made some of our parents quip, "Must be shaving and paying alimony." This lack of dominant talent had led the *News* to predict that Lincoln wouldn't be nearly as strong as they had been in the past, to the delight of parents like Mrs. Hall, who speculated openly that Woodway would go all the way this year.

The horn sounded for the start of the game. Woodway's starters settled on the bench for their introductions, while the others formed a gauntlet through which the starters would run to center court as their names were announced. Mrs. Hall and Mrs. Poston stood and clapped and Alexis Poston did a backflip when Toby Hall's name blared over the public address system.

The arena lights came down just before the start of the game, adding to the drama of the moment. I readied my legal pad for all of the glorious details leading to our expected victory. The ball was tossed and our fans screamed as we won the tip-off.

A quick pass to Toby Hall caused Mrs. Hall to stand up and holler, "Swoosh!"

Toby let go with a long three-point shot which missed badly.

Lincoln fans whistled, laughed, and chanted, "Air ball, air ball."

Mrs. Hall glared across the court and mouthed derogatory words even a non-lip reader could understand.

A zippy Lincoln guard grabbed the ball and drove the length of the court for a layup to the cheers of the Lincoln fans. We inbounded and passed the ball down the court. Toby Hall received the ball on the wing and made a picture perfect jump shot, the ball bouncing high off the rim, into the hands of a leaping Lincoln player, who threw a baseball pass to his speeding teammate for a quick dunk. The Lincoln fans roared and stomped the floor in thundering unison.

This pattern continued. Most of the time our long shots missed and the athletic Lincoln players controlled the rebounds and ran our pants off for layups or dunks, until Lincoln led twelve to nothing.

Coach Riley finally called time-out, and his Woodway players walked heavily to the bench to scattered boos from our obviously stunned fans.

I leaned closer to hear the coach's words. His face was red, and his eyes bulged. "What are you guys doing? This is pitiful. You're supposed to beat this team. You are embarrassing your fans and yourselves. How can you be ranked third in the state with a performance like this? Those guys are running you off the court. I swear if you stars don't get your act together, I'm going to bench you and replace you with someone who wants to play. And, Hall, stop taking those NBA three-pointers. Work the ball inside to a cutter for a higher percentage shot. Now get out there and play smart!"

I quickly glanced at Mrs. Poston and Mrs. Hall for their reactions to this negative turn of events. It wasn't a pretty sight.

Mrs. Hall was in high gear, ranting to all around her, especially her husband, "That is simply ridiculous, telling the best player on the team not to shoot. That coach is going to kill his spirit and make the team lose. I will call a meeting of the parents. Riley is going to ruin this season for the seniors, and I won't stand for it!"

Her husband, a local chiropractor, clamored, "I'll sue that jerk for causing mental trauma to my kid. He won't like answering questions on the stand. I'll break him financially. I've had it with him. We need a better coach. Everybody can see that he's the whole problem."

Mrs. Poston sat quietly, a frown making her face appear especially distasteful, undoubtedly more the result of her daughter's sideline tears than the poor performance of the team.

Our starting five took the floor once again and inbounded the ball from the near sideline. Cameron Fields received a pass and dribbled toward our goal, passing to Toby Hall cutting through the middle toward the basket. He jumped high and let go a gently arching shot that fell through the net for our first basket. Our fans cheered, but their celebrations were short-lived as a Lincoln player inbounded with a long pass to a streaking teammate who made an uncontested layup. As I watched the game, it soon became obvious that our team simply wasn't moving as fast as their opponents. The Lincoln players seemed to have more energy as they hustled to the ball, and the lead slowly had widened to eighteen points when the final horn sounded.

Mr. and Mrs. Hall stormed from the stands, hate written on their faces, and accosted poor Coach Riley before he could get to the safety of the locker room.

"Mr. Riley, I want to talk to you," came the angry words from Mrs. Hall.

The coach stopped, sighed, and looked at her with weary eyes. "Yes?"

She got right to it. "Why did you tell my son to stop shooting? Do you see what you did? You caused us to lose the game because you prevented him from making his points tonight. Your coaching was terrible, simply ridiculous!"

Before the beleaguered man could respond, Mr. Hall chimed in. "I coached Toby in the youth leagues for years, and I know these kids. You can't shut them down like that. What kind of coaching is this? Not any I know, not any that will win, I can tell you that."

Coach Riley hung his head for several seconds and finally responded, "Mr. and Mrs. Hall, please. There is nothing wrong with our coaching. The problem is that the kids didn't follow our game plan. Long outside shots have low probabilities of going in. I teach taking shots with higher probabilities, from the paint. Layups are much better than three-pointers. And with our height, that is a sound plan. As for this game, we knew that Lincoln was fast. If we missed shots, they were more likely to get the rebounds than our players, so we had to play a more deliberate, down low game. But our kids went back to those long jump shots, and it killed us."

Mr. Hall snapped at the coach. "You know, when you degrade the kids, they are going to miss shots. It's better to be positive at all times, tell them they can do it, than to knock them down, like you did tonight."

"It's better if the kids respect their elders and do what they are taught. When they do wrong, they need to be told so and held accountable. That's how they learn. These boys are almost adults. They need to be treated like that, not little children."

Mr. Hall was not finished. He pointed a menacing finger at Coach Riley. "We expect the team to win this season. They have too much talent to loose. If they aren't successful, it will be your fault and I will personally go to the school board about your job. I hope you are very clear on that. I mean it."

The Halls stormed off, followed by Mrs. Poston clutching her tearful daughter around the shoulders.

The woman stroked her daughter's long, highlighted hair and spoke in baby talk, "Don't worry, Darling. Mommy is here. We're going to make it all right. Just watch and see. Tonight I'll take you shopping and we'll buy lots of new clothes."

Lizzie and I sat in the stands, two of the few fans remaining as the cleanup crew started its work. I tried to think of what I would write about the game. Then we got up and walked to the exit.

One of the older men who followed the team had been sitting near us. He rose and moved down the stands, slowing to talk to me on the way out. "You're a student at Woodway, aren't you? I saw you at the games last year."

"Yes, sir," I answered.

He shook his head. "I know the *News* has the team ranked third in state, but I hope you don't have your sights set too high for this season."

"What do you mean?"

He squinted. "Your team can't win against good talent. Not fast enough. Lincoln is only a moderate team and they beat you pretty good. Wait till you go up against the really top teams, like Washington and Bush and Travis. They will run you off the court."

I looked up at him. "Gosh, I hope not. That sounds pretty awful."

He shook his head. "I'm afraid so, unless you find more talent. And that's not likely. Not now that the season has started."

"I really want Woodway to win the region and go to state," I admitted. "That would make our senior year special, something to remember. But that seems impossible now, and knowing it makes me so sad. Is my senior year going to be a total bust?"

Lizzie patted my shoulder. "So what? You aren't big on sports anyway. I bet it will all turn out great. Just give it a chance. Something good's going to happen. I can feel it."

CHAPTER SIX

The next day at school, my mind was on the basketball game story I was trying to write. How could I showcase any player from a disaster like that loss?

I stopped by my locker, and there she was, Alexis Poston, snuggling with Toby Hall, whispering in his ear.

I looked the other way but could hear her words to him. "Come on, Toby. Cheer up. It's only one game. So what? You'll win the next one. Big deal. Don't you think I look pretty in my new clothes? They're designer jeans. They cost three hundred fifty dollars. You got the most gorgeous girl in the school."

It was easy to feel sorry for Toby. After all, he was the stud of the team, the player everyone expected to carry us to the state tournament. But his team had lost the game everyone knew they would win.

Closing my locker, I decided to offer some encouragement. "Toby, I was at the game. Sorry we didn't win. But you did well. A couple of your baskets were great, especially that first one."

He turned to me with a blank look, as though I were a bug or piece of slime. "I don't need your pity. I don't even care what you think, Shoes. Don't talk to me. I don't want anyone to see you near me."

I looked at the floor. "I wish you wouldn't call me that. It hurts."

He shot back, "Well, it's true. Everyone calls you Goody Two Shoes, 'cause you are always worrying about old people and dogs and stuff like that."

"I was only trying to help."

He laughed. "I don't need your help. I don't need anything from you."

Alexis chimed in. "Yeah, Shoes, he's right. You can't do anything for either of us."

I began to feel my eyes fill with tears, unable to say anything more, causing me to turn and run from them.

Lizzie stopped me in the hall.

"What's the matter?" she asked.

My embarrassment was fast changing to pure anger as I spit out my answer, "Those jerks! Toby and Alexis are at it again. They ragged me just for trying to be nice to Toby. Why are they so hateful?"

Lizzie looked squarely into my eyes. "They don't like to be reminded of any screw up. Their parents tell them they can do no wrong, no matter what, and they have to be the best all the time. I even heard that Mrs. Poston hires a tutor to do all of Alexis's homework and papers. She doesn't really deserve that number one ranking. Want to hear something else about Alexis?" Lizzie stopped talking and looked around, before continuing at a whisper. "Mrs. Poston came to the office today to see Principal Newman."

I was getting curious. Lizzie was going to tell me something juicy and awful. I wiped my tears. "Go on."

She continued, "Well, she went in to see him behind closed doors. Then I heard her tell Principal Newman that he needed to change Alexis's chemistry grade from an eighty-nine to a ninety."

I didn't want to believe her. "Why would he do that? Heck, I struggled for my ninety in chemistry, studied all the time. And no tutor for me. Couldn't afford it."

Lizzie went on. "Mrs. Poston said that Alexis wasn't feeling good, but that she knew the material. Then she said that Alexis needed an A to maintain her ranking as the number one senior and that her admission to an Ivy League school depended on her remaining number one."

I looked hard at Lizzie. "And what did he do?"

"At first, nothing. But Mrs. Poston got very forceful and said she had done a lot of things for the school and he needed to remember that. Then she said she wouldn't leave his office till he changed the grade. Finally, he said he would, if Alexis wrote an extra credit paper, which Mrs. Poston quickly agreed to. When she left, the woman was all smiles."

I blinked at my friend in disbelief. "That bitch. No wonder her darling is number one. Who can compete with that?"

We continued to fume about the injustice, walking together to our first class. I was so angry that I wouldn't even look at Alexis Poston, but felt her presence in the room.

Finally the bell rang for the end of class, and Lizzie and I went different ways. The day wore on numbly for me, the dull hurt of the morning still in my gut. Then the bell for last period sounded, and I took my legal pad and walked to the gym for an interview with Coach Riley, hoping I wouldn't run into Alexis Poston or Toby Hall again and that the head coach could give me some good ideas for my story on the game and the rest of the basketball season.

The team was doing warm-up drills, passes, and layups mostly. I settled in the stands, expecting Coach Riley to call me over for a short interview before practice started, since I had called ahead. As I looked around, my gut started to hurt more than before. There were Alexis Poston and her mother and Toby Hall's mother, watching the practice from high in the stands. I turned away from them.

As I watched the players, I could not forget the words of the man after the game: the team couldn't win against real talent; it just wasn't good enough, not enough speed. Suddenly, as I watched the athletes run their drills, I could see the problem for myself—our players needed that extra second to set up for the shot, to get to the rebound, to move into defensive position, and I knew he was right.

I noticed a person standing in the doorway to the gym, intently watching the players. I didn't recognize him and wondered if he was a student from another high school here for some extra curricular activity. He was fairly tall, maybe six feet three or four inches, but not as tall as some of our players, like Toby, who was six feet six inches tall or Cameron, about the same height. The visitor had a medium build, but I sensed he was muscular beneath his clothes, probably from the way his shirt bulged against his stomach and chest. Straight, blonde hair hung partly across his left eye, contrasting with tanned skin. I guessed he was a swimmer. He had a pleasant, friendly face with round, boyish features and a sweet smile. But there was something else that made him appear good-looking. Then it hit me—he had the bluest eyes I had ever seen, so blue they appeared almost backlit, seeming to radiate across the gym.

I continued to watch the visitor, interested in his identity and the reason for his coming to our school. Soon he walked into the gym, toward Coach Riley at the other end. I got up and moved from the stands to find out about this mystery person.

He walked up to the coach, extended a hand toward the man and politely said, "Excuse me. Are you Coach Riley?"

The coach was paying attention to the drills and didn't respond right away, causing the visitor to try again. "Coach Riley?"

The coach finally looked at the visitor. "Yes? Can I help you?"

The young man smiled, and those blue eyes flashed, like blue glacier ice I had seen in pictures.

"Yes, sir. I'm Matthew Blair. Just enrolled here. They gave me your name in the office. I was wondering if you might have room for me on the team. I heard the season just started," he softly said in an accent I thought to be British, but a little different.

Coach Riley looked eye-to-eye at the visitor, responding in a businesslike tone, "The team is full. We're trying to get our chemistry right. I don't want to add any new players. I guess if you were six foot eleven, the answer would be different. But we got several guys your height. You might try the track coach. You look pretty athletic. Maybe he could make a jumper out of you."

Matthew Blair smiled and extended his hand. "Well, thanks, Coach," he said, turning and walking toward the exit at the other end of the gym. After only a couple of steps, the visitor picked up a basketball and bounced it playfully. I glanced back at the coach for a moment, then looked toward the spot where the visitor had stood only a second or two before. He wasn't there but, somehow, was laying the ball high off the top of the glass backboard at the other end of the court. I wondered how he had run almost the entire length of the court in only a couple of seconds. I thought he might have a twin brother who was waiting for him there. But I saw only one new boy.

Suddenly, Coach Riley cried out, "Hey, new guy. Hold up there for a minute." He jogged toward the young man.

I quickly moved closer to them, sensing there was a story in all this.

The coach was smiling. "You move pretty good, lots of speed under control. You have a problem being on the second team? Some guys don't like that, you know."

Matthew Blair flashed those eyes again. "No, not really. Just glad to be a part of the team."

Coach Riley extended a hand. "Good. Look, you're going to need a physical first. Go see the school nurse, and she'll arrange it this afternoon. The clinic is down the street and usually sees our players right away. Then come back and go across the hall to get your gear. After that, come back here as fast as you can for practice. You have a lot of catching up to do. You ever play organized basketball before?"

"Some back home. Nothing really big, though. I worked. Didn't have time for a real team. Played club ball mostly."

Coach Riley nodded. "That's okay. We'll work a little extra with you after practice. Go see the nurse. Remember, get back here as fast as you can, in your gray practice uniform. We'll need all the time with you we can get."

I watched the new guy walk away and wondered how an outsider would fit into the cliquish basketball team. Most of them had played the game together in this community since they were children. I instinctively looked over my shoulder at Mrs. Poston, Alexis Poston, and Mrs. Hall, noticing that Tiffany Malloy and Paige Richelieu had joined their group. All of them were giggling and whispering, watching Alexis hold what looked like a glittering piece of jewelry. As usual, their attention was on themselves.

CHAPTER SEVEN

Our second basketball game rolled around on Friday, an evening contest at Monroe High, north of Houston. I was going to cover the game for the paper, but Lizzie couldn't go. Coach Riley let me catch a ride on the team bus. I wondered if I would ever escape the dreaded yellow monster. The ride took about an hour and a half, and I enjoyed listening to the players chatting about all kinds of things, giving me sources for some juicy gossip Lizzie would love. They were talking about who liked whom . . . and who disliked whom . . . and what parties were scheduled for the weekend, stuff that really didn't affect me very much. But since we always kept each other informed, I wanted to do my duty and share gossip with Lizzie. Anyway, it was kind of fun knowing what was going on in the school.

I sat quietly in the seat behind the coach and his assistant. Matthew Blair sat alone in the seat behind me, seeming unconcerned about not being included in any of the talk.

We drove in Houston's heavy traffic, the slow lane making the trip seem very long. The players' discussions eventually gave way to a nervous silence, the calm before the storm they must have felt coming. The bus finally rolled up to the red brick gym at one end of the school. "Beat Woodway," was posted in bold black letters on Monroe High's sign.

We entered the pentagon-shaped gym. Its mid-court circular scoreboard glowed with lights reflecting off the polished wood floor. Individual padded seats replaced the bleachers found in most of the other high school gyms I had seen. The whole place was done in Monroe's royal blue school color, making it look rich and impressive. Some of Woodway's parents cheered as our team entered the gym in their street clothes, led by Mr. and Mrs. Hall and Mr.

and Mrs. Poston standing and clapping for our players. They always seemed to be around their kids, even for out-of-town games.

I settled in behind our bench to watch the warm-up drills and begin my article on the game, my trusty legal pad in hand.

After a short time, our players came out of the locker room in their red warm-up uniforms. They looked snappy, passing balls around a big circle, doing layups from the left side of the court and then from the right, shooting from the field, and running intricate offensive plays.

The Monroe team came onto the floor in blue uniforms, and its growing crowd erupted in applause, cheers, and whistles. I knew that Monroe was always one of the better teams in the Houston region, mainly because their coach whipped the team into a disciplined unit that defended tightly, rebounded well, and took the high-percentage shot, usually some kind of layup or close jumper. They made the playoffs each year but seemed to wilt against the high-powered, athletic teams with the great players.

The warm-up drills ended and a horn sounded for the start of the game. I looked around and saw that the place was packed. Woodway's player information glided silently around the scoreboard, small square lights forming the letters of the players' names. Then the arena lights dimmed, focusing the court lights on the starting teams.

The game began with a flurry for us, as we won the tip. Cameron Fields took a pass and laid it in for an easy two. The other team inbounded, carefully dribbled down the court, and threw the ball out of bounds, unusual for them. Toby Hall received a pass from his buddy, Cameron, and shot from the corner, nailing a three-pointer. Our fans yelled their excitement. As the game progressed, we seemed to have the better team and extended the lead, sending our fans into a frenzy and quieting the home crowd.

Monroe's zippy guard then took charge, abandoning the cautious game for drives to the bucket, closing our lead from twelve to only four points. I began to feel a lump in my stomach. The Monroe fans made it worse with chants of "DEFENSE," "GO," and "SCORE." The place was rocking, and our players couldn't seem to stop that runt who was hitting everything he put up. Finally, Coach Riley called time-out, but I cringed to see that it was a little late. We were now behind by four points with only fifty-six seconds to go in the game.

The Monroe fans and players were standing, slapping hands, and celebrating the team's incredible comeback and apparent victory. I crumpled the "Woodway Wins" article I had been writing and wondered if Coach Riley could pull a rabbit from his hat.

The horn sounded to resume the game, and we inbounded to Cameron Fields. I crossed my fingers and closed my left eye, not wanting to see too much of the expected loss. Cameron drove the lane and collided with a defender. The referee called a charge on Cameron, adding to the Monroe fans' chaotic frenzy. We had lost that crucial possession to their smiling team, the bench players of which were standing on the sideline and cheering wildly with their fans.

To make matters worse, Cameron Fields was hurt. Coach Riley ran onto the floor, and he and the team trainer helped Cameron to the bench, his contorted expression telling me he was in pain. Coach Riley quickly looked down the bench for a replacement, pointing at Matthew Blair.

The newcomer jumped from his seat and ran to the coach, who hurriedly said, "Now look, don't try anything fancy. Use your speed on defense; keep that guard from driving to the hoop. Try and stay in front of him. Let Toby shoot the ball. Pass it to him. Understand?"

Matthew Blair nodded, before running onto the court. He looked around, and Coach Riley yelled for him to take a position at the top of the three-point arc.

Monroe inbounded to its zippy guard, who carefully dribbled toward the far side, away from the nearest Woodway defender. The crowd hollered, whistled, and yelled as the guard ran precious time off the clock: forty-nine seconds left, forty-eight, forty-seven, forty-six. I just knew that time was going to run out on us as the Monroe guard protected the ball from our players. Coach Riley yelled for someone to foul the guard.

Suddenly, moving faster than my eye could follow, a red streak flashed by the guard, stripping him of the ball. The guard looked around in obvious disbelief, and Matthew Blair gently laid the ball off the top of our glass for an uncontested score, immediately quieting the Monroe crowd, except for scattered calls of "FOUL." But no foul was called.

Monroe inbounded again, and its guard was especially careful with the ball, crouching low to the floor for short, careful dribbles. He crossed the mid-court line and moved from side to side, eating up more time with his team ahead by two points. Only twenty-two seconds remained. The Monroe fans were screaming. The guard seemed in firm control, until a red blur ran at him again, causing the Monroe ball handler to stop dribbling and hold the ball over his head with both hands. Matthew Blair jumped completely over the smaller player and slapped the ball to himself with nothing but clear court ahead for the tying layup. The stunned Monroe fans fell silent, leaving the minority Woodway backers jumping in the stands and cheering in delight.

Monroe called a time-out as its coach stormed onto the court to meet the team, his face bright red and his eyes bulging. He yelled at his players and pointed at Matthew Blair. The entire team turned and looked at Matthew, their eyes wide and mouths open. Then their coach yelled again, and his team turned toward him. He pounded his fist in his other hand, screaming instructions to the players.

The horn sounded for the end of the time-out and Monroe inbounded the ball again, this time to a tall, athletic player who dribbled with his right hand. He moved cautiously down the court, closer to the basket, the clock counting down toward zero. With the clock at eight seconds, he made a powerful pass toward his teammate running near the goal, but Matthew Blair's hand darted into the passing lane and deflected the ball to Toby Hall, who streaked down court and shot from the top of the key. The ball missed badly, but Matthew Blair was there, grabbing the rebound and laying the ball on the glass for a basket as the final horn sounded. Woodway had won by two!

Fans and players streamed onto the court, and it was impossible to distinguish the happy hollering from the cries of defeat. At first, I felt sorry for the Monroe players until I saw one of them make an obscene gesture, and then I was glad we had beaten them on their home court.

Our fans were running up to the team, yelling and offering congratulations, and I was feeling the euphoria of the moment. But my emotions quickly changed because of Mrs. Hall's scowl as she stomped toward Matthew Blair.

"Excuse me, but who are you? And exactly what do you think you are doing shooting the ball?" she demanded.

He turned and looked at her. "I'm Matthew Blair. New to the school. Just joined the team."

Her angry face did not soften. "Exactly. You are new to this team. That is why I want to know why you think you are the star. These boys have been together for years, working hard to become a contender. They played youth ball and were selected throughout school to play on the basketball team. They have earned their right to be showcased now. What right do you have trying to steal the limelight, especially in their senior year?"

He seemed puzzled. "I . . . I'm sorry if I did anything wrong. I really didn't mean to."

She snapped at him "You should have passed the ball back to Toby for the last shot. He was wide open! He would have definitely made it. But no, you had to steal his special moment. Be a showboat, a glory hog."

Matthew blinked several times. "I thought that since I was next to the basket with the clock almost at zero that I needed to put the ball up when I got the rebound. There wasn't time for a pass."

She continued the verbal assault. "You are here merely as a role player, to support the shooters, like Toby. You think that just because you had a couple of lucky plays that makes you the leader? Well, you're wrong. If you don't know that, you're stupid. And I will be more than happy to correct your thinking."

Coach Riley quickly moved between them. "What's the problem here?"

She turned on the coach. "You need to control these bench players. This boy has no business trying to be a star out there. He' been a part of the team for how long, a week? Toby has been in the program from day one and he should be the go-to player, rather than some Johnny-come-lately ball hog. I want you to do something about the situation. I mean it!"

Coach Riley held out a hand. "Now, Mrs. Hall, please. Matthew was just acting instinctively to win the game at a critical time. I can't fault him for doing his best. The clock was almost out of time. He did the right thing out there. He was much closer to the basket than any of his teammates."

She pointed in the coach's face. "You had better watch yourself. There are parents watching you. This team is about Toby and the other starters, not some bench player," she said, before turning to stomp away.

I couldn't believe my eyes and ears. What a mega-bitch she was. I knew she could be very protective of her son, but to criticize a kid who had won the game on his own skill when her son had almost blown it—that was too much, even for her.

I began walking toward the team bus and heard someone call out, "Mary, Mary Lawrence."

Alexis Poston and her mother walked quickly toward me, and I said to myself, "Oh, gosh. What kind of problem are they trying to create?"

Mrs. Poston smiled, not a friendly smile but one telling me she wanted something. "I suppose you are here to write an article on the game. Like you usually do for the school paper."

I answered with a lump forming in my stomach. "Yes."

"I just want to make sure you follow our agreement, the one we talked about the other day at school."

I thought hard, blurting out, "Agreement?"

"Yes, the one where you agreed to write mostly about the starters. You must remember," she said impatiently.

"Yes, I recall the conversation."

She seemed to relax a little. "Good, then I expect that you are going to talk about Toby making the assist that won the game?"

"Toby? But what about Matthew Blair? He really won the game with that buzzer beater."

"Matthew who? He's a nobody. You need to forget about him. I bet he won't even make grades. Most of these transient kids don't. They're too busy going from one school to another. No real foundation. You need to write about Toby." She stopped and turned to her daughter for approval.

Alexis nodded. "She's right, Shoes. You should forget about the strays. Stick with the proven winners, like Toby. That's why he's my boyfriend. I only take the best."

I felt trapped and overwhelmed. "Okay. I'll make the starters the main characters of the story, if that's what you want."

They smiled and bounced away, Alexis's white sneakers contrasting against the asphalt parking lot as she and her mother got closer to their big SUV.

I boarded the bus, and the team members came straggling in from the locker room, chatting happily about the victory. Coach Riley was the last to board, and he quickly counted noses before we took off for home. Matthew Blair sat in the same seat, occasionally receiving congratulations from teammates but not really fitting into any group within the squad.

After we had ridden for about fifteen minutes, Coach Riley got up and sat next to Matthew Blair. "That was an incredible performance you put on tonight, son. You know, you're the fastest basketball player I've ever coached, maybe the fastest I've ever seen in person. You know who Angus McPherson is?"

"He coached his college team to national championships here in the States. Some people say he was the greatest college coach ever."

"That's right. But he was also maybe the most astute judge of talent the game has ever known. He used to say that speed was important, but that the speed had to be under control for it to be effective in the game of basketball. Quite frankly, Matthew, your speed, while incredible, was also in perfect control all the time. I never saw you lose your balance or fumble with the ball. Perfect control, at fantastic speed, that's what you showed tonight." He stopped, studied the young man's face for a few moments, and asked, "Where have you played, anyway? I follow the high school all-star talent around the country, all of the select summer teams that play in the top tournaments, and I've never heard of you. With your talent, you should be front-page news, headed for the pros right out of high school, that kind of thing."

Matthew Blair looked at the floor. "We moved here from Australia, for my mom to get treatment at the big cancer hospital in Houston. We read that it's ranked tops in the world. I played over there, not in the big cities like Sydney. We lived in the interior, and I played in the smaller towns. Not much press out there. It's kind of in the middle of nowhere."

Coach Riley smiled. "You ever lose a game?"

Matthew Blair smiled back, flashing those electric eyes. They were so blue, even in the dim bus light. He didn't answer the question, maybe because the answer was obvious and out of character for his modesty.

Coach Riley rubbed the back of his neck. "Well, you've given me a real problem, I'm afraid. It's funny how there's good and bad to most things, and that is sure true with you."

Matthew Blair looked puzzled. "I'm sorry. What do you mean? What kind of problem did I create?"

"With your talent I've got to start you, and that's going to make some people mad, especially if you do what I think you can do—become the best player on the team, probably by far. Matthew, many of the parents at Woodway are . . . how shall I say . . . real involved in their kids' lives. They try and make everything perfect, you know, grades, sports, extra curricular activities. You are going to replace one of those kids in the starting lineup and, most likely, be the star of the team. But I have no choice. There's no way any coach would sit you. No way."

Matthew Blair smiled again, not a wide grin, but a sweet, half smile, the kind that someone makes when he says, "I hear you and I want to help."

I heard a cell phone ring and saw the assistant coach answer it.

He finished the call, left his seat, and walked to Coach Riley. "We've got a problem."

Coach Riley asked, "What kind of problem?"

The assistant coach looked very serious. "All hell's breaking loose at the school."

CHAPTER EIGHT

We got to the school late, but good old Lizzie was waiting in her trusty sedan to take me home since Grandma didn't drive anymore, and I had no car.

I bounced into the aging car, still excited from our win, my words gushing excitedly, "Lizzie, you won't believe what happened. Monroe was ahead with less than a minute to go, and it looked like we had lost, but this new guy, Matthew Blair, came in for . . . ."

She interrupted my story. "I know, he won the game with a rebound and buzzer shot. But Mary, everything's going crazy. Mrs. Hall and Mrs. Poston have been on their cell phones to everyone they can call, complaining about him being on the team. They want him off, saying all kinds of crazy stuff, like he came too late, after the team was chosen. I've heard from three friends who received calls from their friends. It's all over the school by now. The bitches are on the warpath, and they want their way. I'm afraid they'll get it too. Rotten bitches."

I began to feel sick and shook my head. "They are the nastiest people on the planet. This guy is good, Lizzie, real good, better than any basketball player I ever saw at Woodway or any other school, even schools like Lincoln that always seem to have great players. And he can help us win, I mean, maybe, win it all at Austin, the big dance, the state championship. He really can, Liz. What are those parents doing, shooting the school in the foot just because their precious Toby isn't the best guy on the team? Well, the truth is he's not, not even close. Toby can't play anywhere near as good as Matthew Blair. And the entire school has to suffer for it? That's just stupid!"

Lizzie giggled. "What's he like? They say he's cute. Did you see him up close?"

I was trying to get over my anger, not really thinking about his looks, but forced an answer. "I guess. Yeah, I saw him, sat in the seat in front of his. It's hard to say really. I haven't talked to him or anything like that. He stayed mostly to himself on the bus. I suppose you might say he's cute. But those eyes . . . man, they are so beautiful—a deep blue, not dark blue, but a blue that seems to go on and on, with no end, like the sky or the ocean. Electric light blue."

Lizzie began to laugh and tease me, "Mary's in love, Mary's in love. I'm going to tell everybody."

I snapped at her. "Stop that! I'm not in love, don't even know this guy. I just think he's great for the team, that's all. I'm mad that the bitches are after him. They have hurt so many kids over the years."

Lizzie's face grew serious. "Yeah, they can be real bad at times. But what do you expect from women who would slit a kid's throat so their own kids could move up in the class ranking or get an extra award?"

I felt a chill, causing me to vent, "They are monsters. Killed lots of spirit. Embarrassed people, on purpose. Kept them from their dreams, just so some spoiled brat could get another trophy."

Soon, we had arrived at my house. I thanked Lizzie for the ride and walked to the front door, still feeling angry about the bitches' campaign to rule the school.

Grandma was waiting. "I thought it was you. Just wanted to wait up a little till you got home. Want something to eat?"

"You should be in bed. It's 11:45, way past your bed time. You don't need to wait up for me. Heck, I'm almost grown," I protested.

She yawned. "I know, you're a big girl, almost eighteen years old. But I can't help it. Just seems like I can't rest till I know you're safe at home. It's a parent thing. I did the same for your mother while she lived here. What about something to eat? Maybe a sandwich or some soup?"

"No thanks. I want to stop eating late, to lose some weight. I've been thinking about changing my image, you know, for college. I'll probably start dating at the community college, and I'd like to slim down a little and get rid of these zits too. Sooner or later, boys will be important to me, and I want to be ready, if I can."

She chuckled. "You look fine. You've got a cute shape. I know skinny is in. But plump figures used to be admired. Look at all those classic sculptures. The women aren't slim. Besides, there will be plenty of time for you to change your image for the boys. Don't grow up too fast." She stopped talking and thought for a moment before continuing. "You know, I have some news for you, about that band you like so much, Promise. I was watching the television before you got home, and they had a special program on the group."

I became interested. "Really? What did they say?"

"Well, it was very fascinating. They started out by saying that the band is the most popular of all time, that they have sold far more albums than any other band in history, but that they are a mystery. It seems no one knows their true identities or where they live or any of the details of their lives, like who their agent is or where they come from. The television reporters were doing a sort of investigative report, talking with different people in entertainment and music. But even after the investigation, the mystery remains. They did find out that some strange man, a lawyer maybe, appears to set up their concerts and negotiate their music deals. Then he disappears with no trace, until he surfaces for the next deal. Thought you'd like to know about the program."

"I knew that no one seems to have any details about their personal lives. There have been a lot of articles about that subject and who they might be. Some people have said they are illegitimate children of great musicians, with the talent of their parents, but not wanting to upstage them, since Promise has far eclipsed all other artists in popularity. But who knows? All I can say for sure is that they are the greatest musicians ever and I love their music, like almost everyone else on the planet seems to. They just touch my heart like no other band. I don't know whether it's their lyrics or melodies."

Grandma continued, obviously interested in the television report, "They did say one more thing. It seems that some people speculate they use a lot of their fortune for the poor, different charities and such. But even that is a mystery. No one really knows who they have given money to, how much they have given, or for what purposes."

She yawned, and I yawned back. She gestured toward my room. "Time for both of us to go to bed. You have school," she said, lovingly stroking my head. Then she added, "You look so much like your mother at this age. You are beautiful, inside and out, Mary. You really are."

I lowered my gaze. "It's tough. Sometimes I don't feel beautiful. It seems that the world is full of selfish, hard people waiting to put you down just so they can be on top. The rest of us get the shaft. I'm afraid that my whole life is going to pass and I'll be a nobody, never make a difference, never do anything special, never even have a date. No one will really care about me or think I'm special. It sure makes me sad. I wish Mom was here to hold me, make me feel a little better. I wish she was here right now, tonight."

Grandma held me in her arms, rocking gently back and forth. "I do too, Mary. More than anything."

CHAPTER NINE

Morning came way too early. I pulled the covers over my head, not ready to get up—too many dreams, keeping my mind in turmoil throughout the night, creating a need for more time to work them out. But reality took hold, and I rushed through my morning routine, thankful that I wouldn't waste time on makeup and hair and clothes that had to be perfect. I had no time for that stuff, just a quick wash, comb through the red rat's nest, floss and teeth brushing, and a pair of overalls that held a lot and hid a ton, as usual.

I ran through the house, to the front door, grabbing Grandma's sack lunch along the way. "Chips today, Grandma? And maybe a cookie?"

"No chips and no sweets. You know they make you break out."

I blurted out, "Your healthy stuff will kill me."

"Mary!"

I slowed down to give her a kiss on the cheek. "That's my stomach talking. Forgive me?"

"Always."

I sprinted toward the corner, the place where the yellow monster ate us poor bus riders. Gosh, how I wished for a car, once in a while, to make a bit of an entrance at school in the morning. But Lizzie had to get to school early because of her job in the principal's office, leaving me stranded, well, almost.

As I was riding to school, the kid in front of me had his radio on and I could hear the news: "Early this morning, there was a coordinated bomb attack in several Middle East cities. Preliminary reports indicate that more than two hundred people died. Military forces have responded with tanks and planes, killing scores of suspected militants in various cities in the region

---

43

and arresting many more. Thousands of local residents are rioting in protest, adding to the angry situation."

I turned to the student with the radio, a chill running through me at the thought of living in such a dangerous place. My high school did not seem so terrible any more. "I'm sure glad we don't live there. Those poor kids that do, I feel sorry for them. They live with fighting every day, and the fear they might be killed."

Noticing tears in his eyes, I tried to reassure him. "But we're okay. It's safe here. We don't have to worry in Houston."

He spoke slowly, "My uncle was killed by one of the bombs. He worked as an engineer over there. He was Mom's brother. She's in shock. My dad too. They sent me to school to get away from all the turmoil in the house. I don't know what's going to happen. I'm really confused."

I looked at his radio, still blaring details of the mass killing. "I'm so sorry for your family."

The bus came to a stop at the school, and I walked toward the side entrance, thinking about the poor people of the Middle East and wondering how they provided for their families and protected their children, thoughts that partly distracted me from the stares of the junior bitches.

The day rolled on, classes, lunch, Lizzie, until journalism, all muffled by the fatigue of a sleepless night. I entered the journalism classroom, usually a place I enjoyed, but today just somewhere to get a little rest.

I sat at my assigned table, put my head to my hand, and jumped as Mr. Lawless awakened me. "Mary, I want to give you a special assignment. You may need to take a few notes. It's kind of different from what you have written before."

I worried that Mrs. Poston and Mrs. Hall had gotten to him about the article I was going to write on the Monroe game.

To my surprise, he began in a different direction. "I suppose you heard about the terrible attack in the Middle East. It's on all the news programs. A lot of people died. Almost a thousand were injured. I would like you to do a special article for the school paper on the situation there. Make it a human interest story, something about a person or family living in that region, and how they are affected by the conflict."

"But why do you want a story about the fighting in the Middle East for the school paper? That seems a little heavy for high school kids. Don't you think?"

Mr. Lawless looked at me over his horn-rimmed glasses. "These events are a part of our world, and the students need to have some understanding of them. Who knows? Maybe a Woodway student will read your article and be moved to do something to end the suffering, something really great for the world. It could happen."

"Maybe, but I wouldn't bet on it. I'll do my best. The internet probably has some articles that will help. When do you want it?"

"Great. Can you have it ready for my review by Thursday of next week?"

I thought about my homework and the other article on the basketball game before answering, "I'll get on it right away. I probably can have something for you by then. Hope it will be good enough to publish. I've never done anything political, especially a human interest story."

"I know it will be good. You need to have more confidence in your writing, Mary. Your work is better than you think. It's become the best in the class. You write with a lot of heart," Mr. Lawless said, patting my shoulder.

I smiled, appreciating his support.

My mellow thoughts were interrupted by Lizzie as she ran up to me. Her words flowed breathlessly. "I've got some important stuff to tell you. Guess what I just heard in the office?"

"What? I hope it's not bad," I cautiously said.

She leaned closer and whispered, "Mrs. Poston and Mrs. Hall just finished a meeting with Principal Newman and Coach Riley. They demanded that the new boy . . . Matthew . . . Matthew Blair, that he be removed from the team. Something about his not being on the roster when a certain deadline closed."

"What?" I stopped, a lump forming in my stomach, before continuing, "Is he off the team?" I demanded, not wanting to believe her.

"They had a big argument. The mega-bitches said they would take the matter to the school board if the coach didn't remove him from the team. Principal Newman acted like he was going to agree with them. He really seemed whipped, until Coach Riley said that the deadline didn't apply to transfers from outside the state. They can be added anytime, according to the coach."

I was afraid to hear the end of the story, scared that the principal didn't buy Coach Riley's explanation, but gathered just enough courage to ask, "And who won the argument?"

Lizzie winked. "Principal Newman called me on the intercom and asked for the district athletic rules. I found them and brought the rule book to him. He looked through the book with me standing right there. I was afraid he would agree with Mrs. Poston and Mrs. Hall, but there it was, in the book, the transfer rule just like the coach said. He read it out loud. Matthew Blair was legal since he came from outside Texas."

"Yeah, way to go Riley! That's showing those mega-bitches. We won!" I yelled, feeling wide awake and pumped.

Lizzie's smile quickly faded. "But they aren't finished. I know they are going to make more trouble. The mega-bitches as much as said so as they stomped out of his office."

"How do you know they will cause more trouble? Isn't that the end of it?"

Lizzie cupped a hand to her mouth. "I heard Mrs. Poston in the hall outside the office. She called to Alexis and Toby. They must have been waiting out there. She told them not to worry, that she had something else planned, something that would work. It makes me sick, Mary." She stopped and looked at me, probably for some reassurance.

My juices were flowing full force. I winked at Lizzie. "We might be able to help poor Matthew Blair. Mrs. Poston wants me to write about the stars, and that's exactly what I'm going to do, for everyone to read. When I'm finished, the whole school will think he's the best basketball player in the state!"

"Yeah. You kick some bitch butt, girl," Lizzie said as she gave me a high five.

I felt a surge of creativity. "Ah, the power of the press. Ain't it wonderful?"

We giggled as I took out my trusty legal pad and began to write the story about our team's victory: "Woodway pulls out a come-from-behind win over a tough Monroe squad thanks to the heroic efforts of a new star from across the Pacific, Matthew Blair. His incredible speed and exceptional defense shocked Monroe's usually steady point guard into several key turnovers, leading to Woodway scores by Blair, including the winning bucket. His outstanding talents were recognized by head coach Riley, who said Blair was the greatest player he had ever seen in the district, perhaps in the state. Blair's addition to the Woodway team helps its title hopes. Another longtime basketball observer agreed, saying, 'Woodway's basketball future looks bright, so long as Blair leads the team, but without him, everything falls apart.'"

Chapter Ten

Almost three weeks of games had passed, and I guessed my basketball team articles were a little too strong, at least for some people. Mrs. Hall and Mrs. Poston reacted poorly, one afternoon thunder-footing through the journalism classroom into Mr. Lawless' office and yelling at the poor man, their loud voices penetrating his office walls and closed door. Making matters worse, Alexis Poston and Toby Hall followed their parents, stopped directly in front of me, and stared with looks that could kill a gorilla. As they glared into my eyes, I could feel the heat rising in the room.

Mrs. Poston seemed so mean. "My husband and I have donated a great deal to this school over the years. Our daughter, Alexis, has the highest grade point average in the senior class. In fact, she is a leader here. Our wishes should count for something at this school."

Mrs. Hall's voice became high pitched and staccato as she continued the argument. "He's not even from this area. He didn't grow up with the other boys, and he will probably fail in school, or move away any time. How can you showcase this . . . this outsider? You're the teacher responsible for the school newspaper, aren't you? Then you need to do your job responsibly and order Mary Lawrence to write about Toby and Cameron. They're the real stars, the ones all the other students know and admire, especially now in their senior year. This Blair person is a nobody. I order you do correct the situation, before we go to the school board and do it for you."

"Mrs. Hall, Mrs. Poston, please be reasonable. I recognize that your students are outstanding here at Woodway. But the school paper isn't writing based on popularity. We report facts, and the facts are clear. Mary Lawrence obtained copies of the stat sheets for the last five games, since the time Matthew Blair joined the team. Here, look at these." He said nervously, but without backing down. He then apparently offered the stat sheets to them, as the rustle of papers came from his office. After a few moments, he continued, "You see the statistics? They show that he has scored an average of forty-four points per game, far more than any other player in the state. And he has gotten almost twenty-four rebounds a game, more than eleven blocks, and right at sixteen steals a game. There is nobody close to those stats. Woodway has won each of those five games by an average of twenty-six points, and from what I hear, we could have won by more if Coach Riley had left Blair in the games longer."

Mrs. Hall snapped, "You are making him out to be a super god. He's only an average boy who . . . who is a showboat. That's what those statistics mean! And your biased articles are perpetuating his grandstanding. You are hurting the team, dividing the players against themselves. That can only lead to failure."

Mr. Lawless responded very deliberately, "Mrs. Hall, the team is undefeated since Matthew Blair joined. How can we be hurting the other players or the team as a whole? It's obvious that his success on the basketball floor has helped the team greatly. I would wager that any team would love to have Matthew Blair . . . and his points, rebounds, blocks, and steals."

The mega-bitches seemed unmoved and peppered him with alternating criticism, finally threatening to take me off the paper, to shut the paper down, to expel Matthew Blair, to go to the school district superintendent. I hoped they were full of donkey dung but was afraid that, just maybe, they could do something terrible.

I sat very quietly, wanting them to leave and hoping it would happen soon. Suddenly, Mr. Lawless opened his door and the mega-bitches stormed out of his office, stopping to give me the worst evil eye I had ever seen—something out of a monster comic book, like the hideous one-eyed cyborg. Yuck, they were nasty! Then they pushed their kids in front and stormed out, and I felt the knot in my stomach begin to unravel.

Mr. Lawless and I stared at each other for several seconds before I broke the silence. "Sorry. I didn't mean to cause trouble for either of us. Maybe I got a little carried away in my writing. But they deserved it, always wanting us to write about the stars. Well, Matthew Blair is the star of the team! Plain and simple. Just like you said, based on the facts."

"He is that, at least now. You didn't do anything wrong. The paper is supposed to report the facts. They just don't like them. This new kid is a phenomenal athlete, period. There's nothing wrong with saying that. The city papers are reporting the same things. It won't be long before the state papers follow suit, and then the national media will start reporting on him." He stopped and rubbed the back of his neck.

"You think they can make good on their threats, like kicking me off the paper or closing it down?" I asked, afraid he might stop my articles.

"Not likely. Look, I want you to keep reporting the facts. We'll deal with their pressure as best we can. Okay?" He smiled, and I began to feel better.

"Okay." I hugged him, and he stiffened. I let go. "Sorry, just a reaction."

The bell rang for my next class and I headed for calculus, grateful not to encounter Alexis, Toby, or any of their friends along the way. For the first time in my high school career, I was glad Woodway had four thousand students clogging the halls and classrooms.

Finally, school was over. Lizzie and I had planned to meet in the journalism room after school, and I waited for her there. She was late, and I worried she had forgotten.

But soon I heard her characteristic fast shuffle, and she burst into the room, almost out of breath. "Mary, Mary! Something terrible has happened!"

I was afraid to ask any questions and blinked in silence.

She caught her breath. "Mrs. Poston and Mrs. Hall—they went to Principal Newman. I was in the office at the time."

"What for?"

"They are saying Matthew Blair is gay, that he hasn't been seen at any of the school dances or associating with any of the girls or acting like a normal teen boy would act. They say he acts oddly, like a loner, and that he must be gay, and they don't trust him around the other boys on the team." She stopped for a moment, taking a deep breath, before continuing, her eyes wide, "They demanded that the principal remove him from the team right away."

"What a bunch of bull. They can't beat his basketball talent, so they lie and cheat him off the team so their precious Toby won't be upstaged. Disgusting! Has he come on to any of the other boys? Did they say that?"

"No. They didn't. Just the stuff I told you. But it sounded awful."

"I can't believe they would stoop so low. The mega-bitches aren't going to stop until they get their way and run him off the team, out of the school too, most likely. We've got to do something. But what?" I asked, wanting to scream curse words.

Lizzie looked blankly at me. "I'm not sure there is anything we can do. You remember that girl who challenged Alexis for head cheerleader last year?

Mrs. Poston got her thrown off the squad. Something about her residing outside the district and lying about living with an aunt inside the district. That woman scares me to death, Mary. There's no telling what she will do. She always seems to get her way."

I thought for a few minutes, as we sat quietly. Then it hit me. "We can wait till basketball practice is finished and tell Matthew Blair what's going on. We can warn him so he can defend himself and diffuse the situation. What do you think?"

"It can work, if we tell him right away," Lizzie excitedly responded, regaining her smile.

We gathered our books and hurried for the parking lot outside the boys' locker room, jabbering about how we would tell him. There were other students around, some seemingly waiting for friends, others just talking, and I hoped Matthew Blair would come out the door where we waited.

Lizzie and I sat in her car, listening to the radio. Finally, the team members began to come out. Toby Hall and Cameron Fields led the others, and I pushed Lizzie's head down, not wanting to get into a confrontation with them. They got into Toby's red sports car and sped away, the car's engine hurting my ears as it roared out of the parking lot. I saw other players, but not Matthew Blair.

"Heck, he probably left by another door. Just our luck," Lizzie said with a sigh.

I kept up the vigil and felt better when he finally came through the door, looking for something in his backpack. "There he is. Let's wait here so no one sees us talk to him. He's coming this way."

Matthew Blair walked within a few yards of us, and we quietly got out of the car. "Matthew. Do you have a minute to talk?" I called out softly.

He looked my way, seemingly surprised. "Sure. You are . . . ."

I felt a blush on my face. "Mary Lawrence, and this is Lizzie Murchison, my best friend."

"Sure. You rode with us to one of the games, and you write for the paper, sports articles, I believe," he said, melting me with those blue eyes.

I was flattered he remembered. "That's right. But I'm working on a special article now, a little different. Matthew, we need to talk to you about something. Do you have a few minutes?"

He looked at me in silence, obviously waiting, those bright eyes capturing my attention, before I regained my sense of why we were there. "I don't know exactly how to say this, so I'm just going to do it. There are some parents who are saying really stupid, hurtful things—like that you don't seem to fit in here at Woodway because . . . well, because you don't socialize with any of the kids, you know, at the dances and parties. They're trying to make something mean out of it. Jealously, most likely."

"And?" he asked with a wrinkled forehead.

I continued, wondering how to be diplomatic. "Well . . . you aren't . . . gay, are you? Why don't you ask any of the girls out or go to any of the parties?"

He regained his smile. "Oh, I see. No, I'm not gay, not that that would make any difference. Gay people have the right to go to school and play basketball. They're humans too, with rights like everybody else. I don't socialize because I work and also spend a lot of time at the hospital visiting my mom. She needs me right now, with her chemotherapy. Dad passed away several years ago, so it's just Mom and me. That's the reason we came here, for Mom's treatment, I mean. And since my aunt and uncle live here, we felt a little better about being away from home. In fact, I'm waiting for my uncle to pick me up now, to go to the hospital. After that, it's homework and then work. I'm pretty busy with all that. Not much time for parties."

"That's great!" I stopped and looked at Lizzie, feeling better and glad we had talked. "I mean, we're sorry about your mom, of course, but I'm happy everything else is normal. You know how some people talk. We want you to get along with the other kids here at Woodway, clear up any problems. You know what we're saying."

"I understand. And thanks for the help. It's tough to fit into a new school, especially senior year. Everybody has their friends and groups. I hope you and Lizzie will be my friends," he said with a sweet smile.

I looked at Lizzie again, then turned to him. "That would be great. We'd love to be friends with you. Maybe we can do something. Lizzie has a car."

Matthew Blair peered across the parking lot. "That sounds great. Got to go. My uncle just drove up. See you at the game?"

Lizzie called out as he ran off, "We'll be there. Good luck."

"What a hunk from Heaven," she whispered.

I watched him get into a white sedan and sit in the front seat. An older man at the wheel talked with him before driving slowly away.

Lizzie and I slapped hands. "Lizzie, we've got to get the word out as fast as possible, call all of the best gossips. Wait till I tell people why he can't socialize with the kids. Who will criticize him? Working and visiting his mother in the hospital. What a great guy. That should put a sock in the mega-bitches' horn."

Lizzie chimed in, "And I'll mention this to Principal Newman in the morning. He always asks me what's going on in the school. That should about do it for Matthew. Yeah, Mary. I think we're going to win this one."

We turned and walked toward Lizzie's car. She was humming a Promise tune, "Wailin' on High." I felt the moment and hummed along. When we reached her car, Lizzie turned to me and said, "This calls for a celebration. Ice cream?"

"Sounds great! But not that diet stuff. Yuck, it can gag a maggot," I said, feeling better about everything.

She seemed happy. "No way. The good, fat-filled stuff. I even got some money to buy."

My mood was getting better by the moment. "Terrific! I'm broke, like always. But thank God for good friends with a little cash."

We laughed and headed toward our favorite ice cream shop, and all the while I could think of two blessed things: a state basketball championship and chocolate with almonds!

CHAPTER ELEVEN

Lizzie and I sat in the Lou's Creamery, and I finished the last bite of brown Heaven. I looked to see if anyone was watching, then quickly licked the cup.

Lizzie began to laugh. "Good to the very end. Want another one?"

"No. This was enough. Do we have time to do what we had planned? It's getting a little late. I guess waiting for Matthew Blair took more time than I expected."

Lizzie looked at her watch. "Sure, but we've got to hurry."

We walked quickly to her car and headed to the city pound a few blocks away. The sprawling white building soon came into view, and we pulled into the parking lot. I was eager to see some of my animal friends, causing me to jog into the place.

We entered a long vinyl-tiled hall that smelled like a cross between urine and pine cleaner. There were concrete cages with chain-link fronts, each one containing puppies of different colors, ages and sizes, all of them bunched at the fronts for attention, someone to stop and speak gentle words, or scratch a belly or a floppy ear.

I stopped in front of one cage and opened the gate to pick up a tiny white fur-ball mix, probably a lot of West Highland Terrier with some other small white breed, making it unsuitable for those seeking a purebred dog. The puppy flattened its body in my hand, heart beating wildly against my palm and legs trembling.

I held the part-Westie close and spoke softly, "It's okay little fella. I love puppies, just like you. You're a sweetie, yes you are. I just want for us to be friends."

A few ear scratches and kissing sounds did the trick; the small dog stopped trembling and its heart slowed.

I gently pushed ringlet fur out of bright eyes and saw that the puppy was looking intently at me, making me respond affectionately. "I bet some nice little kid will come and take you home, a good home where you can play in the yard."

I put the puppy back and closed the gate, and he stuck his nose through the chain-link, a tiny pink tongue licking continuously, and followed me with sparkling eyes.

We walked along the row of cages and I eagerly looked for a special little fellow with curly brown fur and a stub of a tail, a terrier mix I had gotten to know. He wasn't there, and I hoped some loving person had adopted him.

"You're kind of late today, Mary. Thought you weren't coming," came from behind me.

I turned to see Mr. James, a grandfatherly type who volunteered at the pound. He was looking at me through pop-bottle glasses, smiling in his usual friendly manner. Mr. James always appeared the same: denim overalls showing his short, round frame; big brown eyes; saggy wide face that reminded me of a Bloodhound; and a full head of white hair that looked like sheep's curly wool. His gentle voice seemed to reassure the puppies, just as it did me. He and I had become friends because we loved the puppies—kindred souls wanting to help creatures unable to help themselves. It always felt better knowing Mr. James worked at the pound.

Turning to the cage in front of us, Number 19, I asked, "The little brown terrier. You know, the active one that likes to lick your ear. He's not here. Guess someone adopted him, a nice family with kids, I hope."

Mr. James looked into my eyes. "Sorry. They took him away this morning, to be put to sleep. Him and his litter. I tried to keep them longer, but they were overdue. Nobody took them in time. A real shame."

"Gosh. He was so cute, liked me a lot. Always kissed my ear. I hope he didn't suffer," I said, feeling a warm tear on my cheek.

Mr. James took a tissue from his pocket and wiped the tear away. "No, he didn't suffer."

I cleared my throat. "You know, if I can just get another two thousand dollars, I can buy that van. They want five thousand, and I've collected three thousand from bake sales at the school. Then I can take a lot of the puppies to the retirement home. That will save them and help the old folks too."

"That's a great project, Mary, good for everybody," he said, putting the tissue in his overalls.

Lizzie touched my arm and softly said, "Mary, we need to leave if we're going to make Green Garden today."

I looked at the big clock on the wall. "Right. We have to go, Mr. James. I'll see you tomorrow. Thanks."

We hurried to Lizzie's car and left for Green Garden nursing home, the image of the lively little brown puppy occupying my thoughts along the way.

About fifteen minutes later, Lizzie and I pulled into the parking lot of the one-storey brick building shaped like an X, with the living quarters radiating out from the common area in the center. We entered, and I thought it smelled a lot like the pound, an aroma I hated. Lizzie and I walked down one hallway toward the rooms of several of the residents I had come to know on my visits. There was Mr. Washington sitting in a wheelchair along one wall outside of his room, not doing anything special, just sitting there alone.

We stopped, and I leaned down. "Hi, Mr. Washington. How are you feeling today?"

"I don't know what to do. Could you tell me what to do?" he asked with a pained expression.

"I would just rest. How does that sound?"

Mr. Washington gazed at the floor and mumbled, "If someone would tell me what to do I would feel a lot better. Can you stay here and talk with me, tell me what to do?"

"Sure. It's going to be fine. Everything will clear up. Just wait and see," I said, rubbing his arm.

He looked up again and blinked several times and his lower lip quivered. "Been a long time since anyone sat a while and talked. Makes me real confused. I don't like that." He stopped and slumped in the wheelchair.

Lizzie tugged at my sleeve, and I patted his arm. "I've got to go now. But I'll be back soon, and we can visit some more. Would you like that?"

"Sure wish I knew what to do," came ever so softly from his bowed head.

Lizzie and I turned and walked to the next room. It was down the hall a little and on the other side. I peered through the partly opened door, and in the dim light I could see Mrs. Cook in a flowered robe, sitting up in bed.

Lizzie waited in the hall while I went in. "Hello, Mrs. Cook. How are you feeling today?"

She looked at me, a smile spreading across her face. "Lena, I'm so glad you came. Knew you would come. Said to the nurse that you would. How's Mr. Cook? Did he get over that cough? Sure was bad. Thought it would kill him."

"It's Mary, Mrs. Cook, not Lena."

"You know, Lena, I sure have been missing you and Mr. Cook. Can we go home now? Me and Mr. Cook got to tend the garden, plant some tomatoes for the spaghetti sauce. He likes that sauce. My special recipe," the wrinkled woman said, her cheeks marked by heavy rouge.

"I bet your sauce is terrific. You look pretty today. Is that a new robe?"

The smile faded. "I wish Mr. Cook would come and see me. Been a long time, I think. Where is he?"

"I don't know, but I bet he's thinking of you right now."

The corners of her mouth fell and began to quiver. "He's not coming. I know it. He never comes, Lena either. Nobody comes. Sure is lonely here; nobody to talk with. Maybe tomorrow," she said, her voice trailing off. Mrs. Cook looked up at me and breathed a tiny sigh that carried faint words I strained to hear, "All gone. Just me left."

Lizzie called to me, "Mary, it's late. We've got to go."

I rubbed Mrs. Cook's back. "I'll come and see you again, real soon."

We walked quickly from the nursing home, Lizzie setting the pace. Soon we were driving home, each in silent thoughts, and I wanted more than anything to come back with the puppies that would bring some joy to Mr. Washington and Mrs. Cook and the others who had given up and were just waiting till the day they could leave Green Garden.

CHAPTER TWELVE

Thank God for the internet. Without it, I would have been lost. My "Middle East" query produced four hundred sixty-seven thousand nine hundred ninety-two articles I could access, if my eyes didn't fall out first. What was I thinking? Four hundred sixty-seven thousand nine hundred ninety-two? Who could read all of that and not go crazy? I decided to start at a good place: article number one, thinking maybe there was a good reason someone had put it there. It was entitled, "Middle East—Crucible of Hope, Cauldron of Fire," by Josylan Merriwether.

Scanning the fourteen pages of the article, I could tell that Josylan Merriwether was smart, probably one of those nerds who made all As and looked like a horse . . . or a frog, and never had a date because she was too busy writing long articles, no time for hair and makeup and trendy clothes . . . gosh, just like me!

But the material was good, thorough and well-researched, something I could rely on with confidence, and I mentally thanked Josylan for making my job easier.

I began to read the article, silently at first, but then aloud: "The Middle East is an anomaly—its most deeply affected victims and its most hopeful citizens being one and the same group, the children. For they are the ones being scarred physically and emotionally by the constant, house-rattling explosions and the openly expressed hatred they do not understand, and those deprived of mothers and fathers and siblings so badly needed but killed by the fighting. These are the same people robbed of an entire segment of their lives, childhood's blissful, innocent lessons, such as playful afternoons at peaceful parks and games important only for their social value.

"At the same time, the children harbor in their innocent hearts hope for this tumultuous land, perhaps the only hope. Most likely, only their hearts are capable of forgiveness and tolerance.

"Take, for example, the plight of Mohmmad Riza and his sister Sosha, of Nablus. They were promising junior soccer players, with dreams of playing on college teams—until their father and coach was killed by a mortar shell that fell on a local market. Now they sit in a tightly boarded house, not allowed to play outside, protected by a fearful mother who cannot forget or forgive the death of her husband or endure another loss.

"And, while many of the children do not understand the reasons for the intense hatred gripping their land, they do understand forgiveness. As little Sosha said, 'I miss my father. But I would forgive the soldiers, if they would stop killing us, and let us play soccer again. My father would like that.'

"The story of ten year old Moshe Solomon is strikingly similar. He was the victim of a bullet that shattered his body. Waiting for a prosthetic leg in a Haifa hospital, he showed no hatred when he said, 'It makes no difference who shot the gun. Bullets have all our names on them. I just wish the shooting would stop so I could play with my friends again.'

"The empty playgrounds are silent but echo powerfully the childish laughs that should fill them. It is this absence of childhood sounds that is so resounding. Attempts by well meaning adults to open various public areas to children, who have no political or military agendas, only the need to be carefree, have failed.

"For example, Aaron Wiseman, an old storekeeper, cleared a rutted, empty lot next to his small store of glass shards and broken concrete, hoping to bring the children out of their homes to play together. He expressed love for them, each day trying to reassure Muslim and Jewish children alike that they could be friends and play together.

"His efforts were not sophisticated, merely simple actions of a loving man, including . . . . Yet, they produced some positive results . . . .

"However, determined militants killed him by . . . and vowed to continue their terrorism, no matter the cost in human lives. The military authorities, equally determined, have promised retaliation for these acts of terrorism. The result is a killing field that has no safe harbor, even for the children.

"And yet, the hearts of these little ones may still be open to messages of peace that could change this land. Perhaps one girl, peering from a partly opened door, said it best, 'I would let you come in, if my father would allow it. But someday, I will have my own house, and then I will let you come in.'"

I closed the article, thinking about Josylan's words, wondering if any of the articles contained success stories. I scrolled through the titles of other articles, hoping to find a more upbeat story, something about places without violence and fear. But they all seemed similar: "The Middle East Gordian Knot of Death," "Human Suffering in a Holy Land," "Palestine and Israel—Lands of Perpetual War," "Jerusalem's Death Squads," and "Ancient Hatred Stalks an Ancient Land."

I laid my head down on the desk, weary of the continuous stories of conflict and killing, thinking that the puppies and old people were not as pitiful as I had thought. At least they had a chance to live. My mind began to swirl: jet planes screaming overhead, helicopters' engines making cannon-like sounds, bullets whizzing by, explosions in the distance, lifeless bodies of puppies stacked high in a trash bin, old people shuffling for cover, and death-filled darkness closing fast, all coming together in some incredible nightmarish soup of the mind.

Several days had passed, and today was the day I would know about my Middle East article, how it had been received by the other Woodway students. I was scared to death, afraid that the other kids would make fun of it, and of me. The article had been published in the *Woodway Gazette* the prior day. But I didn't yet know the other students' reactions because the paper had become available at the end of yesterday's classes. My doubts about the article kept driving my mood downward. My one skill, writing, might be no real talent at all. Maybe I was a total failure.

The article was probably melodramatic or shallow or stupid or plain gushy, failures that would get me stares and jeers from the kids who professed to know the meaning of cool, and tried continuously to tell the rest of us.

I wished Mr. Lawless hadn't made me write that article.

The ride on the yellow monster wasn't normal. It seemed to take forever. Maybe it was my fear of getting to school and facing the criticism I expected, and feared. The other school bus riders, mostly nerds like me, weren't helping the situation. They were usually my cohorts in non-coolness, kindred outcasts. But today, as I bounced in the hard seat, I could feel their mocking stares on the back of my head, and they seemed just as alien as the high school jerks and bitches who lived outside my world.

Finally, we arrived at Woodway, and I didn't know whether to sit in my seat and get killed by the traitor nerds as they walked by and gave close-up stares of disapproval or to get off and be killed by others waiting for me outside or in the school.

As I walked down the hall, I could feel the killer eyes on my back, thinking once again that I shouldn't have written that article for the school paper, that the kids didn't appreciate or understand it, that it would be a source of pain.

And then it happened, hell waiting in the hall. They were right in front of me, like a nest of killer bees—Alexis Poston, Paige Richelieu, Cameron Fields, and Toby Hall—whispering in a tight circle near my locker. I so wanted to keep going past them, but I had to get the books for my first two classes.

I took a breath, fumbled with the locker combination and let the tension out quietly. "Stay calm, Mary," I said to myself.

Their giggling stopped, and I heard a familiar, mocking voice. "Oh, Shoes, saved any lives in the Middle East lately? I bet you saved a whole bunch. Any humanitarian awards headed your way?"

I turned to them. "Very funny, Alexis."

Toby began to laugh, followed by the others, before they finally stopped and Toby said, "That jet lag must be rough, right, Shoes? Oh, you did go over there, didn't you, to get the facts? All that stuff you wrote, you didn't make it up, like everything else you write for that rag? Sure you didn't."

I glared at the jerk. "I didn't make anything up, Toby."

Cameron and Paige looked at each other before Cameron chimed in, sounding like an owl, "Who, you? Oh no. You never make up your articles. Not you."

Alexis continued the verbal assault. "Shoes, everybody at Woodway knows your MO. You try to get sympathy with your 'oh poor me' act. That's your effort for some attention, and it's pathetic. That article is more of the same, a lot of fiction you dreamed up to make people think you're somebody, when everyone is laughing at you."

Toby joined the others. "She's right, Shoes. Give it up. Stop telling lies all the time."

I was getting so mad I could have thrown up on Cameron's fancy sneakers. "You guys think you are so good, well think again. Let me tell you something that is absolutely true and factual. Toby, you and Cameron can't even carry Matthew Blair's jock strap between the two of you. That's how good you're not! And everybody knows it."

Toby and Cameron glared at me in silence. Maybe I had gone a little too far—hitting them where it really hurt. But it quickly occurred to me: nah, I did the right thing; they deserved it.

Books in hand and small victory won, I left them stewing, and, I was sure, scheming. As I hurried to class, sour thoughts made me grumpy toward everyone I saw, even the kids I counted as friends. I wanted to slap someone, to pay the bitches and jerks back for being stuck up and nasty.

Getting some fresh air seemed like a good thing, and I noticed a side door to the outside, some place away from the other students. I pushed it hard, slamming the door against the wall, immediately grateful no one was on the other side.

The door opened onto a sidewalk that went around the building to the teachers' parking lot. I walked away from the building, glad to be free of the criticism. A nearby soccer field looked pleasing, and I could smell the aroma of freshly cut grass. I closed my eyes and breathed deeply, before noticing someone sitting on one of the metal bleachers on the sideline. Though I couldn't clearly make him out, the boy looked familiar. I walked closer and realized it was Matthew Blair, his head down, looking at something in his hands.

As I approached, he seemed to be intently reading a newspaper, the school paper, its red *Woodway Gazette* banner clearly visible. I slowly moved closer, drawn by his attention to the paper, yet, not wanting to disturb him, but my movement must have distracted him from his reading.

He looked my way, his face not radiating its usual smile, and said, "I've been reading your article on the Middle East. It made me think about the people there, the children mostly. This is heavy stuff. How'd you get the information?"

I sat next to him, looking at the newspaper and trying to remember the articles I had used. "From the internet. There are a whole lot of stories about what's going on over there, the fighting on both sides and its impact on the people. One of the articles dealt mostly with the kids and how they are suffering, the ways the fighting is robbing them of their childhood, but also how they may be the only hope for peace. And, I guess, that's what I wanted to write about, you know, the chance for peace, slim as it seems."

He turned back to the article and read for a short time more, before asking, "This man in East Jerusalem, Aaron Wiseman, was he a real person?"

"He was, and the other people were real too, at least according to that article I read from one of the British papers."

Matthew Blair looked seriously at me. "His efforts to bring the children together, did that really happen the way you wrote it?"

I began to feel a little queasy at his questions, thinking he didn't trust me, like Toby and Alexis and the others. Was everybody going to make fun of my work? I closed my eyes and breathed deeply.

After a bit of stewing, I calmed down. "Yes, it's all accurate. But I really don't know if anyone continued his work and brought those kids together. His murder shut everything down. After that, the parents were afraid to let their children out of the houses. Most likely it's that way today. Pretty sad, isn't it? Guess they are all scared to death. Who wouldn't be?"

Matthew Blair read some of the article aloud: "Aaron Wiseman beckoned the children to his small shop, not just the Muslim children from the other side of Haifa Street but the Jewish children from his side as well. The sweet melons from his garden were the candy he hoped to use to get them together to be friends. Wiseman wanted to see them accept one another, to drive the hate from their hearts, so that they would stop killing each other.

"His plan seemed to be working, as the number of children coming to his shop began to grow, attracting the attention of adults whose hearts were filled with hate. One night, his store exploded from a powerful bomb, killing him and his dream.

"Now the children stay behind locked doors, unable to laugh together, their minds filled with fear from the gunfire and bombs that are their teachers. The place where his shop once stood is only rubble, adding to the sadness of a street where the children cannot dance or run or play or sing, made that way by angry hearts that will not soften."

Matthew's attention to my article changed my mind about him. He wasn't questioning me or my writing. I cautiously said, "Kind of melodramatic, right? Too gushy, I guess. People will probably laugh at it."

Matthew folded the paper and placed it in his backpack. "It touched me, Mary. I really hadn't thought that much about the children over there. It must be terrible, the kids being afraid to go out and play and hating each other, being terrified of death all the time. What kind of childhood is that? I wonder who will bring peace. Somebody has to, some person who can change hearts."

I didn't know what to say, thinking that I had no answer, but finally said, "It's awful. Nobody has been able to do anything about the fighting, not our president or any of the leaders over there. It makes me feel so insignificant, like . . . some boob who can't even write a decent article on the subject."

Matthew looked at me, his smile working its charm with those blue, clear eyes. "You aren't a boob. This is a good article, really good. It speaks to me, and I'm sure to others. You never know what it might do. You've got to have confidence in yourself, in the talents God gave you."

I could feel myself blush. "Oh, you're just saying that to be nice. I don't think I will ever make any real difference in the world. I feel like I'm drowning by all the stuff going on. What can a nobody like me do?"

The first period bell rang. We got up from the bleacher and headed for the building.

He opened the door for me, and, as I walked in, he said, "You might be surprised, Mary. You have a talent to write, to share your passion with the reader. That's a real skill, and it can change the world. Don't give up on yourself. You've got to have the courage to win the game. That's really what life is all about."

"What game?" I called out.

Matthew turned toward me, those eyes flashing their energy across the hall. "The one you're in right now."

I began to feel different about my article. Maybe it was better than I had thought. It might even do some good, somewhere, sometime, and the thought of it made me pass by Alexis, Paige, Cameron, and Toby, feeling no resentment toward them or their hard glares.

CHAPTER THIRTEEN

The Woodway basketball team had won sixteen games in a row and was ranked second in the state. School was fun, and many of the students' petty differences seemed to have evaporated. The *Houston News* had asked me to do an article on the team, and I had just finished my eleventh draft, not satisfied with the "facts only" approach used for the school paper.

Mr. Lawless walked up to me, the article manuscript tightly gripped in my hands and my eyes scanning the words in search of better ones.

"How's it going, Mary? You need to have the article finished soon. The editor wants us to e-mail it tomorrow."

I looked at him, feeling the frown on my face. "Okay, I guess. But it's not finished, not the way I want it, at least. I've gotten writer's block."

He tried some gentle guidance, saying, "Why don't you read it out loud? That always helps me. I'll listen and give you some tips. What do you say?"

I smoothed the wrinkled pages and began to read. "Woodway High School's basketball team is riding high in the state polls with a fantastic sixteen and one record, leaders of their district, and ranked second in the state. Led by the brilliant play of Matthew Blair, the team is cruising through its season, with only one game to go, an out-of-town contest against state leader Mountainview in San Antonio this Saturday. Never in the school's history has it had an athletic team ranked so highly and playing so well against other strong squads.

"Woodway's returning lettermen had made the basketball team highly ranked at the start of the season, but an early loss created doubt about the team. Matthew Blair, a six-foot-three-inch walk-on, changed things quickly. His special skill led Woodway to a come-from-behind victory in the second game with athletic defense and steady scoring. In fact, Head Coach Riley has commented that Blair's skills are beyond those of any player he has ever seen in the high school game.

"Yet, questions still remain about the team's ability to win against a very powerful Mountainview squad, led by seven foot Matu Obliqua from Nigeria, the top high school big man in the country with ten blocked shots per game, and by shooting sensation Carlos Vendi, averaging almost thirty points per game.

"Woodway answers with Blair, leading the state statistics charts with an average of forty-two points, twenty-one rebounds, and twelve steals per game. Woodway also has a strong supporting group of players with the play of six-foot-six-inch forwards Toby Hall and Cameron Fields.

"There is such great interest in the game that it has been moved from the Mountainview gym to the Alamo Dome. A crowd of forty thousand is expected from around the state, including university coaches and professional scouts.

"This game could decide the state championship at an early stage in the playoffs, as the winner is expected to be the team left standing at the state tournament in Austin later this month. While Texas has long been known as a football state, basketball is now king in the hearts and minds of many of the state's sports fans. This Saturday, the eyes of the nation will be on San Antonio."

"Too one sided? Maybe too much about Matthew Blair? Give me a chance to rewrite it. I can do it by tomorrow," I pleaded.

"It's a good article, Mary. Factual, interesting. It presents both teams, focuses on the main players, those the readers want to know about. I think it's finished. Did you spell check it?"

"A couple of times."

"Okay. Let's e-mail it. They want to put the article in Thursday's edition. I hear the game's going to be carried on TV. What an event it's becoming."

I studied the papers once more, then handed a floppy disc to Mr. Lawless. "Let's rock and roll."

He took it, and I got up from the table, gathering several books. My back was stiff, making me glad to stretch a little as I walked down the hall.

My locker was a welcomed sight, a place to unload the heavy books. But Mrs. Hall and Mrs. Poston were standing near it, whispering to Alexis and Toby. I didn't want to look in their direction, but Mrs. Hall's attention made me look at her. She had the most puzzling expression, a smile that was not pleasing or happy but more like a smirk, almost as though she knew something I didn't, something not nice or good, but hurtful.

It was hard to look away, and I felt uneasy as I caught sight of her walking in my direction.

"Everyone is talking about your articles on the team, Mary. You sure like that Blair boy, don't you? Well, things have a way of working out," she said in a very smug, assured way.

"What do you mean?" I asked.

She smirked again, almost hissing as she said, "You'll see. That boy isn't the person you think. He won't even be on the team much longer."

I reacted in disbelief. "What? That would be terrible now, just before the playoffs. He's the heart of the team. We couldn't do nearly as well without him. The team would probably lose early."

She looked down at me over her glasses. "That's only your opinion. As I said, you will see. Very soon, you're not going to be able to write any more about Matthew Blair, only about Toby and Cameron. I should have handled this properly long ago, before things got out of hand. But better late than never, as I always say."

Mrs. Hall returned to the others, and their laughing began. She looked at me once more and shook her head, their laughing growing louder.

I closed my locker and walked quickly away with a churning stomach. I knew she meant business and was sure Mrs. Hall could make trouble if she really wanted to. She had proven that many times with others she opposed.

I wondered what she was planning before thinking of my reliable source, Lizzie, always in the know from her job in the principal's office. Off I ran, toward Lizzie and the truth, hoping it wasn't too terrible. I rounded the corner and slowed down to walk discreetly into the office, and there was Lizzie, sitting at the desk, her head in her hands, and I knew it was bad, very bad.

I walked slowly to her. "Lizzie, what's the matter? You look so upset."

Her red eyes told me she had been crying. "It's Matthew Blair. He's going to get kicked off the team. Probably today. Maybe it's already happened."

I found it hard to talk. "But why? What's he done?"

Lizzie wiped her nose, then her eyes. "Mrs. Hall and Mrs. Poston just finished a meeting with Principal Newman. They told him that Matthew Blair was failing calculus, that Alexis had told her mother, and since she has the highest average in the class, a lot of people believe she can be trusted to know what's going on there. Mrs. Hall demanded that he be removed immediately, according to the rules. Mary, you know how hard Mrs. Benson is in calculus.

Most of the kids flunk or make Ds. As hard as it is for me to face, I bet Alexis is right. I hate her for doing this!"

It all seemed like a dream, as though I would wake up and shake the bad thoughts from my head and be glad reality was different. But then, Mrs. Benson, the calculus teacher, came in and addressed Lizzie in her usual, formal manner. "I'm here to meet with Principal Newman, about Matthew Blair."

Lizzie cleared her throat and softly said, "Yes ma'am. I'll tell him you are here. Just a minute, please."

I felt sorry for Lizzie as she stiffly got up and walked to the principal's office door. In slow motion she knocked, opened the door, announced Mrs. Benson, turned, and almost whispered, "He can see you now."

The door closed, and Lizzie put her ear to the wall next to the door. I blinked, my conscience telling me, "No." But curiosity won the internal struggle, and I followed suit. Through the wall, I could hear them well.

Principal Newman explained Mrs. Hall's accusation and asked about Matthew Blair's grade in the class. I closed my eyes and swallowed hard, not wanting to hear the response.

Mrs. Benson wasted no time answering. "Matthew Blair is certainly not failing. In fact, he currently has the highest average in the class, a ninety-eight point six. I was surprised that he understood the material so quickly and thoroughly, but he did. No, Mr. Newman, your information is very wrong. Perhaps jealously played a part in the unfounded rumor."

Lizzie and I looked at each other. We hugged, and I almost let out a yell, until I heard Mrs. Benson's steps and pushed away from the wall, sitting hard in the chair beside Lizzie's desk. Lizzie almost fell on my lap as she flew to her chair, just ahead of the door opening. Mrs. Benson walked past, her posture very erect and businesslike, and I forced a goofy, toothy smile.

Principal Newman came to the door, his face very serious. "Lizzie, see if Mrs. Hall and Mrs. Poston are in the building. If they are, tell them to come to my office immediately, and send for Alexis Poston too."

Lizzie and I gave each other high fives, and she quickly sprang into action, summoning the bitches to the slaughter. Oh, what a glorious moment that was, one never to be forgotten!

CHAPTER FOURTEEN

Lizzie and I were so excited, driving to San Antonio all by ourselves, free to see the sights, walk down the River Walk, shop in El Mercado, visit La Villita, stroll the Alamo grounds, and, yes, even go to the game with Mountainview. We were staying in a hotel on the River Walk, and it was all just too much. I felt like a grown woman, and everything seemed so good. We checked in the hotel and then hurried to get to the Alamo Dome for the afternoon game. I had to be there to see every moment of the contest for the school paper article Mr. Lawless expected.

We entered the arena, and the place was huge, larger than any basketball facility I had ever seen. It was rocking with cheers, applause, foot stomping, and music, the result of competing fans, bands, and cheerleaders.

I looked at the lighted floor far below. It appeared so small in the great building. "Gosh, Lizzie, I'm glad we have press passes. I think we're just behind our bench."

We made our way along the aisle, until we were at section five hundred, then down toward the floor to row four. I looked up and felt sorry for the spectators in the nosebleed section. The players would probably seem like ants to them.

Suddenly, the place erupted as the Mountainview players took the floor, their shiny white uniforms gleaming in the bright overhead lighting. I was stunned by the overall size of the team, with the big Nigerian towering above several other players, most of them taller than anyone on the Woodway squad. They began layup drills, which quickly turned into a dunking clinic that delighted the crowd, their hollers echoing off the walls with each jam.

I watched for a few unbelievable minutes. "Man, Lizzie, they're really good; even their point guard can dunk. Our guys haven't seen any team like this."

One of their players didn't join the others in the dunking exhibition but remained beyond the three-point line shooting long-range buckets.

Lizzie muttered, "Does that guy ever miss?"

The Woodway team took the floor to the roar of our fans, and our band struck up the fight song. The players looked snappy in their red uniforms, moving in intricate patterns while passing and dribbling, then forming two layup lines, and finally shooting from various distances in the field.

The horn sounded for the start of the game, sending both squads to their benches for the announcement of the starting lineups. The Woodway starters sat on the bench while the other players formed a gauntlet onto the floor through which the starters would run to center court. When Matthew Blair's name was announced, the entire place erupted.

Next, the announcer presented the Mountainview starters to the crowd, and their seven footer stood out like some professional player. I could see the highly defined muscles in his arms and wondered if anyone could stop him. The announcer said that they were eighteen and zero, making me think that no one had stopped him so far.

Toby Hall was set to jump against the Mountainview giant, who easily controlled the tip. Their guard quickly passed to their long-range bomber, Carlos Vendi, who let go a high-arching shot that bounced off the rim. Matthew Blair grabbed the rebound and threw it to Toby who shot a jumper that missed, but Matthew laid the rebound off the glass for two.

Lizzie was into the game. "How did he get there so fast? I thought he was at the other end of the court. He's super quick!"

Mountainview inbounded, the guard working the ball down court. The big center set up down low and received the pass, turning and dunking over Toby, to thundering applause.

Cameron took the ball out of bounds and threw it to a streaking Matthew Blair, way ahead of the defenders for an easy layup. Mountainview threw the ball in, repeating the play to the seven-footer, who scored over a double team of Toby and Cameron, our tallest players. Two Mountainview defenders anticipated Matthew's speed, hanging back to defend the fast break. But Matthew moved to the far wing, beyond the three-point line, drilling a perfect shot that put us ahead, seven to four.

The opposing coach called a time-out as our fans exploded in hollers, claps, foot stomps, and whistles, obviously delighted with the game's beginning. I strained to see the Mountainview coach point to Matthew and gesture wildly at his players, his red face visible across the court.

The teams took the floor. The Mountainview squad brought the ball down the court and passed it around the top of the key, until their guard threw a lightning pass to the big man. He faked left and pivoted right, finger-rolling the ball toward the glass over Toby's outstretched arms. Matthew Blair slapped it away, but the official blew the whistle and called goaltending, to boos from our fans. Cameron bounced the ball in to Toby who passed to Matthew for a medium jumper. A Mountainview player bumped him hard, but no foul was called. The ball missed its mark and was snagged by the big center who threw to their shooter, Vendi, for a three that barely moved the net. Mountainview now led by two, and our fans screamed and booed when Matthew's driving layup was disallowed for a charge.

The game seemed to settle into a frustrating pattern: Mountainview passing the ball into its center for close shots which were allowed even though the big man bulled his way over the defender or because of goaltending calls on Matthew Blair; and our team having only one effective offensive weapon, our Aussie, who consistently was bumped or slapped by one or two players without a single foul being called. Still, the game was even, Matthew somehow answering each made shot of the Mountainview team in spite of the hard body contact.

The clock was winding down with the score tied at eighty, sending the crowd into a nervous frenzy. Mountainview's Vendi took another long range shot that missed. Matthew Blair snagged the ball from above the seven-footer. He dribbled quickly down the court, but three Mountianview defenders waited under our bucket, and the other two double-teamed him on the sideline. Matthew passed to Toby for a short jumper from the baseline; a Mountainview player batted the ball off the rim, but goaltending wasn't called. Even I knew the defending team couldn't interfere with the ball as it bounced in the cylindrical area above the net. I screamed in disgust and frustration when we didn't get the goaltending points we should have been given by the refs. The Mountainview guard grabbed the rebound and quickly drove the ball the length of the court, passing to the seven-footer, who backed over Toby and Cameron for a basket and a two-point lead.

Coach Riley called time-out and huddled the team for one last shot. Mountianview positioned three players, including its center, under the basket and two players out high. Our team took the floor. I looked at the clock; only twelve seconds remained. Lizzie and I hugged each other, and I prayed. Cameron inbounded to Toby. Some of the crowd counted the clock down toward zero, while others screamed. Our guard took a pass and almost lost the ball to one of the quick defenders, but the Woodway ball handler regained possession and threw it to Matthew Blair. He didn't dribble or run at the basket but jumped high above two defenders and let go a long shot despite being knocked to the floor. The final horn sounded and the place exploded as the ball found only net. We had won by one point! Bedlam was everywhere. Our team mobbed Matthew Blair; I kissed Lizzie and then the old man sitting next to me; Coach Riley was hugging everyone.

But then it happened—the scoreboard didn't change to give us our three points.

I was confused. "What's happening? Where's our points? Is the scoreboard broken?"

"They disallowed the basket. The ref is motioning that the shot came after the final horn. But that's nonsense. I saw him shoot before the horn sounded. What a bunch of cheaters," the man next to me said after a curse word.

Loud boos filled the arena and our players stood silently and watched the Mountainview team's wild celebration. I felt so sorry for the Woodway guys, especially for Matthew Blair, whose face showed the red bumps from the beating he had taken.

I was boiling, hoping some Mountainview fan would get in my face so I could let him have it.

"This is so unfair. How can the refs do something like that? Aren't they supposed to be fair?" I fumed.

The man next to me answered. "Woodway got hometowned. The local people don't want to see their team lose, even some of the refs. It's prestigious to have an undefeated team. So these refs stole the win from you. It's sad, but it happens, especially when the game means something."

I turned and looked at him. "You know what my answer is? We had the better team, pure and simple. Everyone saw that tonight. We won. I hope we meet them at state. We'll show them and their fans, and those cruddy refs!"

"You're feisty," the man said with a smile. "I like that kind of spirit. Don't see it much these days, especially from a high school kid. Lots of you guys are too cool to get excited."

I turned to him. "I'm not so much feisty as I am determined to win, especially when I should. Somehow a person's got to have the courage to win the game—and we're going to do it!"

CHAPTER FIFTEEN

I sat in the journalism room, thinking about my next basketball article for the school paper, wondering if I should expose the biased refs and the politics in the game, even at the high school level.

Mr. Lawless walked out of his office, sat next to me and said, "You sure look serious. Want to talk about it? Talking out a problem can sometimes clear the mind and relieve tension."

"How would you feel about being cheated and not able to do anything about it? I want to say something, to scream and tell everybody how I feel, how the team must feel, especially Matthew Blair. Those refs let the other team kill him and did nothing. They didn't even call one foul on the other team. It's a miracle he scored anything."

Mr. Lawless sighed, obviously trying to be patient and helpful. "Mary, it's very hard to change the system. Politics, and worse, seem to get into most organized activities, especially if there's fame or money involved, and that includes amateur sports too. You can't beat those biased refs or the coaches who cheat or the kids that take steroids or the crooked people behind the scenes pulling the strings. There is simply too much corruption out there. It's sad because that corruption even invades amateur sports. Some of the officials, who are supposed to be watching, are a part of it or turn a blind eye. Don't split your head open trying to knock down that brick wall, Mary."

"That makes me feel helpless. Can we really change anything, I mean anything that matters? If the world is so screwed up, aren't there any good people who are strong enough and smart enough to fix things? Like the fighting in the Middle East, killing so many people, even innocent citizens—can't anyone bring peace there? Is everything going down the tube?"

His eyes became glassy and distant. "I suppose there comes along once in a while, probably a very long time, maybe only once every two or three thousand years or so, a rare person who does something great, rights wrongs, brings peace, diverts mankind from falling off a cliff, creates lasting hope. But that is a very, very special person, like someone God sends down to Earth to get us on the right track again, straighten out things from the mess we seem to make. Maybe that person will show up some day and make things right."

The bell rang, and I gathered my things for the next class. Hurrying to the door, I stopped to talk to Mr. Lawless again. "I hope God sends us someone like that soon. We need it, real bad."

As the day passed, my mind wasn't on classwork, distracted by swirling thoughts of things and people I disliked . . . or feared: Middle East killers, corrupt refs, puppy murderers, children who forget their elderly parents, Mrs. Hall, Mrs. Poston, their bratty kids. But finally the day was over, and I rushed outside to meet Lizzie.

She was waiting for me in the parking lot. "Hey, Mary. Want to do something before we go to the pound today? Have a little fun first?"

I looked toward the school building and saw Matthew Blair standing outside the gym. "Why's he there? Doesn't he have basketball practice?"

I walked toward him, afraid that Mrs. Hall had been up to her old tricks and somehow had gotten him kicked off the team.

"Hi, Matthew. No basketball today?" I warily asked.

He smiled, making me feel like a friend. "Not today. Coach wanted to give us a day off before the playoffs, to get a little R and R."

Matthew Blair seemed somewhat lost, and I wondered about his plans after school. "What are you going to do now?"

He looked around. "I don't know. My uncle is supposed to pick me up after practice, in a couple of hours. I called him about practice being cancelled, but he can't come now. He's tied up on business. Guess I'll just wait here, probably study a little."

"Would you like to go with us? Lizzie has a car. We were planning to do something, you know, have some fun before we visit the puppies in the pound."

"The pound?" he asked.

I explained, "Yeah, we go there a couple times a week to play with the puppies. They enjoy the attention, like babies."

He hesitated. "Well, I had planned to go see my mom at the hospital. I better wait here for my uncle to take me. Don't want to miss him."

"Could we change our plans and take Matthew to see his mother at the hospital? It's not very far away," I said as Lizzie joined us.

My best buddy was, as usual, super cooperative. "Sure. We'd be glad to. You guys ready to go? My car's over there, Matthew. Nothing fancy, but it gets Mary and me around."

Soon we were driving along Loop 610 toward the Texas Medical Center, Lizzie at the wheel, me in the other front seat, and Matthew in the back. It didn't take long for us to get to the Cancer Center.

"Look at that place. It's like a city, with those tall towers connected by all the smaller buildings. It goes on for blocks. Where's the entrance?" I asked, feeling lost.

Matthew directed Lizzie to a parking lot, then to an elevator that led to a long, brightly lit tunnel, at the end of which was an escalator. We rode it to a large lobby bustling with people.

"Matthew, how do you find your way in this maze? It's like a hundred office buildings put together." I sensed a goofy expression across my face, the kind you know is there when you are completely confused, and quickly tried to smile . . . or make some kind of normal face.

"The colored stripe system." He motioned to a series of painted lines on the floor.

"What?" Lizzie asked, a similar goofy expression on her face, making me feel a little better.

"You follow the colored floor stripe for your location, red, blue, yellow, or orange. Our color is yellow. It takes us to the right building, sometimes using people movers down the long halls."

Lizzie and I let Matthew take the lead, as he walked along a seemingly endless yellow stripe, bringing us to a bank of elevators, a third-floor walkway across a street, a long escalator, two long halls, and, finally, a hospital room. Lizzie and I waited in the hall while Matthew slowly opened the door and walked inside.

After a few minutes, he appeared at the door. "Want to come in? My mom would like to meet you. She's excited you're here."

Lizzie and I followed Matthew into the partially lit room, passing the first bed, its IV-connected patient asleep, and stopping at the foot of the second bed. The cards and flowers did little to make the gray walls seem more inviting.

I felt uncomfortable about what to say, until the patient smiled and extended her hand. "I'm Mrs. Blair, Matthew's mother. Thank you for visiting me."

She had eyes similar to Matthew's, deep blue, only faded, much like blue fabric bleached by the sun.

I shook her frail hand, followed by Lizzie, and Mrs. Blair continued, "You must be friends of Matthew."

She seemed sweet and easy to talk to. "Yes, I'm Mary Lawrence, and this is Lizzie Murchison, from Woodway. We're all good friends at the school."

She smiled sweetly, just like her son. "I really appreciate your bringing him to see me. Usually his uncle does. But their schedules didn't fit together very well today."

Lizzie bubbled. "Oh, we are glad to. Matthew is so nice to everyone. We just wanted to help him, especially since he's new to the school. You know, it can be kind of tough to fit in if you're new."

"We're thankful for your help and your friendship toward Matthew. It has been hard for him to move to Houston and leave his friends back home, especially his senior year in high school," Mrs. Blair said with a sigh, leaning back against a pillow.

Matthew patted his mother's arm. "It's been okay, Mom. The important thing is to get you the best care possible, and that's what we're doing in Houston. I'm happy to be here with you. Our family is together."

She grasped his hand. "You've become the man in our family since your dad died. You take good care of me, come here every day." Mrs. Blair stopped talking and released his hand.

"You need to get some rest. I'll come see you tomorrow," Matthew said, after he had kissed her forehead.

She nodded and closed her eyes. Lizzie and I tiptoed out. We waited for Matthew, until he walked heavily from the room and gently closed the door. None of us said anything, walking along the yellow stripe the way we had come. Finally, we were moving slowly on a long people mover down a white hall.

Lizzie broke the silence as we moved toward the lobby. "I hope she gets better soon, in time to see you graduate. I'm sure that will make her feel very proud."

Matthew turned to her, his eyes having lost their usual sparkle. "She isn't going to get better. The doctors say she has, maybe, a few months. I can't take her home because she's too sick. So we are just going to wait it out here. Do the best we can. Make every day count. I sure appreciate you and Mary visiting her. She gets awfully lonely in that room. The nurses are terrific, like family, but it's real tough in a cancer hospital with all the sick people. Lots of sadness."

I found it hard to say anything, wiping my eyes, before forcing words of encouragement. "Sure wish I had the puppy project going. I bet they would brighten her spirits."

"The what project?" Matthew asked.

Lizzie seemed happy to answer. "The puppy project. Mary is planning to save puppies from the pound by putting them to work visiting old folks' homes . . . ."

"And hospitals!" I added, before stopping to confirm my thinking. "That would save more puppies, maybe lots of them. You see, I've got three thousand dollars from bake sales at the school, in a bank account at the teachers' credit union, since I get a little better interest there. It's actually in Principal Newman's name. I only need two thousand more to buy a ninety-five van to haul the puppies around in. Won't that be great?"

Matthew looked down at me, the sparkle having returned to his blue eyes. "That's a terrific idea." He stopped talking and looked away, his gaze far off, somewhere I did not understand. But soon, he came back to the present. "But what about you, Mary? Aren't you going off to college? How can you do that project if you'll be attending college in some other town?"

"I'm not going off to college. No money for that. I'm planning to attend community college here, so I'll have some time to do the project. Still, it would be great to go away to a major college. But that's silly. I've got to be realistic, so I'll stay here. Besides, the puppies and old folks need me."

We finally got to the car and made it out of the multi-storey parking garage. Lizzie drove us along the building-shaded streets of the medical center and headed for home, and I played with the radio, looking for some good music. After a short time, I found it, a station playing Promise's "Cambio Bay." I closed my eyes, beginning to feel the words and melody sweep me away to some tropical island. I had the sense of gently swaying to an imaginary breeze.

Lizzie explained my weird behavior. "She's goofy about that band. Thinks they are the greatest people in the world. Their songs make her crazy, not dangerous crazy, just a little nutty. You'll have to excuse her."

Matthew laughed. "They are okay. I think some of the other groups are better, like the early rock groups. They were terrific, mainly because they created a whole new type of music. Promise probably learned a lot from some of those artists."

I turned quickly toward him and snapped, "You're crazy! Who could be better than Promise? They are the greatest band ever, sold many more albums, and made lots more money than any other group in history. Everybody on the planet loves them. Some people say they are the richest people in the world, by far!"

"How do you know?" he asked.

I shot back, "'Cause I read everything I can find on them, even from the internet, and there is plenty online, all kinds of articles." I stopped and thought about some of the information I had read. "But it's so strange that they are anonymous. Why don't they want people to know who they are and show off their mansions and exotic cars and custom jewelry? I bet they have expensive stuff all around the world, like a jet and a helicopter, and even a mega-yacht, all kinds of incredible things that make their lives great."

Matthew jumped in unusually fast, as though the discussion had struck some nerve in him. "Maybe they don't have any of that stuff because they don't care about it. Maybe they want people to hear their music and be lifted up by it, rather than focusing on them and a lot of useless things. After all, they aren't really important. God gave them the talents they have. They aren't responsible for any of it. And besides, some of those celebrities are weak people who couldn't do anything useful if their lives depended on it. They're vain, wasteful, frivolous, selfish, and terrible role models. They flaunt all their needless possessions while others go hungry. Promise probably doesn't want to be like that."

I couldn't believe my ears. He was making me mad. "Are you nuts? Promise is the greatest band ever, and they have every right to be rich and adored and happy with all of the most expensive things. You're just jealous, and I think that's very petty of you, Matthew Blair!"

He shut up, and I was glad because I didn't want to hear any more of his crazy talk about my idols.

After several uncomfortable minutes Lizzie calmly said, "Mary, Matthew didn't mean to run down Promise. You two just have different views, that's all. Say, tell you what, I've got three dollars and seventy cents. Anyone got any money?"

I shrugged. "Seventy lousy cents."

Matthew Blair checked the contents of his pocket. "I have two dollars."

Lizzie smiled widely. "Great. Then we have enough for the magic potion that fixes all things. Mends fences. Makes friends of enemies."

I looked at Lizzie, then at Matthew, his eyes radiating their blue magic, and began to feel better, before exclaiming, "Chocolate ice cream with almonds! Okay, okay. I forgive you. We're friends again. But no more bad talk about Promise. Off to Lou's Creamery!"

CHAPTER SIXTEEN

The next day was much better. I wasn't mad at anyone. That ice cream was amazing, but its effects couldn't last that long. The basketball playoffs were beginning and we were a top seed, having won our district. That meant we got a bye to the second round, giving Matthew Blair a little more time to heal before he had to go into battle again.

I breezed through my morning classes and hurried to meet Lizzie over some surprisingly good cafeteria Mexican food. It was cheese enchilada day, and I took mine with onions. Lizzie usually got to the cafeteria first, and that was critical on enchilada day. I could always count on her to get me an order before they ran out.

We happily babbled, our mouths full of the delicious Tex-Mex. "Lizzie, you want to go to the auditorium after this? They just finished the new pipe organ. They say it's huge, biggest in the city. I'd like to see it, maybe for a story in the school paper. You game?"

Lizzie looked serious. "I don't know, Mrs. Poston raised most of the money, and they say she hovers over the thing like she does Alexis. Do you really want to be around her?"

I enjoyed my last bite and licked the fork clean. "I don't care. Today I'm not mad at anyone."

Lizzie gathered up our mess for the trash. That girl was always so good at those domestic things. She returned to the table and said, "That's fine. I'm proud of you. You're becoming more tolerant. Let's go see that pipe organ."

We walked out of the loud room, and I was glad to leave the noise behind. Soon, Lizzie and I had come to the auditorium; impressive with its many rows of red-upholstered chairs running down an incline toward an elevated wooden stage with heavy red curtains the height of a three-storey building. And then

I saw the organ: golden pipes spreading out like an Oriental fan, pipes as tall as a house in the center, smaller ones arranged by size toward each side, to tiny ones at either end; and in the center of the stage there was a console with row after row of knobs and switches, more controls than I imagined were in the space shuttle, surely requiring a Ph.D. in *organology*. I wondered who could play the thing—probably nobody at Woodway, and then I thought it was probably a waste, like so much of the stuff at the school.

Lizzie seemed interested. "Come on. I want to get a better look at that monster. It's twice as big as the one in my church."

I followed her to the stage, climbed stairs, and walked to the organ. There were several other students, teachers, and parents looking in silence at the machine, obviously impressed.

I studied the pipes zooming toward the ceiling, then moved to the console. "It makes my brain hurt to think about all those gadgets. You'd have to know more than a brain surgeon to play it. Too complicated for the normal person."

"Not really, it's pretty basic," came from someone behind us. I turned to see Matthew Blair smiling, his blue eyes sparkling, and I was glad he wasn't mad at me. I wanted us to be friends.

"I don't know. It looks really confusing to me," I responded, turning back to the console.

He walked beside me. "Look, each control produces a unique sound, like different musical instruments in an orchestra, and the keys make different notes. So you can have horns and percussion instruments and woodwinds, all playing different tunes together or in succession. You just have to know which knobs produce what sounds and then learn a little keyboarding, that's all. No big deal."

"And I suppose you are an expert, Mr. Blair?"

Everyone around the console turned toward Mrs. Poston, a smirk on her face. "I don't think so. In fact, I think you don't know anything about organs, just a lot of BS you are trying to snow people with, like all that grandstanding you do at the games. Well, let me tell you something, you have no business here. This instrument is only for serious students and performers, like my Alexis. She started organ six months ago, and she can already play chords and two songs."

Mrs. Poston stopped her verbal attack, and I could feel my embarrassment. Alexis stood at her side, with an expression like her mom's, and I suddenly wanted to slug her.

Matthew Blair beamed that sweet smile in their direction, reinforced by electric blue eyes. He said nothing but moved to the console bench and sat down. Without looking, he flipped a switch underneath the console, and the sound of machinery came to life, accompanied by the sweep of a breeze. He looked at the keys and began to play "Chop Sticks," causing some of the onlookers to laugh.

Mrs. Poston stopped the laughter. "I think that is enough. You are going to break the instrument, and I know you can't pay to repair it. You had better leave, before I call security."

Suddenly, his fingers began to move across the face of the console, activating switches and knobs in some incredible pattern I couldn't follow, only seconds before his hands flew along the keys, and complex music poured from the pipes like a great symphony brought to life by the wave of a conductor's wand. It was classical music, Beethoven followed by Mozart, I thought, but energized into fast-paced, heart pounding arrangements. Other pieces quickly followed, the composers unknown to me, but I could make out trumpets, flutes, French horns, violins, drums, guitars, and clarinets playing together with other glorious sounds I could not identify. The power of the great machine vibrated my body, the low notes producing bone-rattling energy.

The entire chamber, meant for thousands, seemed filled to the walls with glorious music, running the length of the scales so fast I thought the machine was doing it by computer, until Matthew Blair's fingers slowed a bit from the incredibly fast pace at which they had been moving, and I knew this was no music any artificial brain could conceive. It was too brilliant, too creative, too spontaneous to come from anything other than human genius. I could feel the music, causing me to close my eyes and sense my being swept away to some other place and time filled with light, warmth, and energy. The music seemed to rush past me, producing some kind of refreshing sensation, like that caused by a clean wind on a Spring morning. Then the notes started their drive toward an expected climax: high, higher, very high pitched, and down fast to a unified, thundering conclusion that made my eyes spring open.

Thunderous applause and loud cheers immediately replaced the music, jerking me around to see a packed house. Every seat was occupied, and the aisles were filled. The entire school must have been there, but, as I scanned the faces of those I knew, I did not see Mrs. Poston or Alexis, and, instinctively, I knew they were gone.

Chapter Seventeen

"Mary, I am so excited about attending the press conference. Thanks very much for taking me as your assistant. Do you think all the major papers in the state will be there?" Lizzie bubbled as she and I walked to the gym.

I didn't slow my fast pace, afraid we would be late. "I heard all the big papers are going to send reporters, some of the magazines too, not just from Texas, but from around the country. It should be exciting."

The school's security officers stopped us at the gym entrance, and Lizzie and I proudly showed our press passes, compliments of Mr. Lawless and the *Woodway Gazette*. We entered, and I looked at the crowded center section bleachers.

"What a herd. I didn't know there were this many sports reporters in the universe," I said, scanning the empty seats for two together.

There were two seats on the far end of the throng, several rows up, and I hurriedly led Lizzie in that direction before they were gone.

We sat down and chatted, until Lizzie poked me in the ribs and whispered, "Look over there." She pointed with her chin.

I looked in that direction and cringed.

"How did they get in here? I thought this was supposed to be only for the press," I protested, focusing on Mrs. Poston, Alexis Poston, and Mrs. Hall several rows above us and dead center, dressed to kill.

My attention changed to Coach Riley leading the team into the gym from the locker room, to scattered clapping, and a few whistles. The team sat in folding chairs on the court, and Coach Riley stepped to a microphone. "I would like to welcome everyone to this Woodway basketball press conference, a first, I believe, for the school. What a crowd. We have forty-five minutes for questions and answers before practice. You may raise your hands, be recognized, and ask questions from your seats."

Hands shot up everywhere, reminding me of a revival I had seen on television.

Coach Riley pointed to a man on the first row, who stood and said, "Tom Fenton of *Universal Sports*. The number one and number two ranked teams in the country, Mountainview and Woodway, are playing for the state championship this Saturday. It will be carried on national television. How do you keep these kids grounded for a game of that magnitude?"

Coach Riley smiled. "With threats."

Laughter filled the room.

The head coach raised his hand. "Just kidding. No, these are great kids, and they understand the importance of the game. They go about their business seriously. It doesn't take anything special from me."

Hands exploded upward again, and the coach pointed to someone directly in front of him.

A short, jerky man shot up. "Yes sir, Coach, this boy you got, this Matthew Blair, he's averaging more than fifty points in the playoffs, against some tough teams. The kid has crushed those teams—in scoring, rebounding, blocked shots, steals, every phase of the game. Where in the world did you get him? Nobody seems to have ever heard of him before Woodway High School. Can you tell us a little about him and how he came to be on your team?"

Coach Riley cleared his throat and answered, "He comes from Australia. His family moved to Houston after school started. We were real lucky he moved into our attendance area."

The birdlike man wouldn't sit down, following with another question. "From what town? We follow the top players over there too. They play pro ball in Australia, like here, but I can't find any mention of him in the back issues of the Sydney or Melbourne papers."

Coach Riley turned to Matthew Blair. "What town did you live in over there?"

"We lived in Alice Springs, in the interior."

The hands went up again, and Coach Riley pointed to someone on one end of the group, a tall, white-haired man, who stood and calmly asked, "Mr. Blair, why don't you dunk the ball? I've seen you elevate until your waist is even with the rim. You could dunk every time, but you always lay the ball off the top of the glass. Why not dunk, like the other great leapers do?"

Coach Riley beckoned his star to the microphone.

"Dunking is fun, and I enjoy doing it. But I . . . try not to dominate the other team. You know, make them feel bad. If I score off the glass, then we get the points, without slapping the other guys in the face. That's my normal style of play."

Another man asked a question, without being recognized. "But don't you want to break the other team, show them who's boss?"

Matthew Blair smiled, his blue eyes sparkling. "No."

Uneasy chatter rippled through the crowd until a very large man stood and said deeply, "Sam Bethune, *Basketball Times.* Mr. Blair, do you understand that you are saying something completely contrary to what most coaches are teaching in competitive sports these days? I don't know of any coach today who doesn't tell his squad to overpower the other team, dominate them. It's that mental contest that determines the winner. Why don't you agree with that?"

Matthew Blair straightened his posture. "Because you don't need to hurt the other guy to play the game. It's wrong to make the other team feel like losers. They aren't losers. Sports should be fun, something to lift people up, not bring them down. I understand about the mental competition, and I want to have confidence, but I also want to control my emotions as best I can. At least that's my plan. Can't say I always follow it, though."

A man near us stood and spoke loudly, "Allen Ross, from the *Western News.* Mr. Blair, are you interested in a professional career right out of high school? I talked with some pro scouts who said you are ready right now, that you can play at the top of the pro game today, with your incredible speed and leaping ability. Do you have any plans to do that?"

Matthew Blair looked our way, a slight smile on his face, and I silently mouthed his response. "No."

The *Western News* reporter remained standing. "Why?"

Matthew Blair's smile faded. "Because I have other things to do, more important things. Sports isn't my top goal. I'm going somewhere else with my life. I want to just enjoy my senior year here, and basketball is fun for me."

The place erupted in loud talk among the visitors, and I watched the last questioner shake his head and mutter, "What a waste."

Coach Riley held up both hands to quiet the crowd. "Please, you are here to ask about the team and our upcoming game. Let's have relevant questions, rather than personal ones."

Hands shot up again, and the coach recognized a woman in the middle. She stood, raising her voice. "Coach, is it a motivator that all the video shows that Woodway actually won the prior game against Mountainview? That last shot clearly left your player's hand before the buzzer, but the refs disallowed the bucket and you lost the game. Does that make your players more determined to win the championship game against Mountainview or does it hurt their spirit?"

Coach Riley became serious. "We try not to dwell on the past. What is done is over, and we can't change that. We are taking the championship game as a new challenge, a new opportunity."

The head coach was busy listening to another question as I looked at Matthew Blair, wondering how he felt about losing that game and thinking that the question about the Mountainview loss had stirred some emotion in him. I noticed that his eyes were still flashing blue twinkles, but, rather than being their normal round shape, they formed narrow slits, concentrating energy in a way I had not seen before.

Chapter Eighteen

The Austin State Dome was alive for the state championship game. Spectators filled every seat in the futuristic glass arena. Our cheerleaders tumbled in front of the Woodway section to thundering applause from thousands of fans wearing red shirts. The Mountainview cheerleaders were dancing before a sea of white, moving to the beat of their band's toe-tapping music.

The teams had warmed up and left the floor for their locker rooms. I could feel the tension building, as everyone around Lizzie and me chatted nervously: "Could we really beat Mountainview? Was the big Nigerian unstoppable? Was he really seven feet four inches tall, as some experts had said? Did their three-point shooter vow to score sixty points in this game? Could he really do it?"

I turned to Lizzie, feeling my nervousness. "I hope all of that talk is a lot of bologna. Otherwise, my article will be pretty sad."

The Mountainview band boomed as their fans loudly welcomed the team to the court, singing the fight song and pounding out its beat with thunderous foot stomps. The Mountainview team circled in the center of the court, arms locked around shoulders, and swayed left and right. The Nigerian center, Matu Obliqua, towered above the rest, and I thought the bleacher talk must be right—he looked even taller than professional seven footers I had seen on television. The other Mountainview players went into some incredible weaving drill, ending with each player dunking the ball, all of them. Then their three-point shooter left the others and started drilling long shots, one after another as he circled to his left across the floor. After he had made several baskets, I began to count his buckets: "one . . . four . . . eight . . . eleven . . . ," until he finally missed at thirteen.

I looked at Lizzie. "Gosh."

My focus quickly turned to Woodway's red warriors streaming single file onto the court to the school's fight song. Our fans sounded good. "Woodway together, always remember the red; family bound forever, whatever may lie ahead. Woodway forever, crimson shades lighting the sky, for all of us so very blessed, to be from Woodway High."

I started to feel goose bumps on my arms, but I fought to hold back the tears. It wasn't good to let your emotions get out of control—a hard lesson I had learned as an orphan.

The starting horn sounded, driving the teams to their benches for the announcement of the starting lineups. Woodway was announced first, with Matthew Blair given the honor of being the last starter introduced, receiving a standing ovation when his name boomed over the public address system.

Mrs. Hall, sitting just to my left, scowled.

Mountainview's fans began to holler, clap, stomp, and whistle so loudly I had a hard time hearing the announcer say the names of their starters. But when their big man was introduced last, I thought the roof would come off of the great arena.

The teams huddled around their coaches, before taking the floor, obviously receiving last-minute instructions.

One of the television cameras was positioned at half-court. I watched the lens go in and out, pointed directly at the place where the game would start. Toby Hall stood there to jump center against the Nigerian giant.

The ball was tossed, and Mountainview easily controlled the tip, quickly passing to their three-point shooter, who let go a long shot, but Matthew Blair somehow came from nowhere to slap it away as it left the shooter's hand. Cameron Fields snagged the rebound and began to dribble toward our basket, passing to a streaking Matthew Blair for an easy layup. Mountainview inbounded, but Matthew Blair stole the ball from their point guard and hit a three. The crowd was going crazy, keeping me from noticing the time-out called by the Mountainview coach. As his team gathered around him, I could see that their coach was mad, his wild antics telling the entire story.

The horn sounded, and the teams took the floor again.

Before play started, someone called out, "Fight," and people screamed. One of the Mountainview players was hitting Matthew Blair, as he backpedaled, his arms protecting his face. A referee quickly moved between them and sent the Mountainview player from the court. The ref ran toward the Mountainview coach, pointing directly in his face. Loud boos filled the arena and the opposing coach hung his head.

After order was restored, Mountainview's point guard came close to the end line and received the inbound pass. He quickly dribbled the length of the court and passed to Matu Obliqua. The center whirled, his right hand holding the ball high, but Matthew Blair was there, much higher, to steal the ball from the wide-eyed Mountainview center. Matthew Blair was at the other end of the court before any defenders could catch him, laying the ball high off the glass for another score.

Lizzie hugged me. "They can't stop him, Mary, can't score against him either. This is getting ugly, and I love it!"

I hugged her back. "I love it too! I said we could win this game. I knew it!"

We continued to hug each other as Matthew Blair took the game as his; he scored on almost every offensive possession, sometimes hitting long three-pointers and other times streaking to the glass for uncontested layups, his speed unmatchable by any of the defenders; he stole the ball again and again; he blocked almost all of Matu Obliqua's shots; and he got almost every rebound.

Before the first half ended, Coach Riley pulled Matthew Blair with us ahead fifty-six to seventeen. The halftime horn sounded, and, as the teams went to their locker rooms, it was like some huge stereo failure: the Mountainview side was dead quiet and the Woodway side was breaking eardrums.

Someone from behind us put a bear hug on Lizzie and me and screamed, "It's over! They're finished. Mountainview just wants for it to be over so they can go home. They know they can't beat this guy. He's crushed them! What a clinic!"

I peered at the other team and immediately felt sorry for them. Their heads were down, and they moved like old men—no energy, emotion, or purpose. Then I saw Matthew Blair trailing our team off the floor, but there was something very different about him. His blue eyes had lost their sparkle. The tight slits had given way to wide-opened lids, almost like those of a frightened child, and I knew that he was feeling the other team's pain.

CHAPTER NINETEEN

My story about Woodway's basketball team winning the state championship was tougher than I had thought it would be. Gosh, why couldn't I think of anything to write? We hadn't just beaten Mountainview; we had destroyed the previously number one ranked team in the state and in the nation. What was my problem? I got tired of having the creativity of a potted cactus and decided to take my writing outside of the journalism classroom, hoping the fresh air would stir some creative juices.

Out the back door I went, to a small concrete area that overlooked our football practice field. I sat down, enjoying the green grass and pretending it was some romantic country setting that would inspire me . . . in a minute or two, maybe, hopefully.

"Gosh," I said, feeling nothing except writer's frustration.

"What's the problem?" came from behind, causing me to turn and see Matthew Blair walking up. His blue eyes still had that same lifeless appearance I had seen at the end of the first half in the championship game.

"I probably should be asking you what's the problem," blurted from me.

He sat down. "Oh, I don't know. Maybe now that basketball is over, I just have too much free time. You know, no practice. My schedule is kind of off. I'm just chilling till my uncle picks me up for the hospital."

"That's not all. Couldn't be. Something else is bothering you. Want to talk about it? Somebody told me that talking out a problem can help. Want to try?"

He looked down and softly said, "I feel real bad about embarrassing those Mountainview guys. They sure looked whipped after the game. Their fans too, lots of parents and grandparents with long faces. They didn't deserve that."

I felt my nose wrinkle. "You just did your job, extremely well of course, but it was your job to win. And you did that. That's nothing to be ashamed of."

"But it wasn't my job to destroy them, and their pride. To ruin the season for all those people."

I couldn't believe my ears. "Matthew Blair, you just paid them back for beating you up in the first game. For cheating. That's payback in sports!"

He faced me squarely. "Look at me, Mary. Do you see any of those bumps or bruises on my face?"

I looked at the clear skin on his face and shook my head.

He continued. "They all healed, gone. But the hurt I put on those other players will never heal. They will always live with that lopsided loss. What was the final score? I stopped counting."

I swallowed, beginning to see his point. "One hundred and six to forty-three. But Coach Riley played you only a few minutes in the second half, and Toby and Cameron scored a lot. That made Mrs. Hall real happy. I saw her after the game, and she was all smiles, for a change. Even gave me a hug! That was good, right?"

Matthew Blair chuckled. "Yeah, that was a little good that came from the game, I guess." Then he became serious again. "But I let my emotions get the best of me, Mary, and it hurt a lot of people, especially those fans. I could have won that game and let it be close. But no, I had to go all out to show them. I guess the thought of those biased refs in the first game made me mad. But that's not what it's about."

I didn't understand him. "What are you saying? What's the 'it' you are talking about?"

He looked down. "Life."

I shot back. "Life? What about that basketball game? It was a very important life activity. It was important to me, and to our fans, to the whole school, to Houston. Wasn't it worth doing to the max?"

He looked up at me. "It was only a small part of a much bigger game, and I blew it, slammed a lot of people. They didn't deserve that. A person has got to understand that he is given talents by someone else, to use in the best ways possible. And that means helping people, not hurting them."

"But didn't you help Woodway?"

"The smart person can do good things without making others feel like dummies; the rich man can spend his money for poor people without making them feel useless; the great athlete can win without injuring other players. You see, Mary? Talent has responsibility, or else it hurts people, instead of doing some good. And if you do that, you screw up a bigger plan. The real contest is how we play against ourselves. There's always that other side of each of us, pulling us down, wanting us to be selfish or mean or materialistic, and we have to beat that other side. But I didn't do that."

I sat quietly, understanding for the first time what he had meant about "winning the game." It was the game with myself, and I began to see an entirely new life, one not about my red hair or plump figure. I looked at the legal pad in my hands and realized I had been writing the first words of the basketball article: "A packed Austin State Dome saw a great struggle between two powerful teams, one tall and gifted from the Alamo City and the other fast and athletic from the Space City. Rarely, if ever, have the fans been treated to such a sports contest, and the players from both teams will live with the memory that they participated in one of the most incredible basketball games ever seen, at any level. Mountainview's players showed their awesome . . . ."

CHAPTER TWENTY

"Lizzie, come on! We're going to be late," I called out, really getting into the spirit of shopping.

"Okay, okay. I just have to put up my books," she said, a smile lighting her face.

We got into her car, looked at each other and said together, "Mall, here we come."

Lizzie pulled out of the school parking lot and headed for the freeway. Once we were out of heavy traffic and in the slow lane, she whispered, "Want to hear some gossip?"

I whispered back, "Sure, but why are we whispering?"

She giggled. "Cause it's juicy."

I wrinkled my forehead. "Oh, that makes sense. Come on, give. What's up?"

She glanced at me for a micro-second and bubbled. "The head basketball coach from Southern States is coming to the school tomorrow to meet with Matthew Blair. They say he's going to offer a full scholarship and everything, right in Principal Newman's office. Isn't it exciting? States has one of the top college basketball programs in the nation. Even I've heard of their teams. They're great."

"How did you find out?" I asked.

Lizzie giggled uneasily. "The wall, of course. Am I terrible?"

"Yes. Do you think I could listen tomorrow?"

Lizzie raised her hand, and I gave her a high five.

As we drove, Lizzie handed me an envelope. "Happy birthday. How's it feel to be a grown woman?"

I began to turn all mushy inside. "Lizzie, thanks. You're such a terrific friend. But you didn't need to, really. God, you're too good to me. Really."

"Oh shush. We're best friends. Go ahead. Open it," she commanded.

I lifted a white card from the envelope, its simple design appealing to me. On the front cover, two yellow-feathered chicks sat together above the caption, "Friends forever." I turned to the inside and gasped to see chicken parts in a frying pan, above, "Even in tough times."

I hollered, "Lizzie Murchison! Thanks for the twenty bucks."

"Now you have some shopping money, how much in all?"

I pulled several bills from my pocket. "Let's see, fifty from Grandma, ten I had, and twenty from my best buddy, Lizzie. That makes eighty dollars. I'm rich. I can buy all sorts of stuff at the mall. Onward to stuff!"

We laughed hard, until my side hurt, making me settle down. "Lizzie, how long have we been friends?"

She stopped laughing and thought for a moment. "Oh, I guess since freshman year."

I slouched in my seat. "Exactly. We met in freshman English, Mrs. Tisdale, and just hit it off. I invited you to my birthday that year. My mom took us to eat in Kemah, on the water, and we felt like big stuff. Remember? And . . . ."

"Red hair and lard, red hair and lard, I'm a disaster!" Mary Lawrence yelled at her mother.

Nelda Lawrence calmly responded, "You are not a disaster. You are just a teenager. High fashion looks come later."

Mary Lawrence closed her eyes and stomped. "Red hair and lard, and it's all your fault!"

Nelda Lawrence studied her daughter for several seconds. "Okay, it's all my fault. So sue me."

The young Mary said, "I will. Know a good lawyer?"

Her mother laughed and asked, "Isn't that a contradiction, a good lawyer, that is? Aren't they all bad?"

Mary Lawrence whined, "Would you please be serious? I'm talking about me and how I look to other people. That's important! Please be serious."

Nelda Lawrence answered, "I am being serious. I think you're right. So what?"

Mary Lawrence burst into tears. "What? So it's true. I am a total and complete disaster. Nobody will ever love me. I hate myself. Nobody cool is coming to my birthday party, not Alexis or Cameron or Toby or Paige. I'm such a putz."

Nelda Lawrence remained calm. "Your friend Lizzie said she is coming to the party, and your other friend, Agnes, said she would be here too."

Mary Lawrence turned away and cried out, "Agnes? She plays tuba in the marching band! Oh great, a whole herd of fat cows, together for everyone to laugh at. Moo, Moo, Moo."

Nelda Lawrence grasped her daughter's shoulders firmly, the woman's patience clearly wearing thin. "Mary Lawrence, that is a lot of nonsense, and you know it. Look at yourself: you're a very good student, all As in school, a gifted writer who has written poetry and stories, someone with a fun personality who has good friends, and you are blessed with loving parents who adore you. If you aren't grateful for God's gifts, He may take them away. Remember that, Mary."

Mary Lawrence looked up at her mother, feeling ashamed, and hugged her. "I'm sorry, Mom. You're telling me the truth, aren't you? I mean, I'm not a total disaster, right? I hope not. Mom, will you always be here for me?"

Nelda Lawrence returned the hug. "Always."

"Where are we going to eat for my birthday? I'm so hungry."

"Your favorite place, Smitty's on the Boardwalk, for fried shrimp."

"Yeah, fried shrimp and baked potato!"

The doorbell rang. Mary ran to the door. "Lizzie! We're going to have so much fun. We're going to the Boardwalk for seafood, and Mom is taking us shopping after that. They have lots of great stuff in the shops there, and you gotta help me pick out my gifts. Like some neat jeans or earrings or stuff for my room."

Lizzie bubbled, "Oh, how fun. Maybe your mom will let us find some cool songs on the car radio. Mary, have you heard that new band, Promise? They are so totally cool. Everybody's going crazy over them. They say people around the world love them, that they're becoming mega-popular super fast."

Mary Lawrence giggled. "Yeah, I heard one of their songs. Awesome! They are so deep too. I'll buy one of their albums. Will you help me pick it out, Lizzie? And then we can go looking for some other things."

"I hope you aren't planning to dollar me to death," came from Mary Lawrence's father as he walked into the room, a serious expression sending her mood downward.

Mary blinked at him. "What are you saying, that my birthday isn't worth spending money on?"

John Lawrence looked at his daughter over thick glasses hanging low on his broad nose and defended himself. "We need to watch our money. It doesn't grow on trees, you know. My business isn't making what I want, at least not yet. Those big discount stores are selling hardware and lumber so low. It's tough on the little guy, like me. We've got to be careful right now. That's all I'm saying."

Mary blurted out, "But Dad, can't we just have fun, buy a few things on credit, like other families? And stop worrying so much all the time, especially about money?"

He pointed at her. "Credit, for discretionary things? That kind of thinking is stupid, Mary. It will drive us into the poor house. Is that what you want, for me to file for bankruptcy?"

Mary began to feel her eyes become heavy with tears. "No, I don't want that. But, it just seems like some of the other kids have neat stuff . . . and . . . we don't. It would be nice to be able to buy a special dress or some pretty jewelry or that Westie puppy I've been wanting."

John Lawrence snapped, "There will be no dog. We can't afford those vet bills. And the rest of those goods are worthless, just something you will forget about in a couple of weeks. We don't have the money for all that nonsense, young lady."

Nelda Lawrence moved between them and held up a hand. "That will be enough, John. We realize the need to be careful with money, and, for the most part, we are. But today, we are going to forget about that. We have the money for our daughter's birthday. This is going to be a fun day for Mary and her friends."

Mary Lawrence hugged her mother, as John Lawrence shrugged and shook his head. The doorbell rang; Mary's face brightened.

She and Lizzie bolted for the front door. Mary flung it opened, and the girls cried out in unison, "Agnes!"

The newcomer walked in, seeming subdued for such a festive occasion. Mary placed a hand on Agnes's shoulder. "What's the matter? You look kind of sad."

Agnes Grunfeld began to cry. "Those stupid cheerleader tryouts. I didn't make it. I tried my best, really. But I didn't make the squad."

Lizzie patted her on the back and offered comforting words, "It's okay, Ag. You did your best. That's all you can do. Forget about it. There's lots of other things to do."

Agnes dried her eyes with her sleeve, cleared her throat, and said, "I know. But it all seems so unfair. It really hurts, like I'm no good."

Mary asked, "What do you mean?"

Agnes said, "Oh, Alexis, and her buddies, Tiffany and Paige. They made it. But it wasn't fair. They had a private coach there, and he was buddy buddy with the judges. Seemed to know them. Talked to them a lot. And I just knew Alexis and the others would make it. And sure enough, they were the first ones chosen. I really wanted to make the squad, and I was just as good as they were, better on my flip-flops. It's just not right!"

Mary and Lizzie looked at each other, before Mary turned to Agnes, wanting to help more than anything else at that moment. "It's going to be okay. There will be sports and choir and band and parties, lots of other stuff for you to do, some really good things. Let's just be friends and have tons of fun today. And we can be real mad at Alexis and Tiffany and Paige and hope they fall on their rears. And who knows? Maybe they will, in front of everyone at the football game."

The three laughed and bounced into the living room, led by Mary pulling them toward her smiling mother and knowing that this would be a good day, one to remember forever.

"Mary? Mary! You okay?" Lizzie asked.

My mind returned to the present. "Fine. Just thinking, that's all."

Lizzie seemed concerned. "You sure looked far away, like you didn't even know where you were. It kind of worried me for a minute."

I smiled and tried to reassure her. "Don't worry, I'm terrific. Who wouldn't be on her birthday? This is going to be a very good day, with my best friend, one to remember."

Lizzie pulled into the mall parking lot. "We're here. Where do you want to go first?"

I didn't hesitate. "The cafeteria. They have great fried shrimp!"

CHAPTER TWENTY-ONE

The next day, I wore my new jeans Lizzie had helped me pick out at the mall, not the two-hundred-dollar designer ones, but a nice pair anyway, and I felt pretty spiffy, at least better than when I wore those overalls. Maybe that little bit of rouge had helped. I was feeling so good that I didn't even notice the bitches when I got off the yellow monster.

Lizzie came running up and cupped her hand around my ear. "Mary, he's here, in Principal Newman's office."

I was confused. "Who?"

"You know, the head basketball coach from Southern States, like I told you yesterday, to offer the scholarship to Matthew Blair," she impatiently explained.

I said, "Oh. Oh! Is it over? I hope not."

She quickly responded, "No, but we have to hurry and see our friend—you know, Mr. Wall."

I began to jog for the principal's office, dodging students clogging the halls. In a few minutes, we were in Principal Newman's outer office, and Lizzie looked around before beckoning me to be seated in a chair. Matthew Blair came into the room shortly after we were settled.

He stopped and looked at Lizzie. "I'm supposed to meet someone here. Am I early?"

Lizzie sat very straight in the secretary's chair, appearing quite professional. "No. He's in the principal's office, just him and another man. Principal Newman said you could meet in private there. He's using another office. You may go in."

Matthew Blair nodded at me, walked to the office door, and knocked before entering as two men stood up and greeted him warmly. Then one of them closed the door. Lizzie and I sprang from our seats and pressed our ears to the wall next to the door like a couple of suction cups. The connection was great. I could hear them very well.

"Matthew, I am Coach Steve Coy, and this is my assistant, Coach McDermot, from Southern States University. I take it you have heard of our basketball program?"

"Yes sir. I believe your team finished second in the national tournament this year."

"And we finished second the year before too. We are always among the top teams in the country. That is why we are here. I guess you have received a lot of letters and calls from other schools, right? That's normal for the top high school players."

"Yes sir, quite a few," Matthew Blair answered.

The coach's voice was commanding. "Well, forget about them. They can't offer what States can. Have any pro agents called?"

"Yes, a couple. One has been a little insistent, even came by the house."

Coach Coy snapped, "Ignore those jerks. They'll only screw up your college eligibility. Don't sign anything. I will get you a good agent at the right time."

The coach stopped for a moment, following with a different tone of voice, low, slow and sure. "Son, I believe in getting to the point, so I'll be very blunt with you. We have studied you carefully, have a lot of tape on you and a number of scouting reports, even a computer analysis of your skills. And I have to tell you that, quite honestly, you have the most incredible talents we have ever seen. I mean the absolute best. Of even the top players we see in college or the pros."

"Well, thank you, sir," came the modest sounding reply.

"Don't thank me. Thank your mom and dad. Son, I'm not trying to flatter you. I'm just stating facts. You are only six foot three inches tall, but you play like an eight-footer, higher than any player we've measured on the computer. Your vertical is, honestly, off the charts. No telling how high you can really leap. A ten-foot basket is obsolete for you. And your speed . . . well, it's almost superhuman. Do you know how fast the top players are, the really great ones?"

"Not really," came the reply.

"Matthew, we know from the computer that a player of that caliber is about nineteen percent faster than the average professional athlete. We can determine an athlete's speed very precisely from putting video of him on the computer. It tells us exactly how fast an athlete is, as compared with a model of a normal pro player. And we can do that with any athlete."

The conversation stopped, and I wondered if we had been discovered, almost making me leap backwards.

But then the head coach continued, "Son, do you know how fast you are, by our computer, that is?"

"No sir."

"You are twenty-eight percent faster than the average professional athlete. They are moving in slow motion as compared to you. Even the great players aren't capable of keeping up. You are like some unique product of nature, different from everyone else. God knows what you could run the hundred in. I'm sure it would be a world record, probably much faster than the current one. Or you could probably shatter the high jump record or score a touchdown each and every time you ran the football. But those things are meaningless, 'cause they can't offer you the financial potential that I can, at least when you count the entire college and pro basketball package we can put together."

There was one of those pauses again, followed by deliberate words from the head coach. "I want you to come to States and play basketball for us. You will start right away. But I'm willing to pay for it. You can have anything you want, new car, money, apartment, just name it. I can give you anything, in addition to a full scholarship."

"But I don't really want those things," came the reply.

"An honest man. I like that. Then come for the scholarship. You will also be on television a lot. Next season, six of our games will be televised, and that's before the tournament. What do you think about that?"

"I guess I hadn't really thought about that," Matthew Blair said, sounding sincere.

"I want you to think about it real hard, right now. This could be a very big deal for you, the biggest opportunity of your life. And when you finish at States, we can pull some strings and get you on the pro team you want. Where do you want to play? We can make it happen. Just say the word."

"Well, sir, quite honestly, I really wasn't planning to play basketball in college."

The coach reacted harshly. "What! That's crazy. What are you talking about? You surprise me, you really do. You don't look like a stupid kid. Son, let me make this very clear: there is no other athlete like you, anywhere on the earth, and that translates into very big things, money, gobs of it from rich alumni, and fame and power. Even high elected office, if you want. Would you like to be a senator in Washington? Your adoring fans will elect you. No opponent will be able to beat you. Do you now understand what I'm offering you, how big this can be?"

"Yes sir, I understand. But I have other plans. Money and fame and all that stuff aren't important to me."

There was a longer silence, much longer, finally broken by the head coach's whine. "Son, please, be reasonable. You are just immature. You don't understand about the real world, how tough it is out there. I'm offering you a great life, something very rare, even for the gifted high school athlete. Take the other basketball players at this school, for example. They made all district first team, right? But that is only because you led the team to the state title. In reality, not one of them is good enough to get even a partial college scholarship. They will have to get regular jobs and go to work morning to night and hassle with some boss who tries to make their lives tough for his jollies. But you can escape all of that, live like a king, have anything you want, including beautiful women, as many as you want. Do you like pretty girls, Matthew? We got the most gorgeous babes you have ever seen. They all want guys with lots of money, and you will be rolling in it. They're kind of snotty, but really beautiful, and they love celebrities. They're all yours, as many as you want, whenever you want them. I can make that happen too."

"Sir, I appreciate the fact you think so much of me, but I'm really not interested. I have other plans that don't involve playing college ball."

The coach's tone turned angry. "You are turning me down, the head coach from one of the top universities in the country? My offer means nothing to you? I know what you are planning: going to one of those no-name Podunk colleges to make it a powerhouse. Well that won't happen. It for sure won't. Listen to me. We have strong political power around the country. Do you know what will happen if you go to one of those nothing schools? We'll turn it in to the regulatory boys, and they'll find some infraction and put the school on probation for years. That means no television, no championship, no national tournament, no scholarships. The basketball program will go to nothing. Everyone will blame you. Your college playing career will go down the toilet. You will fall into a black hole and no one will care about your pitiful little team, no matter how good you are. The coach will be fired, and the whole program will go up in smoke. We can do that, son. As harsh as it all sounds, we have that kind of power. It's happened before. The college game is littered with programs that tried to challenge us and got stepped on—hard, very hard. They never knew what hit them. That means you play ball with us, or you don't play at all. And if you think you can turn us in for breaking the rules, it won't happen! Nobody has been able to do it. We're bullet proof—one of our people is in a high place in the government, and she makes us untouchable."

Matthew Blair's voice was strong and sure. "You weren't listening, sir. I told you I wasn't interested—in playing basketball, anywhere. I meant what I said. I'm not going to play a kid's game after high school. I have other plans, much more important plans than that."

I was so proud, I almost peed in my new jeans. Yeah for Matthew Blair and honesty and honor and all that good stuff. I gave Lizzie a contorted high five.

Matthew Blair opened the door, Lizzie and I still bent over with our ears close to the wall and hands entangled.

He laughed. "Ladies, you are looking very pretty today, a bit shorter than usual, but very pretty."

I could sense myself blush, loving every moment of it. I watched him walk away, so very tall and sure as he went. We stood up, and I straightened my jeans, feeling that, maybe, there was some honesty in the world and hoping that, somehow, it would spread from Woodway High.

CHAPTER TWENTY-TWO

All day, I proudly walked the halls of the high school, feeling that, in my new jeans, I probably looked a little like a spring roll, a bit overstuffed but still kind of good. At least I was on the menu, and that made me happy, until Lizzie caught me just after the last class had ended.

She came running up to me, almost out of breath. "Mary, you better come right away. She's trying to screw you."

"Who?" I asked, mentally scrolling through images of the bitches.

Lizzie caught her breath and frowned. "Mrs. Poston. She's with Principal Newman now, trying to take your bake sale money away."

I couldn't believe my ears. "What? The puppies and old folks and sick people need that money. Why would she do that? How?"

Lizzie and I ran for the office, and for the first time today, I didn't like my new, stiff jeans, my old overalls being much better for running. We arrived at the principal's office, and there she was, Mrs. Poston, politicking with Principal Newman.

He saw me and beckoned toward us. "Mary, I'm glad you're here. There is something I need to discuss with you. Do you have a few minutes to talk with us?"

I blinked, not knowing what to say, and walked slowly toward the two adults.

He cleared his throat. "It seems that Mrs. Poston has brought a matter to my attention, and . . . well, it involves you. The money you raised from bake sales at the school, I know you planned to use it for a community project. Something about, what was it?"

I found my ability to talk. "Puppies, saving puppies from the pound to visit retirement homes and hospitals. I was going to use the money to buy a used van to carry the puppies around in. I raised three thousand of the five I need to buy the van."

He nodded. "Yes, I remember now. That sounds like a fine project. But Mrs. Poston reminded me that any money raised on school premises must be used for school functions. It's . . . ."

Mrs. Poston interrupted. "The rule. That money can't be used for a nonschool activity, according to school district rules. It must be used for a school purpose."

I stuttered, "But, but, what about the puppy project? That's worthwhile. It's not like I'm going to blow it on myself or on some stupid thing. The whole idea is to benefit our community. To help people."

Mrs. Poston was wound up. "Makes no difference. Money raised on school property must be used only for school activities, period. No exceptions. Besides, there is an important school activity in need of that money."

I asked, "What?"

Mrs. Poston looked at me over her gold-rimmed glasses. "The cheerleader banquet. We have only fifteen thousand dollars, and we need at least eighteen. The catering is costing more than we expected."

I couldn't believe what she was saying. I wanted to hit her, real hard right on her pointy nose, but realizing that would do no good, I turned to Principal Newman and pleaded, "Please, don't let this happen. Those puppies need this project, just to live. And the old people and the sick patients need it too. They're lonely and hoping for something that will show them love, give them some happiness in their lives. I just have to earn two thousand dollars more to buy that van, and the project will be off and running. Please, Mr. Newman. Don't let her take that money. It took me almost four years to raise it. It's all I have. I even spent my own money to buy cupcakes and cookies to add to the money I raised. Please!"

He looked at me with a sympathetic expression. "I'm sorry, Mary. There is really nothing I can do. Mrs. Poston is right. The rules are the rules, and I must follow them. It's my job to follow the school rules."

I could feel the heat rising from my ears, and I glared at her with what I hoped was the most hateful look I could make. But she seemed only to enjoy it, looking back over those glasses with an expression that said, "Gotcha."

I turned and ran, tears coming down my cheeks, out the side door to the parking lot, just wanting one of the bitches to get in my way and receive a well deserved punch in the nose. I threw my books down hard. "I hate this awful place!"

"What's the problem?"

I wheeled around, hoping it was one of the bitches. "Not now, Matthew! I'm not in the mood for any funny stuff."

He began to melt my hard heart with those electric blue eyes, just looking at me sweetly without saying anything. How could I be mad at that?

"Okay, you think I'm a flake or a psycho, like everybody else does. Come on, say it," I sputtered, feeling a little ashamed.

He responded softly, "I don't think anything like that. Want to tell me what's got you so upset? It's free."

I looked up at him. He seemed so tall, but he really was tall to someone only five feet four. "I can't believe how selfish and stupid some people can be. She took my puppy money, all of it, for the cheerleaders, like their banquet is really a big deal. Talk about frivolous things not to spend a lot of money on, that has to be at the top of the list."

He wrinkled his forehead and asked, "Who?"

I became agitated and snapped, "Stupid Mrs. Poston! That's who!"

His wrinkles disappeared. "Oh, I see. She took your bake sale money for the cheerleader banquet, the money for the puppy van. That's terrible. I'm really sorry. You're right. What a waste."

I was still mad, my snapping turtle act not quite over. "Sorry? How sorry? You got three thousand dollars to give me?"

He shook his head.

I responded harshly, "Then you're being sorry isn't really helping, Matthew. Now you can see why I'm so upset. I've got every right to be! There's no way I can get that money back any time soon. I can't even afford a decent college. And before I can make more, a lot of puppies will die and lots of lonely people will suffer more than they need to."

Lizzie honked for me to come. I turned and ran toward her car waiting in the parking lot, knowing I was being rude, but not caring, only wanting to hurt someone, and poor Matthew Blair was the person in harm's way just then.

Chapter Twenty-Three

I was so glad it was Saturday, not having to go to school and see Mrs. Poston or her precious daughter, Alexis, head cheerleader, first in the class, Miss Perfect. She needed a good punch in the nose; they both did. I couldn't believe I was still so mad.

The doorbell distracted me from my hard thoughts for a moment, before I yelled out, "Grandma, please answer the door. I don't want to see anybody, not even Lizzie."

My grandmother shuffled toward the front of the house. Within a few minutes, she was at the door of my room, a puzzled expression on her face. "There is the most interesting gentleman at the door. He looks like a butler."

I was becoming confused. "A butler? How do you know that?"

She continued. "The way he is dressed, very proper in a three-piece dark suit. And he is extremely formal, almost courtly. Mary, he asked for you."

Interest was fast replacing my anger. "For what reason?"

Grandmother said, "Well, I don't know, dear. He wants to talk with you in private."

I became suspicious and slowly asked, "He's not a weirdo, is he, some kind of serial killer?"

She smiled reassuringly. "Oh, I don't think so, dear. He's much too . . . ."

I finished for her, "Courtly. Right. Let me get my baton, just in case. It can be a weapon. I broke my nose with it when I was twelve."

She frowned. "Yes, I remember. Your mother wasn't happy about that at all. Well, please be careful, dear. We don't want you to break it again."

I was frustrated with her trust of this stranger, thinking he was either a peddler or a pervert, probably both. Old people were entirely too trusting for their own good. I picked up my shiny metal weapon and proceeded to the living room, stopping in the doorway to admire a gentleman straight out of some fashion magazine, tall and well-groomed, slightly gray hair combed straight back, spit-polished black shoes, a starched white shirt, and a pin-striped black suit with matching vest. A red- and blue-striped tie stood out against his shirt, and a gold watch chain hung gracefully in front. Upon approaching him, I noticed he smelled better than any perfume I owned. He looked perfectly . . . well, courtly.

I tried to hide my weapon behind me, sensing it wasn't necessary. "Yes sir, I'm Mary Lawrence. You asked to see me."

He extended a manicured hand with a gold and diamond ring and spoke very properly, "How do you do? I am Anthony Michaels, an attorney. May I have a word with you, Miss Lawrence?"

"Sure. You can sit down, if you like," I carefully answered, realizing he wasn't a peddler or a pervert.

He accepted my invitation, sitting with very good posture and feet together, before saying in the most correct manner, "I represent a group who have asked me to visit you."

I didn't understand him and asked, "A group? Of what?"

He smiled and responded, "People, Miss Lawrence, a group of people."

I continued to be confused and felt a little stupid for it. "But what people would want to send an attorney to see me? I'm nobody important. Is this about that van I said I would buy? Well, I can't do it now. No money. Sorry. Maybe later."

His smile broadened a bit and he explained carefully, "A group of very special people has heard of your work trying to use stray puppies as companions for the elderly and the infirm, and they wish to help. As their attorney, they asked me to visit you and extend an offer of assistance."

"But who are these people? A charity or something?"

He looked squarely at me, his smile now pencil thin. "Musicians of some acclaim, known by the stage name of Promise."

I dropped the baton on my toe, and the pain made me know this was no dream. "Promise. Me, Mary Lawrence. Promise has heard of me? But how?"

He said, "I do not really know. They are animal lovers. Perhaps your work with the puppies somehow caught their attention."

"Is this some sick joke? Promise? You mean the world famous band that has sold more albums than any other group in history? That Promise?" I asked, my disbelief rising.

His smile had gotten wider. "That Promise, indeed."

I felt my heart beating fast and cleared my throat, before asking, "What do they want to do for the puppy project?"

He opened a thin black leather briefcase, took out some papers, and studied them. "They wish to establish a charity of which you will be the trustee. A major law firm, whose fee will be paid entirely by the benefactors, will guide and advise you in such capacity. The charity will be endowed by a gift from Promise and it will be directed to fulfilling the puppy project as envisioned by you."

I was getting into the spirit of things and asked, "How much do they want to donate? I can buy that ninety-five van I was talking about for five thousand. Is that too much?"

Mr. Michaels looked at me oddly, like he didn't believe me, and said, "One hundred and twenty-five million dollars in immediately available funds."

I thought I had misunderstood him and blurted out, "One hundred and twenty-five million U. S. dollars?"

He placed a paper before me, some sort of legal document. It had a number that overshadowed the words: a "125" followed by a whole lot of zeros. Then I saw my name, followed by "Trustee of the Mary Lawrence Puppy Trust."

Before I could read the document, he added, "And there is one more benefit, a fully paid scholarship to the college of your choice. Promise feels you will be best suited to serve as trustee if you have a college education."

The room started to swirl a little, and I called out, "Grandma, could you come here a minute? I need you."

CHAPTER TWENTY-FOUR

"Mary, I can't believe graduation is only two months away. You heard from any colleges yet?" Lizzie asked around a mouthful of tuna sandwich as we ate lunch in the school cafeteria.

I sighed and answered, "Yeah, a couple, but I think I'm going to stay here and go to Poly."

Lizzie stopped chewing. "But aren't you going out of town, away from Houston, now that you received that scholarship money? You talked about wanting to get away."

I looked at a cup of peach yogurt, feeling disinterested. "Things have changed. I'm thinking I need to stay close to home, take care of some responsibilities here. Besides, Poly is a great school."

Lizzie whistled and rolled her eyes. "Yeah, if you have an IQ of two hundred. It's a good thing you're in the top ten percent. Otherwise, forget it. You heard they turned down Janice Mason, and she has real good grades, and a solid SAT too, thirteen twenty, I heard."

My mind was on other things, like making outlines of puppies with the yogurt and wishing I had a good old-fashioned hamburger and . . . the senior prom. "Lizzie, you got a date for prom?"

She seemed very casual in her response. "Paul asked me, just a friend thing. We haven't made any big plans, maybe dinner on the bay first, then the dance. You?"

I was beginning to feel sorry for myself. "Nah. Probably better that way. Costs too much. And for what? One stupid night nobody really enjoys anyway. And besides, Promise is scheduled to give a concert that night in Moscow. It'll be on radio, and I want to listen to them. They'll probably do some new songs. I'd like to hear them."

Lizzie leaned close. "You should go to your senior prom. You can listen to Promise on the radio any time you want. They play their songs all the time. Say, I heard Mrs. Poston rented the country club for a separate dinner and dance for Alexis and Toby and their friends. Some big name DJ is supposed to do it. They say it's all set up, that the invitations went out a week ago."

I sighed again and said, "Guess my invitation's in the mail."

Lizzie laughed and made a face. "Mine too. Still, if you get a date, let's go together. Cause we're best friends, and we'd have a great time together. You know how crazy we can be. What fun."

I looked at her and rolled my eyes. "Sure, like they're lined up to date a fat carrot-top. I don't think the new jeans are doing the trick, Lizzie."

She made another face. "Something might come along. Heck, it's your senior year, and good things happen to seniors."

"Like a big hamburger, I hope," I said, rubbing my stomach.

We laughed, not a wimpy little giggle, but a hearty bellow between best friends. I silently thanked God for Lizzie.

Janice Mason walked by our table, and Lizzie bubbled at her, "Hi, Janice, we were just talking about you. Sorry about Poly. Bummer. But congrats on your scores. They'll get you in most any other school."

Janice was tall and slender with dark eyes and black hair. She had a formal beauty about her, like a nice princess rather than a snotty movie star.

While pleasant, she wasn't overly friendly, but she stopped to chat. "Thanks. State accepted me into the honors program. I'm happy about that. At least I'm not going through what poor Mathew Blair is right now."

Lizzie and I looked at each other, before I asked, "What are you talking about?"

Janice answered, "Well, they calculated the senior GPAs for final graduation rankings and he had the top score, ninety eight point seven six, a full point and a half higher than Alexis Poston. But her mother went crazy and protested to Principal Newman. She said Matthew wasn't enrolled long enough to be named the valedictorian; he's two weeks shy. What a shame, and he's such a nice guy. Who ever knew he had a brain like that? I just thought he was a super jock."

My curiosity was aroused. "How did you find that out, Janice?"

She answered, "Mom is good friends with one of the counselors."

My curiosity began to be replaced by a sick stomach. "The mega-bitch struck again. If she can keep the smartest senior from becoming valedictorian, we're all doomed."

Janice smiled in a sly, knowing sort of way, looked around, and said, "Matthew will still be listed in the commencement program as the graduate with the highest GPA though. He just won't be the valedictorian. Everyone will know what happened. Most people probably already know."

Lizzie and I gave each other a high five as I cried out, "There is some justice in the world, and it's creeping into Woodway High."

Janice said goodbye and went on her way, leaving me thinking about important things: justice, right over wrong, good food, like hamburgers, and, yes, that darned old prom.

The bell rang for the end of lunch, leaving me hungry and wishing the day away so Lizzie and I could get in her car and go looking for some fun, and maybe something tasty to munch on before our planned visit to Green Garden Nursing Home.

The rest of my classes passed more slowly than I liked, but finally, they were over, and I grabbed homework books from my locker and ran to the parking lot, glad to be free. Lizzie wasn't far behind, and I heard her chattering as she ran up to me, "Hey, Mary, let's do something. Want to go to the mall? What about the ice rink? Can't we skip Green Garden today?"

I looked at her, feeling disinterested in all that stuff. "What about a snack, maybe a small burger, with cheese and pickles and tomatoes and lettuce and lots of great sauce and . . . ."

"Ladies. How are you doing today?"

I turned to see blue electricity pulsating from Matthew Blair's eyes, friendly and warm. Suddenly, I forgot what I was talking about.

Lizzie started acting all flirty and crazy. "Hi, Matthew. We were just talking about doing something after school. Want to go along?"

He answered, "I'd like to, but Mom isn't doing well today. My uncle is coming early so we can go to the hospital right away."

"We hope she does better soon," I said, turning to Lizzie for solemn confirmation of my statement.

But her serious expression quickly turned goofy, causing me to say, "Lizzie, what's the matter? What are you up to?"

She grinned at Matthew. "Have you got a date for the prom?"

I could read her meddling little mind like a newspaper headline. "Lizzie Murchison, don't. Don't you dare! I mean it. I'm not kidding."

She ignored me and persisted. "Well, Matthew, do you?"

He answered, "No. I really hadn't planned to go. I've got to work."

I chimed in, trying to stop her, "Good idea, Matthew. The prom's not that big a deal. Besides, it costs too much, way too much."

Lizzie asked him, "Is it a little steep for you, Matthew? You know, a person doesn't have to go crazy on the prom. You can save money if you don't rent a tux or a limo. We could use my car, and we wouldn't have to eat at a fancy place."

I shot back, "What is this 'we' stuff, Liz?"

She turned to me, speaking forcefully, "Hush, I'm trying to put this together. It'll be fun, for all of us. Stop raggin' me."

Matthew laughed uneasily. "I think I could scrape together enough to go to the prom. But I bet everybody has been asked by now. I waited a little late. My fault."

Lizzie was unleashed. "Mary doesn't have a date. What about you two going with me and Paul? We'd have a great time, dinner on the water, then the dance, and finally down to Galveston to make a fire and watch the sunrise. It would be so much fun. Come on, Matthew, it's your senior year. I bet your mom wants you to go. You know, do some fun social thing in high school before you go out into the big, bad world as an adult."

I was paralyzed, frozen by embarrassment. But he got those electric eyes working, and their blue glow began to melt me, driving my resistance away.

He looked at the ground for a minute. "Sounds like fun. Yeah, let's do it, if Mary would like to go with me, that is," he said with the sweetest smile.

I cleared my throat and tried to respond, Lizzie smiling widely in obvious triumph, but nothing came out at first. Then I coughed and said, "Okay."

That was all I could say, my mind swirling: I was going to prom; it was my first date in high school; the guy was great, a jock . . . and a brain; and he wasn't part of the jerk establishment. Lizzie was right, we were going to have a great, wonderful, fantastic, memorable time—probably the best of my entire life!

Chapter Twenty-Five

Next Saturday came fast, the day we had planned to buy my prom dress, and Lizzie and I were off into shopping Heaven. She drove to the mall, and it seemed like so much fun, more fun than I could remember there before. Lizzie began dragging me to every dress store in the place. After a while, all the shopping seemed like work, but like a good teen shopper, I kept going. To my surprise, instead of getting worn out, I felt wired, energized by the hunt for that perfect dress, the one that would make me look like a prom goddess . . . well, maybe just a nerd having fun. But that was good enough for me.

All that activity eventually made me hungry, so I asked, "Hey, Liz, want to stop for a slice of pizza? Maybe a giant pretzel?"

She fired back, "What? At a time like this? Waste your time and money on food? My goodness, girl, we've got to go on, keep searching. What if Alexis buys that perfect dress right out from under your nose? Wouldn't that be terrible?"

I hissed, "Yeah, right. She doesn't shop at the mall. Too ordinary for her. Only the best for our little Alexis, only the most expensive place in town, like Amore."

Lizzie saluted. "Yes, of course. Three thousand for a prom dress. Not here. Only at Amore."

We began to laugh, and Lizzie led the way to the glorious Pappa Sunseri's Pizza Kitchen, home of the biggest, cheesiest slice in the mall. We finally sat down with lunch, and as I devoured a mouthful of pepperoni on thin crust, Lizzie and I watched one of the televisions in the food court.

The national news came on: "And this has been one of the bloodiest days in Middle East fighting. Bombs rocked Jerusalem, Baghdad, and Gaza City, killing at least one hundred and fifty people and injuring many more. The authorities promised a military response, and even now tanks are rolling into areas of suspected militants. Troops are making sweeps, arresting suspects amid protests from mobs in the streets. Prime minister . . . ."

I couldn't watch the horrible scenes from the bombed buildings, turning my attention to the cooling pizza slice on my plate. "Lizzie, when will the killing ever stop? Can't anyone think of a way to bring peace? Maybe no one is smart enough. It's so sad, all those people dying and being injured for life."

We ate without talking, my mind on the orphans and widows and the people who would never come home again, until the entertainment news came on: "In the music world, mega-band Promise has canceled its upcoming Moscow concert for undisclosed reasons, offering the stunned fans a makeup concert, something special. Speculation is running wild about what it might be, maybe a new album dedicated to Russia. But sources close to the situation have speculated that the band might be planning a very special live performance dedicated to various countries in that region. Whatever the truth might be, odds are high that the concert will be a worldwide smash success, like everything Promise does. In London, ..."

I turned to Lizzie. "Why would they do that? I was looking forward to that concert."

"You are going to be at the prom that night, remember? You can catch their next concert. Finished? Ready to start shopping again?"

We jumped up and headed for the next store, and I was feeling full and great, thinking about my prom dress. We looked at everything in the mall, store after store, dress after dress, until I was ready to buy anything, even a burlap bag, to get some rest. Then we saw it, a black number, ruffly and long, just the thing to hide my—well, full figure.

"Mary, this is the one. Just your size. Go try it on," Lizzie bubbled as she held the dress up to me.

I took it to the dressing room and, miraculously, it fit perfectly, no bulges or zippers that wouldn't zip. And the price was good too, only a hundred and ten dollars, on sale. I hurried out of the dressing room, still in the dress, to get Lizzie's approval.

She motioned for me to turn around. "Mary, that dress is it. Makes you look very sexy."

I stopped and said, "What? Lizzie, I may look okay, maybe even a little good, but never sexy. That's not in my genes. Sexy is inherited, you know, and I didn't get it. My mother wasn't sexy, only pleasing, and that was enough for my dad. I'm just pleasing in this dress. So what do you think?"

She became stern. "I said sexy, and sexy it is." She turned to the sales lady. "We'll take it. We're going to the Woodway prom, and my friend found this perfect dress."

I was uncertain and questioned the sales lady, "What do you think? Does it fit properly? Are there any bad bulges?"

She studied me for a moment, while I held my breath, before answering, "It fits you very well, flatters you figure nicely. It's also made of a comfortable material, light and flowing. I think you will enjoy wearing the dress at your prom."

I began to bubble too. "Oh that's great. We'll take it."

As we checked out, the magic of the dress began to combine with other emotions, and I barely paid attention to Lizzie's chatter, focusing instead on other thoughts: Promise, the canceled concert, their next one, how I would look in the new dress, what the other kids would think of me, Matthew Blair, the prom, our dinner that night, and Galveston —to watch the sunrise on the beach. My mind was swirling with all kinds of feelings, some happy and warm, others uncertain and chilling.

Then I realized that I was afraid, but of what I couldn't tell, things unseen in the future, things I could feel but not understand.

CHAPTER TWENTY-SIX

Monday came too fast. I wasn't ready to go back to school, still feeling a little scared and uneasy.

Sitting at the breakfast table, Grandma must have sensed something wasn't right. "Are you okay, Mary? Sure are quiet this morning. What's the matter?"

"I don't know. Nothing I can put my finger on. I'm just feeling a little insecure. Maybe it's the end of school. You know, graduating and starting something new, a different part of my life. It's kind of scary, I guess."

She smiled. "Change is never easy, but it comes, no matter whether we like it or not. Things have a way of working out, though. We have each other for moral support, and that's good."

I smiled back. "And Mother and Daddy to look out for us from upstairs. I hope they are, that Heaven is real. Don't you?"

She hugged me and softly said, "I believe that it is."

I wiped my eyes and headed for the door. "Got to make the yellow monster. Don't want to walk. I'll be home after school. I might be a little late. Got to visit Green Garden and the pound today."

"See you when you get home."

Soon I was bumping along in the school bus, still insecure. But the familiarity of the school made me feel better. Lizzie was waiting for me in the parking lot, a sad expression on her face.

I ran to her. "What's up? I can tell something is wrong."

She pulled me aside, away from the other kids, and placed her hands on my shoulders. "I just heard some bad news, Mary. You up to it?"

I lied. "Sure. What happened?"

"Matthew Blair's uncle came to the office this morning and talked to Principal Newman. His mother died last night. Matthew is taking her back to Australia for the funeral. I feel so bad for him, such a rotten break, and in his senior year. She won't see him graduate. He won't have a parent there. Isn't that sad?"

I swallowed and sighed. "Yeah, I know how he must feel. It's a heck of a bummer. Is he coming back? I sure hope so."

She nodded. "Yes. His uncle said he wanted to graduate from here but that he would be gone about two weeks. Principal Newman said that would be okay, since he's at the top of all his classes."

We walked together toward the soccer field, and Lizzie sat with me on the freshly cut grass along one sideline. The grass smelled clean and seemed so peaceful. From across the field, I could hear a radio, probably a student's, from the rock music blaring through the air.

The song finished, followed by the announcer. "The super group Promise has just released its new album, *Freedom Road,* and it's projected to become super platinum by this weekend, anticipated sales to be one billion copies worldwide. Only those incredible artists could achieve such a feat. From their latest album we have the title song, of the same name, the first Houston station to play it, and that's why we're the number one rock station in the Space City. And now, 'Freedom Road:'"

> *When someday your eyes close, to bad things left down here,*
> *All the tremblin' and hurtin' gone; your heart feelin' no fear,*
> *I'll be lookin' up, smilin' for those I know,*
> *Dear ones not with me, but ridin' that freedom road.*
> *I'll be waitin' for the day, when my eyes close just the same,*
> *Wantin' to ride with them, to the place there is no pain;*
> *And we'll be thunderin' together, feelin' no heavy load,*
> *Laughin' and singin' along that freedom road.*
> *Everyone we've loved, they will all be there,*
> *Ridin' close together on that highway in the air,*
> *God's free wind a blowin', and His sun showin' how to go,*
> *All along that highway, thunderin' down freedom road.*

I turned to Lizzie, my eyes feeling wet, and said, "Do you think Matthew Blair may be listening to that song?"

"I don't know, Mary. Where do you think he is?" She asked, tears now on her checks.

I closed my eyes, swaying to the song. "Probably some place far away by now. But wherever he is, I hope Matthew hears that song. Maybe it will make him feel a little better."

I opened my eyes to look across the field once again, before closing them to focus on the Promise song, hoping it was true, that one day I would be with my mother and father on a place like Promise's freedom road.

CHAPTER TWENTY-SEVEN

The school days passed quickly, much faster than I had expected, the time spent ordering my cap and gown, sending out graduation invitations, wrapping up classes, turning in books, getting my final GPA and class standing, and planning for prom. It all was like some blur on a roller-coaster.

Then one Friday, Lizzie came running up to me as I was cleaning out my locker, grateful that it was the end of the week and that I could sleep late tomorrow. "Mary, Matthew will be back Tuesday! His uncle called and told Principal Newman. Isn't that great?"

"Fantastic! I can't wait to tell him that he has been nominated for most outstanding senior boy. Won't he be surprised."

The smile quickly left Lizzie's face, and she cupped her hand to my ear and whispered, "Mrs. Hall is trying to politic Principal Newman to pick Toby as outstanding senior boy. She came to the office and told him all about Toby's accomplishments: good grades, athletics, cheerleader escort, and . . . ."

I could tell she was holding back and impatiently said, "And what, Liz?"

She looked around and moved closer to my ear. "That he had something Matthew Blair doesn't have, perfect attendance, like that makes him the most outstanding boy in the class."

I backed away and stared hard at her. "That bitch, that mega-viper. I can't believe she would use his mother's funeral in Australia against Matthew. I'm going to punch her in the nose. I don't care, Liz. I'm going to do it. Someone should have done it a long time ago. I mean it!"

My best friend put both hands firmly on my shoulders. "Now, Mary, calm down. That will only get you in trouble. And besides, I don't think Principal Newman bought any of her stuff."

"How do you know?" I quickly asked.

She looked around, before answering. "Because he told me something important."

I shot back, "What?"

"How he evaluated the candidates," She answered with dazzling eyes.

"And?" I blurted, knowing there had to be more.

She continued slowly. "He said that the outstanding senior boy should not be someone who was just good, but someone who was the most outstanding person in the class. Someone with the top grade point average, someone who led a school activity to greatness, someone who had overcome significant adversity, someone who had outstanding talent, such as the ability to play the organ like a virtuoso, someone like . . . ."

I was following her like a puppy dog. "Like Matthew Blair. Right?"

She pointed at me. "Bingo. Not that he said Matthew's name, but I got his drift loud and clear. Now, isn't that the best punch in her snotty nose Mrs. Hall can get? And you don't get in trouble for it."

"Can't you just see her face at graduation when they announce the winner? What a sight, shocked into terminal ugliness."

Lizzie's eyes became wide. "This calls for a celebration. Let's go to the mall."

I was feeling even better than before. "I've got a better idea."

Her smile fell a little. "What is it? Don't tell me. I know."

I sung to her, "Chocolate ice cream with almonds!"

We ran to her car, chatting all the way, passing other students, and I didn't really care about any other discussions or activities at that moment, only our planned celebration.

Soon we were driving out of the parking lot and onto the road leading to good old Lou's. As we drove, I turned on the radio and pushed the buttons until I heard a music station. They were playing some classic rock tune, which I liked, but not as much as I liked the Promise songs.

Finally, the song ended, followed by the news. Lizzie started to change stations, but I stopped her as the announcer said something about Promise: "And today, the entertainment world was stunned by the news that Promise will perform next month in the Middle East. These mega-artists will be doing a concert in East Jerusalem, where almost continuous fighting has taken the lives of many citizens, Israelis and Palistenians, alike. Security is a major issue, and local authorities have warned that they cannot guarantee the safety of the band. This concert is also unusual due that the fact that many of the people in that region do not have the financial resources to attend such a high profile event. We will provide more details as they become available."

I couldn't believe the announcement. "Gosh, Lizzie, why would they do a concert in the Middle East? They could get killed. It sounds crazy. There must be some mistake. Maybe it's just a rumor. I hope so."

"I don't know. It sounds nuts. That's a terrible part of the world. There's probably not even any place big enough to hold a concert like that." She stopped and shook her head. "But I guess we'll see."

We turned onto another street and I saw Lou's Creamery ahead, but for the first time in my life, it didn't look special to me. Dark thoughts had taken hold of my mind and stomach, mixed with fear. I knew that I would be safe in Houston. But there was something else, something I couldn't understand. It felt almost like someone I knew, a relative, was going there, to be placed in danger, maybe to die.

CHAPTER TWENTY-EIGHT

I thought Tuesday would never come, and the yellow monster's driver must have conspired with someone, taking longer than usual to get to school. I ran from the bus, looking for Matthew Blair, wanting to hear him say we were still going to the prom, and to offer my condolences for his mother.

I didn't see him anywhere outside the building, making me run inside with my radar on.

Down the main hall I ran, no Matthew Blair in sight. I worried about our information being wrong. Maybe he had changed his mind about coming back to Houston. The thought of the prom was quickly fading from my mind.

Finally I gave up and walked to my locker, my stomach feeling upset, continuing to wonder if Lizzie had heard the information about Matthew Blair correctly and worrying that, maybe, his family in Australia had persuaded him to stay there. My locker was still a wreck, the product of a year of messiness, and I rummaged through notebooks and papers looking for a clean legal pad.

"Are you that ace reporter everyone has been talking about, the one headed for a major newspaper or magazine?"

I whirled around to see those electric blue peepers beaming at me.

Excitement took hold, and I hugged him. "Matthew! It's so good to see you. Oh, I'm very sorry about your mother. But it's terrific to have you back." I hugged him again and didn't want to let go.

He squinted. "Thanks, but she's all right now, no more suffering anymore. Mom and Dad are finally together."

I couldn't contain my emotions, reaching up as far as I could on my tiptoes and gently kissing his cheek. "You know, I bet they are looking down on you right now, feeling so proud that they made such a fine son."

The corners of his mouth turned upward. "Say, we're still on for the prom, right? It's this Saturday, and Lizzie told me she's going to get her car washed and make reservations at a seafood restaurant on the bay. I'm looking forward to it."

I smiled and quickly responded, "Yes. And I got the most beautiful dress. I think you're going to like it. It's really terrific."

"I'm sure it's fantastic. I can't wait to see you in it," he responded with that sweet smile.

I closed my locker, and, as we walked down the corridor, I could see Mrs. Hall and Mrs. Poston huddled with Alexis and Toby just ahead. When we passed them, I felt their hard stares, and it suddenly hit me: someone had told them that Matthew would be listed in the graduation program as having the top GPA and that he had been selected outstanding senior boy. Their evil eyes said it all. No one had to tell me that they knew.

He left me at my first class, and I felt wonderful, ready to tackle the finals in calculus and history and all the rest of my classes and looking forward to the rest of school.

The day flew by, and Lizzie was waiting for me after the last class. "Okay, time for us to hit the gym," she firmly said at my locker.

I tried to reason with her. "Now, Liz, what's the fuss with the gym and all that stuff? After all, the prom is this Saturday, and how skinny can I get in such a short time? Why don't we do something else? You know, something fun."

She put her hands on her hips and frowned. "Mary Lawrence, I am ashamed of you. You are on the threshold of becoming a sexy babe and you want to give up now? Matthew Blair will want to ravage you."

I looked at her, folding my arms in front of me. "I don't think so. He doesn't look like the ravaging type. Too nice."

"Yeah, I think you're right. But you still need to look like a dish for him at the prom. Think how proud of you he'll be," she said with a laugh.

Lizzie grabbed my hand and dragged me to the car, and I felt like I was being led away into some form of slavery. As we drove to the torture chamber, I could envision the terrible machines, the lump in my stomach growing tighter as we got closer.

Within a few minutes we were in our shorts at the gym, me dreading those darned breath-killing exercises. Lizzie obviously didn't mind the activity because she was skinny and in shape. But for a burrito like me, it was tough to run and row and cycle and sweat like a coward at the dentist.

Lizzie was making the rowing machine smoke, and I was on the treadmill next to her. "Lizzie, is this enough? We've been doing this for . . . at least ten years!"

She spoke in puffs of breath between rows, "Stop it. We've been here only for twenty minutes. We got to go for at least an hour."

"Well, it seems like ten years. I'm dying!"

As the time passed, I hung in there: elliptical machine, rowing machine, treadmill, bike, all surely made for torture by some thin sadist, for an hour and thirty minutes. And I had to admit that when Lizzie and I looked at ourselves in the dressing room mirror, I looked pretty good, not really like a burrito anymore, more like a chicken enchilada, which wasn't too bad since some chicken enchiladas were even low carb!

Saturday finally came, and Grandma and I fussed with the black prom dress. "Do you think it fits okay? I hope it's as pretty as the others, Grandma. Does my stomach show too much? What about my hips?"

Grandma reassured me. "It is lovely, Mary. Fits you perfectly. You are going to be the prettiest girl there. And since you lost that weight, you have an adorable figure."

The doorbell rang, and Grandma left me to think about the slimming effect of the magical garment. She soon returned with a clear plastic box containing the most beautiful corsage I had ever seen, deep red flowers with long pedals and yellow centers.

She handed the box to me. "Aren't they exquisite, Mary? The delivery man was very excited about the flowers, said they had come by air from overseas, that they were some special variety of orchid, very special, not grown here."

I studied the flowers as I gently lifted them from the box. "Gosh, I wonder where they come from. Pin them on me, Grandma."

We looked at the corsage in the mirror, and for several seconds, Grandma and I gazed together on my image, the delicate red flowers glowing on my dress more beautifully than I had thought possible.

The doorbell rang again and I turned in that direction. "Matthew! Grandma, could you get it and let me make an entrance? Please."

"A girl has got to make him wait, just a little. It's in the female handbook somewhere," She said, patting my arm.

Grandma shuffled to the front door. I waited for several long minutes, happy voices from the living room beckoning me. Finally, I had to go, and I walked slowly toward them, wondering if this was the way a bride was supposed to walk on her wedding day.

There he was, Matthew Blair, looking tall and handsome in his dark suit, his blue eyes flashing at me as I entered the room.

He turned to me. "You look very pretty, Mary. That dress is just like you described it. Really terrific."

I walked up to him, feeling very good and self-confident, suddenly remembering the unusual corsage. "Where did you get these flowers, Matthew? They're fantastic, more beautiful than anything I have ever seen before."

"They're from my home, in Australia. I wanted you to have a special flower for an important night."

"But they must have cost a fortune. You need to save for college, Matthew, not spend a lot of money on a corsage," I protested.

"I work, remember?" He studied the corsage, before saying, "I can't think of a better way to spend my money than on our prom night. Right?"

I was putty in his hands. "Right."

Matthew looked at his watch. "I guess we need to go. Our dinner reservations are in twenty minutes."

I was hungry and jumped on his nudge. "Lizzie said we're eating in Kemah, on the water. That makes me think of one thing."

"What's that?" he asked.

"Fried shrimp!" came out.

Matthew laughed. "You mean prawns on the grill? Makes me hungry too."

I said, "No, just good Gulf shrimp, fried crisp, the best way to serve them."

"Okay, Gulf of Mexico fried shrimp. Ready to go?"

He held the front door for me, and we bounced toward Lizzie's car—its clean, shiny exterior appearing more impressive that I remembered.

Matthew let me in first, and Lizzie bubbled, "Mary, you look fantastic, and that corsage, it's so beautiful!"

I thanked her and greeted her date, Paul Tamalino, who was driving. Then we were off, on the night of my life, with my best friend and a hunk of a date I had only dreamed of, and silently, I said a little prayer of thanks, hoping Mom and Dad were watching and smiling.

We headed south on the Gulf Freeway, exiting onto NASA Road One, then in front of the sprawling Lyndon Johnson Manned Spacecraft Center, to Highway 146, and south over the Kemah bridge, the yacht and sailboat lights shimmering on the waters of Galveston Bay.

It was all so romantic, causing me to turn to Matthew. "I appreciate the special flowers, but I really didn't want you to spend a bunch of money on me. We said we weren't going to blow a lot on prom, remember? You're going to need some money for college, even if you get a scholarship."

He looked at me, but his mind seemed to be somewhere else, before he blinked and said, "I'm not going to college, Mary. Got other plans after graduation."

I leaned away. "What, no college? But what are you going to do? I bet you made a perfect score on your entrance exams. You could go anywhere."

"I bet you got a good score too. Am I right?" He seemed a little embarrassed.

I didn't want to brag in front of Lizzie and lowered my voice, "Fourteen sixty, good enough for Poly. Yeah, I guess that's good."

He wrinkled his forehead. "Poly?"

"It's one of the best academic colleges in the U. S.," I explained. "Probably the best in this part of the country. But be serious. Why in the world aren't you going to college, with your super brain?"

He looked out of the window, toward the lights on the bay, before turning back toward me. "I want to do something else, a special job. There won't be enough time for college. I know that sounds stupid, but it's the plan I have for the future. Thought about it for a while."

"What kind of job is that? Must be awfully important to keep you from going to college," I asked.

He didn't respond, again focused on the lights decorating the night waters of Galveston Bay.

Finally we were at the restaurant, and Paul stopped in front of Smitty's, its neon sign painting the night in red and blue hues, and Lizzie exclaimed, "We're here. Everybody hungry for seafood?"

The next two hours were incredible, filled with broiled crab fingers, golden fried shrimp, buttery baked potato, and creamy cheesecake. I couldn't tell whether the company or the food made me feel so good, then gave up and stopped trying to figure it out.

After we were finished, I was glad to walk a little, hoping to work off some of the wonderful meal. As we strolled along the boardwalk in the cool salt air, I felt a little full, but very good—the food, boat lights, and sea air combining into some fantastic feeling of well-being.

We finally arrived at the car, and Paul jumped in the driver's seat to take us to the prom at the Bay Resort on Clear Lake.

It only took us about fifteen minutes to get there. We parked, and Matthew opened the door for me in a very gentlemanly manner, making me feel special. We walked inside to the sounds of rock music streaming from one of the ballrooms.

Lizzie turned to me before we entered the ballroom, nodded toward a long, white limousine visible through a large lobby window, and said, "I bet that's Alexis and Toby's carriage. I'm sure they're inside the ballroom, making their appearance before being whisked off to the country club for their private party."

"Who cares? I'm having a great time. You?" I asked with a shrug.

She giggled. "Terrific! Better than I deserve."

We found a table, Matthew receiving handshakes and pats on the back before we reached it. I felt so proud to be his date and enjoyed the approving stares of my classmates.

We sat down, and he wasted no time, turning to me with a wink. "Want to dance?"

The DJ was playing a fast song, too fast for my comfort level. "Gosh, Matthew, I don't know. I'm not a very good dancer."

He stood up and held out his hand, those blue eyes shining. "Come on, Mary. Who can really dance? We all just move to the music. Let's go for the gold. What do you say?"

Matthew led me to the center of the floor, unbuttoned his jacket, and started slowly with a few rocking steps, first side to side, then front to back. Then he let go with hip swivels, quick turns, and fancy footwork, and Lizzie cried out, "Wow, he dances as good as he does everything else."

He quickly changed steps, moving only his bottom half in complex gyrations while keeping his torso immobilized, then, suddenly, reversing himself with fast, controlled shoulder and head movements. Soon, almost everyone around us stopped and watched his acrobatic leaps and moves.

We stayed on the floor, dance after dance, and I could swear that he never duplicated any set of movements, always doing something new and more incredible than before. And somehow, I danced too, feeling pretty good about my moves.

Finally, I was exhausted. "Can we rest for a few minutes? I'm pooped."

"Why don't you take a breather. I'll get us something cold to drink," he said with a laugh, leading me to our table.

I sat down, threw off my shoes, and breathed deeply. "This feels great."

Watching him walk away, I was glad to have some rest and massaged my toes.

Lizzie plopped down next to me and whistled. "Man, can he dance! Where do you think he learned all those moves? Maybe he teaches dance in a studio somewhere. You think that's his job?"

"I don't think so. From what he says, his job sounds more important than that. Who knows, anyway? Is there anything he's not great at?" I asked, shaking my sweaty head.

Lizzie poked me. "Look over there. Alexis and Toby, still hanging around. It must be more fun here than at their stuffy country club and they don't want to leave. Too bad, what a waste of money for their parents."

We laughed, and I noticed Matthew talking with the DJ. He finished the conversation and walked our way with a couple of soda cans.

"What were you talking to him about?"

He settled beside me "Oh, I just asked him to play some songs I like."

I could feel my forehead wrinkle. "What about the Promise songs he was playing?"

"They're okay, but I like other groups better. Some of the early rock groups may have been the best musicians ever."

I couldn't let that statement go unchallenged, even from him, and shot back, "Nonsense. They were good, but Promise is much better. They've sold many more songs. It's not even close. They sold more than eight billion albums and that's . . . ."

He held up his hands. "Look, all that numbers stuff is fine, but I just like other bands, and I'd like to hear some of their songs. It's my prom too. Truce?"

My scowl was being replaced by a smile, those electric eyes making me mush. "You're right. Truce."

The speakers blared, and Matthew led me to the dance floor again, seemingly energized by the music.

We danced all of that song and all of those that followed, until the DJ announced the final song, a new Promise number from their album, *Freedom Road*. I caught my breath and was glad the song was a semi-slow tune:

> *Need your heart, got your love*
> *On my way to the place above;*
> *Through the night, past the fight,*
> *Your love burns inside, so bright,*
> *Warmin' the cold out of me,*
> *Helpin' to lift me free;*

Your love is deep within my soul,
Pushin' me to reach my goal,
Ridin' down the twistin' road,
Feelin' good where'er I go;
Lightin' up the darkest night,
Your love in me; everything's right.

Need your heart, got your love
On my way to the place above;
Through the night, past the fight,
Your love burns inside, so bright,
Warmin' the cold out of me,
Helpin' to lift me free;

Never forget your face or love,
Given from the Man above,
Special gifts just for me,
To heal my wounds and help me see,
On my ride through the storm,
All the way, you keep me warm.

We moved across the floor, my head resting on his chest, and the music spoke to me, as though, somehow, speaking to my feelings at that moment. I raised my head to look at Matthew, expecting to see his reaction to the unusual song, but his eyes were closed and his lips moved only slightly, mouthing the lyrics. The song ended, and the DJ said goodnight.

Lizzie rushed up, Paul in tow. "Let's go to Galveston. I know just the place down on the sand on West Beach. We can build a fire and walk in the surf and roast marshmallows until the sun comes up."

I looked at Matthew. "You game?"

"Prom's not over. Never been to Galveston before."

Lizzie was wound up. "Great! There's lots of sand and warm water down there. Come on, let's boogey."

Soon, we were driving south on the Gulf Freeway, everyone quiet along the way. The highway went past the bright refinery lights of Texas City, over the Galveston Causeway, to Sixty-first Street, where we turned south across Offats Bayou to Seawall Boulevard. Paul drove us west until we went down the wide ramp at the end of the concrete seawall that protected the city from hurricanes, leading to Stewart Road, barely above sea level and built on the sand bar that was this island in the Gulf of Mexico.

Lizzie began to give Paul directions. "Now look for the sign for a pocket park at Fourteen Mile Road. There it is, up ahead."

Paul turned onto the narrow asphalt road toward the Gulf, the smell of its salty water filling my nostrils. The pay booth was closed, allowing us to drive directly to the parking lot.

We stopped, and Lizzie jumped out. "Now you guys go start a fire while we get into something more comfortable. No peeking."

Paul led Matthew to the beach, and Lizzie and I changed into shorts. We joined the boys, who had gathered driftwood into one of the fire pits in the sand. The wood began to glow, as small twigs caught fire underneath larger pieces, making a fire whipped by the sea breezes. We sat around the blaze, and I reached toward the warm light. The waves broke on the shore, gently driving white foam toward us, a full moon illuminating the beach. Lights shone from far offshore.

Lizzie ran down the beach and called to Paul, "Come on, let's find some seashells. Maybe a Sand Dollar."

Matthew and I continued to huddle near the fire, and he looked toward the sea. "What are those lights?"

"Shrimp boats mostly, but some oil work boats too, going to the rigs."

He responded, "I like this place. Sure is peaceful. You come here often?"

"Not a lot, just when Lizzie and I want to get away and have a little time to ourselves. But I love it here. It's funny, though, how some people make fun of Galveston, saying the sand isn't like California or the Bahamas or Florida, that the beach has been washed away by the storms and can't compare to those places. But it's beautiful to me," I said, filling my lungs with the salt air.

Matthew shrugged. "Yeah, some people just don't see the beauty around them. Those places are fine, but this beach is as pretty a place as I've ever seen. Has its own charm, a kind of simple beauty. I'm glad you brought me here."

I looked at him. "Sounds like you've seen some of those places. You traveled much, Matthew?"

He looked at the fire. "A little."

I leaned against his arm and grasped his hand with both of mine. "I'm really glad you asked me to the prom. It made my senior year wonderful, much better than I had thought it would be. It's funny how things have a way of turning out for the best when they didn't start that way."

We sat in silence, the crackling of the fire and the roar of the sea taking my thoughts away for a few moments, before I asked him, "Why are they doing it, Matthew?"

He turned to me. "What?"

I continued. "Promise. Their concert in the Middle East. Why do you think they are doing it? It's crazy. How does a concert like that help their careers as great musicians?"

Matthew peered at the fire, not responding.

I pressed the question. "Don't you care what happens to them? I know they aren't your favorite band, but don't you worry about them as people?"

He spoke slowly and deliberately, "Of course I do. But maybe they aren't worried about their careers. Maybe they are trying to do something more important, something beyond themselves."

I let go my grip and leaned away. "What? But they are the greatest band ever. Their music speaks to people around the world. That's why they sell so many albums. What's more important than that?"

Matthew looked directly into my eyes, his blue electric gaze going deep inside me. "Bringing peace and saving lives."

I found it hard to say anything, but my love of Promise caused me to blurt out, "But aren't they doing that with their songs now? It's stupid for Promise to put all that at risk. The place where they are going to do the concert, East Jerusalem, that's one of the most dangerous places in the world right now. The Palestinians want it back, and there's violence almost every day, bombings, rocket attacks, and assassinations by death squads. What will happen if they get killed over there?"

His eyes were bluer than I had ever seen them. "Hearts may change. People could accept each other. Children might live to grow up. Maybe good minds will build the land up, rather than destroy it. Suffering could end. All that is possible if someone can win the hearts of the young people away from the people who preach hate. They need a message of hope from someone they believe, someone they admire, someone who can touch their hearts in a special way. Maybe that will stop the fighting."

"And you really think Promise can do that when so many others have failed, even great people, like presidents and world leaders?" I asked.

He looked toward the lights in the Gulf, but even from the side, I could see those blue eyes glowing in the partial darkness. "I don't know, but they must think there's a chance, at least enough of a chance to risk their lives."

I pulled my knees to my chest and hugged them against the chill of the night wind, trying to make sense of what he had said, both of us sitting in silence and peering out to sea for a long time.

The ocean gusts began to calm, and I noticed slight hues of orange and yellow streaking the low sky just above the horizon. The rising sun dimmed the lights in the Gulf and cast a shimmering glow on the surf.

I glanced at Matthew as he focused somewhere far out on the waking sea, his eyes not quite so blue as they had been, and I noticed something unusual about him—a small tear in the corner of his eye, sparkling from a ray of the warming sun.

CHAPTER TWENTY-NINE

Graduation finally came! From the noise, I could tell that the auditorium was filling with family and friends of the seven hundred and fifty graduating seniors and hoped Grandma had found a good seat. The sounds from the auditorium had grown to a level above the music of the pipe organ.

Principal Newman came walking down the line that the seniors had formed in the hallway, giving instructions, "Please remember, the top ten percent should be lined up according to class rank. Everyone else should be lined up alphabetically. Check your position in line to make sure you are in the right place. If you have any questions about your proper position, ask one of the teachers."

I looked at the people in front of and behind me in line, remembering their names from the list passed out in school. Everything looked right. I was number fifty-nine and, feeling very good about it, handled the honors cords hanging around my neck: a silver one for top ten percent graduate, a red one for honors graduate, and a blue one for journalism honors graduate.

A commotion behind me in the line attracted my attention. Principal Newman was searching one of the boys, Nate Antonio, a school prankster.

I asked the girl behind me, "What's that all about?"

She said, "The principal is looking for something."

I was puzzled. "What's he looking for?"

She looked back, before answering, "Mice and other stuff to mess up the ceremony."

Turning my attention in the other direction, I saw Matthew Blair standing at the front of the line, Alexis Poston behind him with the most disagreeable expression on her face. She had turned her back to him and had folded her arms firmly across her chest. Two of the boys just behind Alexis began to pat Matthew on the back and grabbed him around the neck.

Suddenly, they were play-wrestling with him until Principal Newman called out, "Gentlemen, let us be dignified for the occasion."

They stopped, and one of the boys gave Matthew's mortarboard back to him. He placed it on his head and caught sight of me, giving a "thumbs up" sign, which I returned.

I could see his cords: a silver one, a red one, and a gold one—for being the number one ranked student in the class. I felt so proud of him.

The processional bellowed from the pipe organ, sending the line forward to loud applause. Finally, my section of the line entered the auditorium, and I scanned the huge crowd for Grandma but thought it would be impossible to find her, until she popped up from her seat, waving and smiling broadly.

I waved back and mouthed, "I love you."

The excitement felt terrific, and I saw it in the faces of many of my fellow students and of most of the guests, this special day obviously meaning a great deal to so many people. And then, I saw Mrs. Hall and Mrs. Poston sitting in the center of the front row, their faces looking very sour.

The president of the school board was the master of ceremonies and moved crisply through the program: introductions of dignitaries, presentations of special awards, commencement address by a Houston city council member, something about making the correct choices as an adult, and recognition of valedictorian, Alexis Poston, and salutatorian, John Lee. Finally, it was time to recognize the graduates, and the school board president called on Principal Newman to do the honors.

He stepped to the podium, adjusted the microphone, and began. "Ladies and gentlemen, we now turn to the reason we are here, to honor the graduates who have worked long and hard for this important day. Initially, we recognize the top ten percent of the graduating class in order of class rank. Woodway's number one ranked student, graduating with highest honors, and named outstanding boy graduate, is Matthew Adam Blair."

The place erupted in applause and whistles as Matthew walked across the stage, shook the principal's hand, and posed for a picture. His blue eyes were shining so brightly as he walked off the stage. But the applause remained at a deafening level, preventing Principal Newman from announcing the next graduate.

The applause increased, accompanied by a chant, "Number one! Number one! Number One!" And, rather than subsiding, the chant grew louder, causing many of the seniors to look up into the stands, obviously surprised. Suddenly, I understood: the guests were recognizing Matthew Blair not only as the top student but also as the fantastic athlete who had brought glory to Woodway High. Finally, Matthew Blair stood and motioned for the crowd to quiet down, but they responded by standing and clapping wildly. Their chant filled the place more loudly than the organ had done and overwhelmed the clapping.

"Number One! Number One! Number One," thundered throughout the massive room. Most of the graduating class stood, began clapping and joined the chant, leaving poor Matthew Blair helpless in the grip of those who obviously admired him so much that day.

I had the most unusual feeling: that his mother and father were watching over their special son, smiling broadly, feeling very proud, and chanting too.

CHAPTER THIRTY

Monday came, and there was no school, something unusual for me but a part of my life after high school. Still, my work ethic had taken hold, pinning me to the dining room table, surrounded by notes I had written on the pages of a legal pad. I never realized there were so many hospitals and nursing homes, shaking my head as I scrolled down the long lists in the local phone book. The puppy project was going to be harder than I had thought, at least it seemed that way now that I had time to do some serious planning. I wondered how many drivers and vans it would take to transport the puppies to all the places where their licks and wags would provide loving attention needed by the sick, the dying, and the forgotten.

"Mary, someone is here to see you," Grandma said, interrupting my thoughts.

I looked up. "Lizzie?"

"No, not Lizzie. Someone else. I think you will be pleased."

I could feel my forehead wrinkle. "But I didn't hear the doorbell."

"He knocked."

My spirits soared. "He! Is it . . . . ?"

Grandma almost squealed, "It is!"

I ran to the living room, and there was Matthew Blair, smiling and looking so handsome in a red letter jacket.

"Matthew! I thought you were gone. What brings you here?"

"I just wanted to stop and say goodbye before my uncle takes me to the airport."

"Thanks. That's really great of you. I . . . I guess I was kind of hoping you would stay. That maybe you had changed your mind."

He didn't respond right away. "I wish I could, Mary. But I've got a job to do."

"Yeah, I remember what you said, something special. I bet it's far away. Am I right?"

His voice was especially soft. "Yes, it's a long way from here."

"It's stupid, but somehow, I wish I could go with you. That's unrealistic though. Will you stay in touch?" came in words hard to say.

He smiled slightly. "You can count on it." Then his smile faded, and he said, "I wish you could come too, Mary. But it's not possible. The puppy project, remember? A lot of people need you right now. Besides, we'll be connected. You'll always be my girl."

I looked up into his eyes, swept away by their endless blue. Words seemed almost impossible, but unnecessary, as emotion pulled me to him. Our lips met, and for just a moment, my world was complete, no emotions of emptiness or loneliness or resentment in my thoughts during that peace.

Then it was over, and he turned and walked out the front door to his uncle's car. I watched them drive away, my heart sinking. My emotions began to change, as I felt that, somehow, we would be connected no matter where life took us, and that thought made me smile.

CHAPTER THIRTY-ONE

The next day, I was hard at work on the puppy project again, having completed a call with an attorney at Wilson, Black and Caruthers, a big downtown law firm paid by Promise to set up the non-profit trust for the program. We had scheduled a meeting later in the week to go over details of the trust, and I was beginning to become aware of all the legal stuff I would need to know to act as trustee. It seemed like a lot of technical stuff that made my brain hurt. I was so glad I wasn't going to be a lawyer.

The telephone rang and Grandma answered it, before coming to my room. "Mary, it's Mr. Lawless, from the school."

I wondered why he had called and walked to the living room to take the call. "Mr. Lawless, it's good to hear from you. What's up?"

He seemed almost apologetic. "I hate to bother you, Mary, especially now that you are officially a graduate. But the *News* called and asked a favor. They will be covering the concert of Stormy Gold tonight at the Music Hall. They wanted some input from the teen perspective for their article. Of course, since you did such a good job on your sports article for them, the editor wanted to know if you could cover her news conference this afternoon. I guess they will publish your material in a larger article after her concert. Do you think you could go to the Energy Tower at three this afternoon? They will have a press pass for you."

"I guess so. But I don't have a ride down there."

"They will pay you $250 for the article, plus expenses, like a cab."

I was warming to the idea, glad to have the opportunity to make some spending money and write for a major newspaper. "Sure. I'll do it. Sounds like fun."

"Great. This is kind of a big deal, her being such a major star. I'm sure the editor will be appreciative. You can e-mail the article to him. His name is David Rogers. His e-mail address is drogers@hnews.com. Thanks, Mary. Stay in touch."

"I sure will, Mr. Lawless. Goodbye."

At two that afternoon, I was riding in a cab toward downtown, wondering what it would be like to see a real pop diva in person. I wondered whether she would be gracious or snotty, friendly, guarded, intelligent, or just plain dumb. I arrived at the hotel and entered its soaring lobby, looking for the Grand Ballroom. It wasn't hard to find, as I followed other people up the escalator to a mezzanine, to see security people, like at the airport. I picked up my press pass, walked through the metal detector and joined a lot of other people inside, deciding to sit in a chair near the center of the room.

The place seemed to fill up quickly, and I guessed there must have been a couple hundred reporters there. I looked at my watch: 3:00 PM on the dot. I was glad to be on time, guessing they would close the doors when the news conference began.

I waited, noticing many of the others talking on cell phones or reading newspapers or magazines, as the time slowly passed.

After about twenty minutes, I turned to a man next to me and asked, "Were we early? I thought the news conference was set for 3:00 PM?"

He laughed. "You're right. But what's new? She'll be here when she's ready, whenever that might be. You new to this kind of thing, young lady?"

"Yeah. This is my first one. I really don't know the ropes."

He shook his head. "Well get used to it. These stars are pretty arrogant, don't mind taking their sweet time. But don't you be late. She's probably fussing about the wrong bottled water being in her suite. You know what I mean."

I really didn't but tried to pretend. "Sure."

More time passed without an entrance by Stormy Gold: three thirty, three forty five, four o'clock, four fifteen. Finally, I turned to the man next to me. "I hate to leave, but I've got to get home. Maybe she isn't coming."

Suddenly, from unseen speakers, a man's enthusiastic voice blared, "Ladies and gentlemen, Miss Stormy Gold!"

A door opened on one side of the room, and a tall, blonde woman made a grand entrance to claps from the audience, her long dress flowing behind as she walked to a raised platform, where she sat in a large, elegant chair behind a microphone. Each hand had rings that sparkled in the overhead spotlights focused on her, and around her neck was a necklace of polished gold with large shimmering stones. Stanzas from several of her songs blared from the speaker system, and I winced at her tinny, little-girl voice, quickly remembering why I seldom listened to her songs on the radio.

The applause and music ended, and she removed the microphone from its holder. "It is so good of you to visit me today. I have just thirty minutes for the news conference. Please keep your questions brief so that everyone will have a chance to ask something important."

Hands shot up, and Stormy Gold recognized someone on the front row. A man took a microphone "Miss Gold, how does it feel being in Houston for your concert?"

She smiled with large red lips. "Hot! I thought I was in hell for a minute."

Some of the audience laughed, before hands shot up again. She recognized a woman sitting in front of me. "Yes, Miss Gold. That is a lovely dress you are wearing. Is it true that the Paris designer Pierre Gaspar does all of your clothes?"

Stormy Gold said, "I don't let anything else touch my body. I could satisfy the national debt with what I pay him. But he is a genius, don't you think?"

She stood and twirled, the long dress swirling elegantly around her, to claps and whistles from the audience.

Hands filled the air again, when she pointed to a man standing to her left. "Miss Gold, could you tell us a little about your planned World Theme Tour?"

She smiled more broadly than before. "Of course. I leave next month for Paris, then it's off to London, Berlin, Athens, Tokyo, Sydney, Los Angeles, and finally, New York. It's a tremendous amount of work, of course, but my fans demand it, and I am a slave to them. What else can I do? I will be performing new songs in each city, so that my fans can enjoy my artistic scope."

Then, something weird happened. Somehow, my hand shot up. Stormy Gold pointed to me, leaving me speechless for several uncomfortable seconds, before I asked, "And what about Jerusalem, Baghdad, Cairo, Tehran, or Gaza City?"

The star noticeably wrinkled her forehead, a frown quickly replacing the red smile. "What?"

I was too far down the road to stop. "I mean, what about those cities? Would you consider doing a concert in any of them?"

Stormy Gold leaned forward. "Why in the world would I want to do that? I'm a world-class performer, not a soldier. Besides, who can pay me to perform in those places? I've got an agent, a public relations firm, a jeweler, staff, a personal trainer, two chefs, three mansions, a fleet of limos, many lawyers . . . and Pierre to pay for. There's no money in playing the war zones of the world. Honestly, dear, you need to get real."

Laughs erupted from the audience, and the man next to me shook his head and looked at the floor. My embarrassment was too much to bear, driving me from the room at a fast walk. I ran down the escalator, through a large glass front door, got a cab, and dove in, hoping no one from the press was following to take a picture for a tabloid—the dumb Texas girl who pissed off the pop diva and made a fool of herself. I cringed at the thought that this was no way to begin adulthood, and a writing career.

The cab ride back home was filled with different emotions racing back and forth in my mind, mostly about celebrities. What did it take to be a celebrity, talent or luck; did character play a role; did you even need to be honest; and what was celebrity status, anyway; did it give the celebrity certain rights others did not have, could not get?

My mind turned to what Matthew Blair had said to me: a person must win the game, the one against his bad emotions and selfish thoughts. Then it became so clear. A celebrity was a person celebrated by others. I thought, but by whom? Suddenly, I realized that there was only one such person who counted, only one opinion worth having, only one celebration which had any real value, that of the God who was over the entire universe. Only His celebration of a person's life meant anything at all. My mind began to accept Matthew Blair's reason for Promise doing the East Jerusalem concert, and I realized that the band members were the true celebrities.

Several days later, my life was back to normal, preparing for college and working on the puppy project. I was so busy trying to understand legal documents that I barely noticed the phone ring.

"Grandma, could you get it?"

After a couple of minutes, she was at my side, smiling widely.

I looked at her. "Who was that? Lizzie? Please tell me it wasn't another lawyer."

"I have a surprise for you." She beamed at me.

"What is it?"

"He's on his way here. Said he has a few days off and wants to talk to you . . . about something very special."

"Who are you talking about?"

She giggled. "Matthew Blair!"

Chapter Thirty-Two

My mind was a blur from all of the emotions of the past week. I rubbed the gold band on my left hand. My wedding was a little confusing, and I couldn't really believe Matthew and I had been married in such a short time. Grandma was great, working with Lizzie and me, just like Mom would have done. Still, it was so hard to let him go after that, especially since I didn't even know where he was going.

The television announcer's comments about Promise turned my thoughts to the East Jerusalem concert. "Grandma, are you coming to see it with me?" I called, needing her support.

She entered the living room at a fast shuffle. "Yes, I want to see them too. Have I missed anything?"

I looked at the television. "Not yet. Just a lot of talk from the announcer and some Middle East expert. The World Broadcasting Network is covering the concert. I hope Matthew can see it, wherever he is. Maybe he'll call later." I stopped, my thoughts swirling between my new husband and the band I loved. "It's crazy, there's no warm-up group. Wonder why. Maybe no other band is brave enough to play that area of the world."

I popped my knuckles, and my grandmother did her usual, "Don't do that!" routine.

"I'm nervous. You think the police can protect them? It scares me that Promise is over there. Even their government officials get murdered, and they have bodyguards, lots of them."

A well-dressed man appeared on the television screen with a microphone in his hand. "This is Ian Whiteside reporting from the concert venue, in the hills of East Jerusalem. What a curious place for a major concert, but considering the available facilities in this area, it is probably the only venue capable of accommodating such a large crowd. The local officials have set up a stage located on the highest of these hills, scarcely fifty meters from where I am standing. While police are evident all around, security experts have cautioned that it is impossible to provide completely adequate protection for the band and its fans gathered here tonight. Speculation has run rampant about the band's motives for performing this unusual concert. Money has been flatly ruled out, since Promise is estimated to be worth at least two hundred fifty billion United States dollars. Whatever the real motive, the world is watching with great interest this incredible, history-making event in a war-torn land. And now we go to my colleague, Winston Collins, in downtown Jerusalem."

The scene changed to a room where two men sat before a large television screen showing the concert site, looking very stiff and tense.

The younger man said, "This is Winston Collins at WBN concert central at Jerusalem University with historical sociology professor, Doctor Otto Mier. Now, Doctor Mier, I am sure that our audience is puzzled about the band's reason for electing to perform here at this time. Many experts have speculated various motivations, but they all seem unsatisfying. What is your assessment of the situation?"

A round-faced, white-bearded man with thick glasses hanging low on his nose responded, "Very difficult to say at this time. Virtually all well-known celebrities have avoided the Middle East, most openly expressing fear for their personal safety. Many others, of course, see no personal gain from visiting the poor people who live here. I understand that the group is doing this concert for free, but that the WBN has paid somewhere near two hundred million pounds for exclusive rights to televise the event worldwide. However, even that huge sum is insignificant compared to the vast wealth of the artists. Additionally, Promise could make even more money doing concerts in more secure cities. Therefore, monetary gain does not seem to fit this situation."

Winston Collins continued. "Quite, quite, but, Doctor Mier, wouldn't you agree that some overriding motive is at work here, perhaps altruism?"

Doctor Mier nodded. "Well, of course, but the exact motive will not be known until there are further developments. Are these band members pro Israeli or pro Palestinian? Do they desire to aid the survivors of the deceased? You see, the social situation is very complex and difficult to discern."

Winston Collins pressed an earpiece to his skull and announced, "We are now going to Michael Thatcher in downtown Baghdad. Michael, are you there?"

Static filled the television screen for several seconds, giving way to a clear picture of minarets outlined in bright lights.

A tall man spoke directly toward the screen, "Yes, Winston, we are here in the center of Iraq, and the oddest thing has happened. People are everywhere in the streets, watching the event in front of large televisions placed along the sidewalks. This is a most incredible sight: armed American soldiers standing next to young Iraqis, waiting for the appearance of the supergroup, Promise. It appears that their mystique extends even to the heavily controlled youth here. And, while security is very tight, there is a pervasive sense of calm, something not felt in a long time. You can tell it in the peoples' eyes. There appears to be no anger or fear, only excitement and wonder. And we now turn to our colleague, Celeste Blasedale, in Damascus."

The scene changed again, this time to another city with a prominent mosque, confirming the region of the concert. A brown-haired woman clothed in a long dress buttoned at her neck and a headscarf spoke with a low voice into a microphone, "This is Celeste Blasedale, waiting for the appearance of Promise with literally thousands of locals on the streets of Damascus, people who have left their homes to be with others in some incredible, indescribable celebration of the spirit. Perhaps you can hear this vast throng singing various songs of Promise, filling the public places with their music. Many soldiers are among them, and they are singing too. This is a most fantastic happening, something I have never before seen, or even thought could happen."

The picture changed to the room at Jerusalem University, where the commentator, Winston Collins, had been joined by a woman, to whom he turned and said, "Our team is now complete, as Doctor Adie Solomon is with us. She is a professor of linguistics. Doctor Solomon, it is said that many of the local peoples understand ethical concepts only if they are expressed in their native languages, that their religious books were intended to be read in the original tongues of the authors. Do you feel that Promise, as widely loved as they appear to be, can move the local citizens with their English songs?"

She leaned closer to the microphone and, with a strong, deliberate voice, said, "I would have thought that many of the young people would be unmoved by English songs. But tonight's unusual spirit among the thousands of youth watching the Promise event has changed my mind. This outpouring of emotion may well show that the group's unprecedented appeal transcends language and cultural barriers. Additionally, ..."

Winston Collins turned toward the television monitor, interrupting her. "Excuse me, Doctor Solomon, but something is happening at the concert site. The stage lights have come up. Promise may be about to make their famous motorcycle entrance. We now take you there for the beginning of the concert."

I leaned closer to the television, clutching my hands so hard I realized my fingers were aching. "Shit! I wish this thing was over. I wish Matthew was here right now. I need him."

Grandma reacted, saying, "Mary Lawrence, do not curse in this house. Get hold of yourself."

I felt only partly sorry. "You know, I really think I have a right to be a little tense. A lot has happened to me in eighteen years, and a lot of it isn't very good. I'm born a blimp in a skinny world; my parents are killed by a drunken bum who is now out of jail on probation while they are in their graves forever; I'm an only child with no brother or sister to help me get over their deaths; the boy I love has gone to who knows where; I'm not sure when I'll see him again; I attended a school full of overachieving, mean piranhas; the band I adore is in a place where they might be killed. Maybe I've developed a hard shell, but it's necessary to keep out more hurt."

My grandmother placed a soft hand on my arm, her gentle touch softening me, but just a little, and she said, "Some of that is so, but remember, a hard heart never solved anything."

Watching the screen intently, I noticed four figures move slowly onto the lighted stage, but the camera seemed far away, giving a picture I wished were a close-up. They were dressed in long white robes, not the outfits I had seen Promise wear at the Millenium Dome concert. I relaxed. "That must be the warm-up band."

The WBN commentator quickly corrected my understanding. "This is Winston Collins at concert central again. Doctor Mier, Doctor Solomon and I are now watching Promise come onto the stage to begin the program. But this is very unusual. They are not wearing their normal costumes, black leather jeans and vests, I believe. Doctor Mier, what do you make of the white garments the band members are wearing?"

The professor answered deliberately, obviously thinking carefully as he spoke, "Most extraordinary. Those clothes . . . historically they signify that the wearer is offering himself, as a sacrifice for the benefit of others. Such a ritual has not been practiced for, oh, perhaps two thousand years."

Their discussion stopped as another commentator appeared on the screen. "This is Ian Whiteside at the concert venue. These hills are filled with tens of thousands of people in attendance, nervously waiting for the concert to begin. All eyes are focused on the band. Any minute we expect the music to start."

A camera panned the site, and I could see that his description was accurate. People stood shoulder to shoulder, forming a vast patchwork-like blanket covering the low hills all around the stage, as far as I could see. The camera quickly turned back toward the band, but the artists seemed too far away to see their faces clearly.

Without any introduction, I could see Tam hold his guitar high above his head. The band's leader looked across the audience, before his hands quickly began to move along the instrument, producing a pleasing rock melody, and Promise broke into their first song, something I had not heard before. The title was displayed in a caption on the screen, "Walk With Me Tonight,"

Walk with me tonight, across this land we love,
Through the places given to us, from the hand above;
Children of a power, none of us can see,
This land's for everyone, for her and him and me;
Walk with me tonight, brothers in every way,
Family of our God, who weeps most every day,
When the life He's given to us, is stolen before our time,
From dear ones we miss so much, family of yours and mine,
In the name of different things, said to be from God,
But really things of men, who never had His nod.
Walk with me now, away from words of hate,
It's the only way to get through Heaven's gate,
Understanding love, from each of us given,
To others in this land, tryin' to keep on livin'.
People like you and me, we're really all the same,
People lovin' each other, no matter what the game.

I watched Tam's hands make the guitar wail with energy and passion, the words carried on some incredible power that even I could feel thousands of miles away. The camera came in for a close-up on him, but his eyes were closed, as though he was creating the music from some place deep inside, somewhere in the farthest corners of his heart. Then the last note sounded, high and trailing off slowly to the end of the song, and the camera produced a wide, far-off picture again.

The band followed with a series of new songs: "All of Us Together," "Children Seeking Life," "Hate Is Not in Heaven," "Everyone's Jerusalem," "Born to be Brothers," "A Mother's Song," and "Be With Me Tomorrow." With each song, I felt the message Promise was sending, washing away my self-pity and calming my emotions.

"I'm sorry. You were right," I said to Grandma.

As always, she was sweet. "About what?"

"Being so uptight and hating so much. Your advice was on the money. Mom and Dad don't want me to be like that. Matthew doesn't, either."

She patted my arm, before turning to the television again. "Oh, look, they are doing something special."

I focused on the screen. Tam was walking to the front of the stage, where he stopped and looked slowly across the great audience. Then, I noticed something unusual: he wasn't wearing those wild sunglasses I had seen him wear at the Millenium Dome concert or in the magazine pictures. The camera came right on his face, and I gasped. "Grandma, his eyes, they're so incredibly blue, almost a blue light. Just like . . . ."

Tam looked directly into the camera, straight at me, and suddenly I knew his identity. I placed both hands on the screen, warm tears rolling down my face. "I love you."

Tam looked across the crowd. "This is the last song, and we do it for all of you, so that you will live together in peace."

He held the instrument high above his head, as I had seen him do before, and looking straight ahead, Tam placed his other hand on the strings. Without saying anything further, he brought the guitar to life, his hands causing the tall speakers to reproduce the most glorious music, lifting me with the notes racing up the scale. The words of the final song soon came forth:

> *There is life and goodness, for everyone who be,*
> *This life from our God, Who wants all people free,*
> *There is no wish of death, from the eyes that always see,*
> *We can live in peace; a single family.*
> *Do not doubt these words or that love is the key,*
> *I promise this is true; I promise it will be.*
> *For all who practice love today,*
> *I promise, you will live free.*

The band followed with an incredible instrumental, and the camera panned the audience, many holding hands or having placed arms around others' shoulders, singing the words as if they knew the song, but it was clear that the words flowed from their hearts rather than their minds, as they seemed carried away, eyes closed and bodies swaying to the music.

The lyrics resumed, but this time Promise was singing in some other language I did not recognize. Suddenly, a message rolled across the bottom of the screen, "Doctor Adie Solomon, at concert central in Jerusalem, indicates that this language is ancient Hebrew, the language of Moses and the Old Testament, not spoken in almost three thousand years."

I listened carefully, frozen to the screen, wondering why they would sing in this ancient tongue and how they had learned it.

The language then changed to something different, but equally puzzling to me. The message tape reappeared, "Doctor Solomon now says that Promise is singing in classic Arabic, the language of Muhammad and the Koran."

While I could not understand a word of the song, I could feel its energy in this language and quickly understood the power that had led much of the world to follow the great religion of Islam.

Soon, the language changed again to some other tongue, and a new message tape quickly caught my attention, "Doctor Solomon says that the band is now singing in Aramaic, the language of Jesus Christ and his disciples two thousand years ago."

While the band's music pounded powerfully from the television, the combined voices of the audience were equally powerful, like some great crowd unified in a common understanding and purpose, similar to countrymen singing their national anthem. I soon found myself singing with them, as though I were there. The camera gave a close-up picture of part of the audience. Their tears showed the power of Promise's music, many of whom only days before had, most likely, been enemies but now were spiritually united.

Suddenly, there was a blinding flash on the screen, and it went blank.

"Grandma, what was that?" I cried.

She didn't answer, her full attention on the white television screen. Maybe she didn't want to answer me.

I moved beside her and leaned in her lap, and she held me tightly.

The scene changed to the room at Jerusalem University, where the WBN correspondent looked confused. "This is Winston Collins at concert central. There has been some untoward event at the concert site, but I do not have any explanation for you at this time. Perhaps it is something as innocent as technical difficulties or a power failure. Our correspondents at the concert venue should be in touch shortly. Ian, Ian Whiteside, are you there?"

A frightening silence met the request for communication, and I began to tremble. "Grandma, they're all right, aren't they? Please tell me they are. God, please make them all right. Matthew!"

She didn't answer, and my trembling grew worse.

The WBN correspondent held his earpiece tightly to his head, before slumping noticeably in his chair. "Ladies and gentlemen, I regret to inform you that I have just received word from our colleague at the concert venue, that . . . that a suicide bomber has detonated high explosives at the site. Preliminary reports indicate that many are dead, including all members of the band Promise. I am very sorry to have to deliver this dreadful news to you. I am sure we all share a sense of devastation at this horrible development."

I closed my eyes and hugged Grandma as hard as I could. "No, no, no. Why, God? Please tell me it isn't true."

I felt all of the energy flowing from me, and breathing came very hard. As I cried, there were other sobs in the room. I opened my eyes to see Grandma crying too.

Chapter Thirty-three

Grandma and I sat hugging each other for what seemed a very long time, until the afternoon turned to evening and I had no more tears to cry.

I know she wanted to be strong for me, but it was soon clear that I needed to be strong for her, and I said, "We probably should go to bed. It's not late, but I feel exhausted and I bet you do too. There's nothing we can do. Maybe tomorrow something good will happen. Who knows? We can turn on the television in the morning and see."

Grandma nodded, wiped her nose with a tissue, and shuffled off to her bedroom. I had told a white lie, but one intended to do some good, so it seemed like the right thing to do.

I turned toward the screen again and listened to the endless string of experts, some trying to explain what had happened, others trying to justify it. To me, it was all the same, the members of Promise were dead, and the boy I loved was gone forever.

All the talk became a mishmash of unimportant gibberish. The only thing that mattered, that would ever matter, was that the most selfless, most talented, greatest people ever had given their lives for some cause I didn't really understand, some feud going back thousands of years and made incredibly complex by current events no one seemed able to control.

I must have watched the television for hours, my painful eyes telling me a good deal of time had passed. Finally, Grandma's door opened and she moved slowly into the room, rubbing the back of her neck. "Mary, how long have you been up?"

"All night," I said, messaging the corners of my eyes.

She stood beside me, looking at the television. "Has anything new been reported? I guess it's too much to ask whether the band survived, whether the news people made a mistake."

"Afraid not. The WBN confirmed they all died last night."

Grandma shuffled toward the kitchen. The welcome smell of freshly brewing coffee began to fill the air, the first pleasant thing I had sensed for hours. Soon, Grandma was at my side, handing me a steaming cup of coffee, while I focused hard, but mechanically, on the television.

We sat together without speaking, until the scene changed from a single announcer to a picture I had not expected to see, people, thousands of them, standing together.

I turned up the volume and heard: "This is Winston Collins in Jerusalem. We have now established links to venues throughout the region, and the most incredible thing is happening. Hundreds of thousands, perhaps even millions, of local residents have come into the streets, holding each other, walking and talking together, as though there were no conflict, no hate among them. Israelis and Palestinians, Jews and Muslims, men and women, some wearing Stars of David and others wearing the traditional headdress and scarves of Islam, but all together as I have never witnessed. This picture is from East Jerusalem."

Grandma and I watched the scene change to another place filled with a vast number of people, as before. Winston Collins continued, "And now we are seeing downtown Baghdad, where the people are in the streets as well, but this time they are locals and American soldiers, standing together and talking. What an incredible vision it is, ladies and gentlemen. Our link to Gaza City is now up, and we take you there by satellite. As you can see, there are thousands of people filling the streets, some holding hands and others arm in arm, and very many of them talking, hugging, and shaking hands. We have been bracing for violence, but none has been reported, and the local military authorities are said to be meeting with Palestinian leaders at this very hour. We are . . . wait a moment. I have just been handed word that a major announcement is about to be made in Bethlehem, and we now take you there."

The television scene changed to the steps of a low stone building, where men stood together, some in military uniforms and others in the local headdresses I had seen before.

One of the men stepped to a microphone and solemnly said, "Members representing the various peoples of the region have reached agreement.

All violence has ceased. We have agreed to negotiate the resolution of our differences. All armed groups are to immediately lay down their weapons. The military will immediately pull back. We will begin the rebuilding process at once. Today, representatives of all concerned peoples and of the United Nations, meeting throughout the night, approved the new nation of Palestine. Palestine and Israel will share the holy city of Jerusalem as their capitals. With God's help, we will preserve the peace and build lives worth living."

Thunderous applause erupted from the onlookers, followed by powerful chants: "I promise it is true; I promise it will be."

Grandma and I looked at each other before I turned back to the television and saw the leaders embracing.

Grandma hugged me. "You see, Mary, something very good did happen. Promise's deaths were not in vain. They saved many lives, and brought peace."

My eyes didn't feel scratchy any more, and I cleared my throat. "I should have seen this all along. Stupid me. Now it's all so clear. The most talented people on Earth did it. They succeeded where others had failed. But I shouldn't have doubted that they could. They went there to do this exact thing. And Matthew made the peace happen, just like he did so many other incredible things. He came to solve problems others could not solve, save lives, and bring peace to hearts that would not soften, just like he said."

CHAPTER THIRTY-FOUR

I heard a knock on the front door. "Who could that be? Maybe Lizzie. Grandma, could you get it? I can't get up right now."

She walked toward the door, and I heard her greet someone, followed by a man's voice. I turned stiffly to see that lawyer, Anthony Michaels, standing behind her.

His face lacked the smile I had seen before "Excuse me, Mrs. Blair. I apologize for bothering you, especially now, but I was instructed to come here today for a specific purpose."

I felt exhausted but found the energy to say, "That's okay. What do you want to see me about?"

"Undoubtedly, by now you probably know that your late husband was one and the same person as the leader of Promise, Tam. I understand that he had kept his identity secret, from even you. However, he intended to reveal that secret to you, by way of special message from the concert. He asked that, in the event of his death, I come to see you for two reasons. First, he requested that you maintain his secret. He felt it better for the fans to focus on the band's music, rather than on the members' personal lives." Anthony Michaels stopped, seeming to wait for my response.

"Of course. I will keep the secret, just like Tam wanted."

He nodded and continued. "Second, he asked me to deliver something to you." Anthony Michaels opened his leather briefcase, removing a CD case, which he handed to me.

Before taking it, I asked, "What is this?"

He answered, "I believe it contains a song of Promise."

"But why would he want me to have one of Promise's songs? They're being played on all the radio and television stations."

"This is an unpublished song, composed just for you. It has not been played publicly."

I took the case from him and opened it, reading the title written on one side, "Mary's Song."

Tears began to block my vision, and I slumped into a nearby chair.

Mr. Michaels said goodbye, leaving Grandma and me, the CD clutched tightly in both my hands.

Finally, I regained control of my emotions and released my grip of the plastic disc, handing it to my grandmother. "I'd like to hear the song now. Would you put it in the CD player for me?"

She slipped the disc into the machine and pushed a button, my eyes fixed on the box as though it were alive. The melody of a single guitar flowed from the speakers, reminding me of Tam's incredible music, soon accompanied by drums, a keyboard, and a base guitar. I closed my eyes, carried along by the new instrumental, until Tam's voice opened them suddenly,

Wherever I go,
Whatever I see,
Across the reach of time,
No matter how far
Away I may be
You'll be there,
By the side of me,
Part of my soul,
You will be mine.

We'll cruise the mountains,
Thunder the sky,
Feelin' no heavy load,
Singin' and dancin'
Way up high,
Forever together,
You and I,
Along His freedom road.

I closed my eyes as the guitar continued its instrumental magic, lifting me out of the emotional darkness, toward some place only my soul could reach, far beyond the pain fast falling away. The image of Tam in concert came to me, and I could see every detail of him, but without his wild sunglasses, revealing eyes so very blue, like the clear sky beyond which freedom road surely existed.

Part Two

Tomorrow

CHAPTER THIRTY-FIVE

Memories, vivid mental pictures flashed through Mary Blair's mind from twenty years in the past. Her mental focus was so intense she scarcely noticed the jetliner's descent to her African destination.

Mary's attention turned to the uniformed flight attendant, as the tall black woman prepared the passengers for arrival in Addis Ababa. "Seats in the upright positions and tray tables locked, please, ladies and gentlemen. Remember to turn off all electronic devices. We are about to land."

Mary studied once more a small photo album, turning its pages to read notes she had written on the backs of the pictures. She closed the precious booklet, placed it in her purse, and peered out the window of the airplane, the ground slowly coming toward her. Mary studied the sunburst architecture of the terminal. Many passenger jets rested along the concourses, planes with the colors of different carriers from around the world.

The big jet softly touched down on the runway, and the passengers next to Mary leaned slightly forward as the brakes slowed the plane. The aircraft taxied to its resting place, and the passengers exited through the jet way, into the brightly lit concourse, many into the arms of people appearing to be friends or loved ones.

Before she could enter the people mover leading to the baggage claim area, Mary saw a tall, elegantly dressed black man, who greeted her with a broad smile and an extended hand. "Mrs. Blair? I am Doctor John Tafari, personal adviser to President Iyasu. The President sent me to collect you and your luggage for transport to the capitol. Do not worry about your things. They are being brought to our limousine. It is waiting for us just outside this area, on the taxiway."

Mary shook his hand. "Thank you for meeting me, Doctor Tafari. I didn't expect such a grand welcome. But you shouldn't have gone to the trouble. I could have taken a taxi."

He responded in a low, resonant voice. "You are a most important journalist. A lesser welcome would not do. We wish to recognize you properly. If you will follow me, our limousine is only a short distance from here."

She walked with the man, his formal manner making her feel very special. They entered an elevator and descended to the first level, exiting only a few meters from a tinted-window white limousine, a pleasant looking man in a dark suit standing by its open rear door. The man bowed slightly as the two entered and closed the door gently behind them.

The extended vehicle glided away from the terminal, and Doctor Tafari settled into his leather seat, studying Mary before saying, "Welcome to Ethiopia. It is an honor to have a world-renowned correspondent of your stature visit us. President Iyasu has given instructions to make you feel completely at home during your stay here. Whatever you may require, please do not hesitate to ask."

She returned his smile and said, "Thank you. From the pictures I have seen, Addis Ababa is a beautiful city. I've not been here before."

Her host gestured with both hands toward the window. "We have a short drive to the capitol. I believe it will be even more impressive in person."

They drove through low, green hills, white cattle grazing across lush pastures as far as Mary could see. The fields began to end, and she observed a small town ahead. The car slowed as they drove along a four-lane boulevard leading into the town. As they proceeded, she observed low concrete and brick buildings seemingly teaming with business, neat one-storey brick homes with green grass lawns and sidewalks, small cars traveling along clean concrete streets, a park with children climbing on extensive playground equipment, people fishing in a clear lake, and a small airport where a jet was taking off.

"What is the name of this town?" Mary asked, her attention focused on a rail terminal loading grain into waiting boxcars.

Doctor Tafari answered, "Alawa Erithere. It is a rural community serving as an agricultural center. Local farmers grow various crops in thousands of hectares around the town, and the produce is brought here for storage and distribution throughout Ethiopia. This was a pilot project, the model for hundreds of other towns just like it across the country. Now, we feed ourselves and even export wheat, fruit, other grains, and cotton to all parts of Africa. And do you see those interesting looking windmills ahead?"

Mary saw row after row of steel towers, each tower having three long blades at the top, rotating slowly but powerfully, the entire group covering the side of a tall hill to their left.

Interested, she asked, "Are those wind-driven electricity generators? I've heard of them but never saw any up close before now."

Doctor Tafari smiled. "Indeed they are. You are well informed, Mrs. Blair. All of our rural towns have them. Ethiopia imports no energy. We are energy self-sufficient. Our people lack no modern electrical conveniences, even air conditioning, computers, and television. The great farms throughout Ethiopia are irrigated by pumps driven by this system of electricity, making them especially productive. Quite modern, don't you think?"

She smiled back. "Yes. This is very impressive, Doctor. It seems your people are modern in many phases of their lives."

He beamed his approval of her compliments.

They left the town and drove alongside vast fields of neatly planted trees, row after row, tended by many trucks moving slowly along roads between the rows.

Doctor Tafari pointed out the window. "Citrus trees, orange, grapefruit, and lemon, about one hundred thousand hectares, I believe. A great deal of vitamin C for our children."

She inhaled deeply through her nose. "Yes, I can smell the aroma of the lemons. It's wonderful, almost like a lemon pie."

Doctor Tafari began to laugh, prompting Mary to ask, "Did I say something funny?"

He responded, "No, not at all. I was just thinking that we also have another place that produces an aromatic crop. But you probably would not like it as much. When you drive through, it can be very pungent at times."

She asked, "What is the crop?"

He looked at her. "Garlic."

They both laughed, Doctor Tafari's low, melodic tone adding to the pleasing sense Mary enjoyed.

After several miles, she could see the outskirts of a great city on the horizon, its skyline appearing similar to mountains in the distance.

The limousine reached the city. Extensive structures, wide concrete streets, treed esplanades, and soaring buildings became distinct. "I assume this is Addis Ababa? What do you call this section of the city?" she inquired.

Slowing a bit, the big vehicle entered the urban area, and Doctor Tafari's deep voice responded, "This is the financial district, housing the offices of many companies doing business in northern Africa. Our own energy and mining companies have offices in that tall glass building on your right. They take up all sixty floors, and European companies have offices in the fifty-storey polished granite building next door. American securities concerns occupy that seventy-storey shiny steel building on the other side of the street."

Mary studied the man-made canyon, its buildings going on as far as she could see. The car turned onto another wide boulevard and stopped at an intersection while a group of uniformed children crossed in single file, an adult leading the way and another at the end of the group.

Doctor Tafari explained, "Our primary education has come very far over the years. The children are learning as much here as in America or in Western Europe. Those students are from one of our elementary schools, most likely on a field trip. Each school has its own uniforms. The children enjoy the school spirit of their special raiment."

She turned to her host. "Your English is excellent. Where did you study?"

He sat up straight and said, "At Promise University here in Addis Ababa. I took my doctorate in political science there."

They soon passed a campus-like setting of many low beige brick buildings situated on grass-covered hills with stands of trees between the structures. In the center was a tower with a clock in the top. It looked very peaceful, yet important.

"What is that place?" she asked him.

He answered, while looking out the window, "Promise University, named for the benefactors who gave the funds for its construction. That was a long time ago, about twenty years. The university has become the cornerstone of our education, turning out agriculturists, engineers, doctors, and teachers, who have helped build Ethiopia. In the early years of the university, professors from your universities came here and taught agriculture, helping us develop hearty strains of crops strong enough to withstand the droughts we had experienced for many years. They saved thousands of our people from starvation. Those strong bodies became strong minds. Now, we can help ourselves. Promise University is a great blessing to us."

The limousine sped along a river, its banks green with thick grass. A paved walkway bordered one side, and there were shops and restaurants all along the way. Well-dressed men, women, and children casually walked along the path, and the businesses seemed to be filled with customers.

The road came to a fork, the river following one way while the limousine went the other, leading to a series of tall red brick buildings with red tile roofs.

Doctor Tafari did not wait for a question from the visitor, even though she was interested in the complex. "This is the Northeast Africa Medical Center. It does cutting-edge research in communicable diseases, drug resistant strains, immunology, and cancer. In fact, the cure for AIDS was discovered here several years ago. You may have heard about it."

"Yes, I read about the discovery in several magazines and newspapers. It was exciting news. The lead researcher received the World Science Award for his work."

The host seemed proud, as he added, "Doctor Entibe Mugabe. His work saved millions of people across the continent, and throughout the world. Do you know how many children were orphaned in Kenya alone from AIDS, children left on the streets because they had no family?"

"No. Is it a large number? I'm afraid to guess."

Deep emotion obviously flowed through his squinting eyes. "More than one million. Children left to die because there was no one to feed them, to wash them, to heal their sores. But mercifully, the cure stemmed that tide." He stopped for a moment, regaining a slight smile. "The Center is an extension of Promise University. The first professors came from Poly-Technical Medical School in Texas, instructing our students and treating the sick from all over. It has been an incredible development for Ethiopia . . . and for all of Africa."

Mary observed the limousine pull onto a long road, the lanes separated by a flowered esplanade, abundant explosions of colors running all along the way. The extended vehicle slowed to maneuver the curves and stopped in front of a grand building sparkling with shiny earth-toned marble fascia.

The driver exited quickly and opened the back door for the passengers, Doctor Tafari extending a hand for his guest. "This is the Executive Office Building. President Iyasu is waiting for you in his suite."

He led her through tall wooden double doors, into a marble foyer. An elevator whisked them to the top floor. An attractive black woman greeted them, bowing slightly and extending her hand. "Mrs. Blair, I am Helen Tongo, President Iyasu's secretary. He gave instructions to bring you in as soon as you arrived."

Doctor Tafari stayed behind as the secretary led Mary to another door.

Mary stopped before entering, turned to him and said, "Thanks for the tour, Doctor. Ethiopia is beautiful. You have a great deal to be proud of."

He nodded, and the secretary knocked, before opening the door to reveal a large man with ebony skin, dressed in a charcoal pin-striped western suit with a red tie, sitting at a massive wooden desk.

He smiled and quickly rose to greet his guest. "Mrs. Blair, so very good to see you here in Addis Ababa. I was hoping your plane would arrive on time."

She shook the man's powerful hand, and he gestured for her to sit in a leather chair in front of the desk.

He sat beside her. "How was your trip? Not too tiring, I trust."

"It was very nice, but first class is always pleasant," she said.

He seemed pleased, continuing his greeting. "Excellent. I have given instructions for your complete comfort. You will be staying at the Palladium Hotel, not far from here. Many of our visiting dignitaries find it to be excellent lodgings."

President Iyasu studied her for several seconds before he said, "I am very pleased you agreed to come here and write an article on Ethiopia's progress. Your articles on the development of other third world countries, Haiti, Sudan, Afghanistan, and Somalia, came to my attention. You received the World Literary Prize for that work. It was most impressive, very comprehensive, and compelling. You learned your writing craft well."

Mary felt her face blush. "Thank you, but the content of that series of articles came from the people themselves and how they had used the gifts from a special source."

He leaned toward her. "I know, gifts from the late members of Promise, just the same as with our people. That is the story here as well, but with Ethiopia, of course, we were a little behind the others, mainly because their unfortunate deaths interrupted the full impact of Promise's generosity, but only for a short while. Their executors continued the group's work, finishing the university, medical center, and other projects, which quickly began to help our people. And I suppose your tour of the city indicated something of our progress?"

"Yes. Doctor Tafari showed me some of your grand buildings. They are as modern as any in the United States."

His excitement was rising as he spoke. "Our other cities are just as modern. Take, for example, our main port city of Mitswa. It has state-of-the-art container facilities at its docks on the Red Sea, allowing us to handle construction equipment, farm machinery, and vehicles for countries throughout the region. And our literacy rate has risen from only twenty percent to almost ninety-five percent, the result of schools built throughout our rural areas from the generosity of Promise. Today, our mines produce copper, chrome, tin, and clays for goods made around the world. And they are automated with robotics and conveyor systems running for miles to the port storage bins, millions of tons of capacity."

"But, President Iyasu, while I am interested in Ethiopia's progress, you offered me a special story, if I would come here and talk with you."

He looked intently at her, before gazing out a large window for several moments. "Indeed, I did. You generously came all this way. I suppose I should make good on my offer." The president stopped talking, rose, and walked to a picture of a man and a child. "This is my father, the former president of Ethiopia. The people called him Big Iyasu, or just Big I, mainly because he was a very large man, bigger even than I am. This boy is me when I was about ten. My father's parents died of disease when he was a child, and he survived on the streets, eating scraps, and fighting just to live. Fortunately, a kind Christian missionary found him and took him home to be raised with the missionary's family. Later, when he was grown, my father worked in the mines and became a leader in the labor movement. He wanted me to become educated and escape the hard work he endured for many years. We were great friends. The special story really involves him."

Mary's interest was aroused. "And what is this special story? Does it involve an unusual accomplishment of your father?"

"Yes. But there is more to it, much more. Mrs. Blair, did you ever wonder how it was that peace came so quickly to the Middle East after Promise's deaths, in only about a day?"

"I did wonder about it, but not very long. I suppose that my thinking focused primarily on peace finally coming rather than how quickly it came after their concert."

The president settled in his chair, hands clasped together. "The timing was actually very meaningful. There was a reason that peace came so quickly in the Middle East, and that reason is the special story I am going to tell you. At that time, my father was the president of Ethiopia and I was a young man on his personal staff. We were holding a meeting with the top militant leaders from the Middle East. They had asked for the meeting in Addis Ababa. I remember it quite vividly . . . ."

I sat beside my father, President Iyasu, Big I, as he conducted the meeting with the militant leaders, Mohammed Riza, Al Ben Zalawi and Sharif Atta, each wearing a different colored and styled headdress of his people.

"Gentlemen, welcome to Ethiopia. You have asked for this meeting, and I agreed. You offered us aid, for our help. As president of the country I feel obliged to hear you out. What do you have in mind?" my father said, welcoming the visitors that day.

Mohammed Riza seemed the spokesman for the group, saying, "You are aware of our holy war against the infidels from the West. The Americans responded with their army, and, quite honestly, they have been more forceful that we expected. I had thought that they would merely leave the Israelis unsupported after our attacks of September 11. But this American president is more determined that I had planned. His army has disrupted our efforts and killed many of our freedom fighters. We have no safe place to train and develop our weapons."

My father responded, "Yes, we are aware of the Americans' resolve. I think that it has even surprised the leaders of some of America's allies, those who wished to . . . how shall I say . . . escape your wrath."

Mohammed Riza squinted. "Many of the allies are cowards, like most of the American leaders. But this American president is different, more of a fighting rooster, I think. That is much of our problem. And this infidel band, Promise, has also been a thorn in our side, pouring money into poor countries, which has stabilized the peoples, making them less likely to join our cause. Even today, they are performing in Jerusalem. But they will pay for their interference with their lives. However, I need your help to overcome the Americans. But we are willing to offer something in return."

President Iyasu seemed curious. "What would you ask of us?"

Mohammed Riza leaned closer. "A place to train our fighters and prepare our chemical and biological weapons, free from the American troops and agents. Ethiopia is a perfect place, near our land. From here we can send our freedom fighters throughout the Middle East, Europe, and other lands, even to America. And we can also deliver powerful weapons perfected here—chemical agents to paralyze, blind, and kill millions and genetically altered germs to infect millions more. There will be no cure, and millions of Americans and Europeans will die. Victory for our cause will soon follow. But we need safe haven to accomplish these tasks."

The president asked, "And your offer to Ethiopia in return?"

Mohammed Riza sat up straight and said, "Wealth, from the vast oil reserves we will control one day, when we rid our land of the Western infidels. At that time, the entire region will be under our control, from Kashmir to Spain, a single state. We will reward you with great oil wealth to spend as you see fit, free from our power. Ethiopia will not be harmed by our fighters, though other African lands will be part of our state." He stopped talking and leaned back in his chair, took a long knife from his belt and laid it at his throat. "We came so close in the nineteen-forties. So close."

President Iyasu turned to me, as though asking for clarification, which I could not provide, and then asked, "What are you referring to, Mr. Riza?"

The long-bearded visitor pulled the knife across the base of his neck, producing a slight cut from which fresh blood oozed. "Our leaders collaborated with the Nazis in Berlin, offering advice and help on eliminating the Jews. And we would have killed all of them, and the Christians too, had Hitler not foolishly turned against Russia."

At that moment, there was a knock on the conference room door, and I rose to answer it. My sister was there and asked, "Can you see if Father could spare a moment to see Ishi? She is very excited about something and insists on seeing him right away. You know how besotted he is with her."

I walked to my father and whispered in his ear, "Ishi is asking to see you. Could you break for a few minutes?"

President Iyasu rose. "Gentlemen, if you will excuse me for a short while, my granddaughter beckons. Please enjoy some refreshment while I attend to her for a moment."

He and I joined my sister and walked to another part of the presidential mansion, coming to the residential quarters. I opened the outer door for him, and he led the way to my sister's suite down a long hall. A bright-eyed little girl of seven was waiting for him, and when he came in view, she shrieked and ran toward him. "Grandfather, please come see the television. Angels are singing, and I want you to see them."

The massive man picked up his granddaughter and received kisses in return, to his obvious delight. "Angels, you say. And how do you know that?"

"Because they are singing just like you sing to me," my niece answered with a grin.

The president carried her to a large television, my sister and I following. We all sat on a couch, and the president watched for a moment, before saying, "Those people are that band, Promise, performing a concert in Jerusalem. It's been in all the papers. They aren't angels, Ishi."

The child climbed in his lap, looked up into his eyes and said, "I know who they are, Grandfather, everyone does. But they are also angels, and I did not know that until I saw them on television tonight."

He tickled her. "And how are you informed that they are angels, my little one?"

"Grandfather, it is as I told you, they are singing just like you sing to me every night before bed."

The president wrinkled his brow. "Like I sing to you?"

She rose on her knees in his lap, eye to eye with him. "Yes, Grandfather. The songs you learned in the missionary home, the ones you sing to me over and over. They are singing of love, Grandfather, of love and peace, from God, who loves us all and wants us to love each other. Angels sing of those things, don't they, Grandfather? Isn't that what you learned as a little boy from the Christian missionaries?"

He held her close to his heart, obviously moved in a way only she could do. I saw his eyes glisten, and he kissed Ishi on the top of her head. "Yes, my darling, angels do sing of such things. Thank you for reminding me of that."

He lifted her from his lap, placed the child on the couch next to him and said, "Why don't you watch the rest of the concert. I must finish this meeting. Then we will talk of these angels and of love and other wonderful things."

I accompanied my father out of the room, back to the men waiting for his answer that night.

Mary's mind swirled with ideas. "What an incredible series of events. But how did those occurrences bring peace to the Middle East in a single day."

The president said, "My father rejected the militants' proposal. They became angry and threatened the people of Ethiopia and his family. He instructed me to immediately take certain, decisive actions regarding our visitors. I was also told to send a special message to their followers in the Middle East."

Mary asked, "What happened to those visitors?"

President Iyasu smiled slightly. "Their names were well publicized in the media. The 'Elusive Ghost Myrtars,' I believe the papers called them." He stopped, studied Mary for several seconds, as though to see if she remembered, before leaning toward her and saying, "It became clear to my father that those men were the heart of the extremist movement and that without them, it would die. He knew the opportunity was his to do something to end the terrorism. Did you ever hear anything about those men after that time?"

She thought for a moment. "No, they seemed to just fade away."

President Iyasu leaned back in his chair, a hard look on his face. "Exactly. They spent their remaining years in jail here, unable to lead their fighters and create any more terror. That was part of my message to the militants in the Middle East—no safe haven for them or their activities, no support for their cause. Their leaders would remain in our prison for life. But perhaps, most importantly, there would be no new hearts to turn to hate, because of Promise."

"It is all so clear now. With your father's communication to the terrorists and Promise's message reaching millions of young people that night, the militants must have known that their hope of changing the world through terrorism was over. Peaceful negotiation was the only way. Of course they would agree to immediately lay down their arms. What an incredible story, Mr. President, worthy of our best efforts to bring it to the world."

President Iyasu was smiling broadly, clearly glad that his special story had moved Mary to bring it to life.

He rose and walked to the large window through which he had earlier gazed, studying something far off, before turning to Mary, the remnant of a smile on his face. "Do you hear that thunder? It is from the high mountain in the distance. Ras Dashen it is called, the tallest point in Ethiopia."

She joined him at the window. "Yes, I can hear it, very distinctly now. But the sky looks so clear. There are no storm clouds that I can see. It seems unusual, thunder from such a clear sky, that is."

He continued to peer at the mountain. After a short time, he turned to her. "Do you believe in legends, Mrs. Blair?"

She was puzzled at his change from pragmatism to mysticism but tried to be polite. "In some, I suppose. Why do you ask?"

His affable expression was gone, replaced with intense eyes, as he said, "Our people long ago found hope in a song passed down from generation to generation, for many years: that when there is thunder from clear skies around Ras Dashen, it is a sign of God celebrating with our ancestors in Heaven."

She was puzzled and asked, "Celebrating? What are they celebrating?"

He looked into her eyes, the wide smile having returned. "Our freedom, from so many years of suffering, from a time when our people starved and had no hope, when the children cried and there were no parents to hold them, when there was no medicine to cure illness."

The room became silent, only the sound of the distant thunder falling on her ears.

Soon, the president spoke again, "I wanted to build a monument to them, right in front of this building, to Promise, for the gifts they gave to our people. But I could not. How can there be a monument to someone who is completely anonymous? I do not know their names or where they came from, not even of their leader, Tam, I believe his fans called him. He was their inspiration, and I would have built the monument if I had known just his true identity. But perhaps Tam's identity shall forever be known only to his immediate family . . . and to God."

Mary again turned her attention to Ras Dashen, the thunder from deep blue skies surrounding its snow-capped peak filling the room more forcefully than before, pounding her body like some powerful hand, and she thought to herself: Tam's identity, known only to his family and to God? Yes, and, of course, also to me.

CHAPTER THIRTY-SIX

Mary Blair sat comfortably in the overstuffed chair in the Addis Ababa International Airport VIP Lounge, scanning her notes for the Ethiopia article. She was pleased at the mass of facts, descriptions, and quotations gleaned during her week-long visit, feeling confident the article would be published by a magazine with worldwide circulation.

The sound of an incoming call on her satellite phone distracted her pleasant thoughts. She noticed the number on her caller ID and said to herself, "Matt." She pushed the "talk" button. "Matthew. Everything all right?"

"Terrific, Mom. When are you going to be home? I've got some stuff I need to talk with you about."

She answered, "I'm at the airport now, change planes in London; then it's home to Houston. I should be there tomorrow night. What do you need to discuss?"

Matthew Blair responded with excitement. "The music people want us to do a second CD. The first one is selling good, real good. Should hit a million in a couple months. Mom, they say our new songs are even better. What do you think of that?"

She became very motherly and serious. "I think it's great. But you don't want to drop out of college, do you?"

Silence came from the phone. Then Matthew said, "I was just thinking that after we make it as musicians I can go back to college, after the tour . . . ."

Her tone was sharp. "What tour? Matt, we've been over this before. You know I want you to finish college first. Your father . . . would have wanted the same for you."

"You know, Mom, you're always tell me about my father, about what he would want me to do. But I never knew him. It's tough to understand someone who died before you were born. I wish I had known him, just a little."

There was a pause on her end of the conversation, before she softly said, "But you do know him, son, very well. Just look in the mirror, at your blue eyes, or listen to your music. That will tell you a lot about your father. You're just like him."

"Mom, I understand how important college is, especially for someone who made good grades. It seems everyone expects me to become a doctor because I was valedictorian. But there is some feeling pulling me in another direction. I think I was born to do something else, and I need to talk to you about it. I really do."

Mary sighed. "All right, we'll talk about it when I get home. Until then, don't make any commitments to the music people. Love you."

"Love you too."

She pushed the "End" button and gazed off in space, remembering her husband. Her thoughts turned to their son, and she smiled.

Mary began to hear a song in her mind,

> *Some day in my twilight time,*
> *When stillness shall close my eyes,*
> *And men put me in the ground,*
> *Do not raise your cries,*
> *Or look for me in that place,*
> *Or stay there long to stare.*
> *Look for me in another land,*
> *For I will not be there.*
> *When you feel the thunder*
> *Or see lightnin' pierce the sky,*
> *There is where I'll be,*
> *Wailin' way up high,*
> *. . . .*

Mary caressed her phone and felt the smile broaden, as she said softly to herself, "Matthew, what am I going to do? You are so like your father."

She closed her eyes, the music continuing in her mind, and she visualized her son and his father together on a brightly lit stage, singing and dancing and flashing incredible blue eyes toward a vast audience clapping, moving, and singing with the music. She sensed it was a scene from God.

CHAPTER THIRTY-SEVEN

Mary Blair had been home for several weeks. She had finished the Ethiopia article and was researching a story about a condemned murderer. She was at the prison for an interview with him and found the experience unpleasant.

He looked across the metal table and spit on the floor, before saying, "I ain't no kid butcher, am I?" Marquez Cabillo, asked, his voice having a machine-like whine as it came through the intercom on the thick glass.

Mary Blair studied the inmate for a few seconds before answering. "I don't know, Mr. Cabillo. I haven't seen the evidence. But the jury did, and they thought you committed those murders, all thirteen of them."

Marquez Cabillo rose from the wooden chair and looked at the floor, turning to walk to the rear concrete wall and back. "Them knifings was real bad. But if a man don't know whether he done them . . . that kills the soul. You can't make your peace with God. Can't ask the Virgin for help. My family can't neither. It's hurt my mother the most. She comes every week and just cries out there, holdin' her Rosary. Cries the whole time. I'll be glad when they give me the needle, to stop my mind from thinkin' about them kids. The pictures at the trial, of them bloody kids. They is in my mind all the time, lookin' at me, right into my eyes." He stopped and peered at the ceiling. "They is watchin' me right now. Wish I could make them go away."

Mary Blair sighed. "I'm here to investigate your case and do a story on it. The magazine wants to know, so it can tell everyone the truth. It's unusual for an accused serial killer to take the stand and say he doesn't remember whether he killed thirteen children, that he might have murdered them, but that his mind is so confused from drugs he doesn't know. Some defendants say they didn't mean to kill someone, but drugs made them do it. Your case is different, though, very puzzling. There are people saying you may be innocent, that the real killer is still out there, waiting for you to be put to death before he strikes again."

Marquez Cabillo buried his face in gnarled hands, rubbing his forehead before stopping to grasp the skin in a hard grip that distorted the flesh. Mary Blair winced at the pain the man had to be causing himself.

"Mr. Cabillo, we're going to talk to all the witnesses, and I'll do everything I can to write the story before your execution date. But I need your help to get the facts."

He looked at her but said nothing for at least a minute, then, almost apologetically, whispered, "Facts? Don't remember none, except them dead faces. Can't say they are mine. Maybe."

She persisted. "But you must know something. Did you ever meet any of those children? Their parents? Do your friends know any of them?"

His expression changed from bewilderment to something Mary did not understand. Marquez Cabillo squinted at her, the force of his hands having left red streaks on his forehead. He spoke in a growl-like manner, "They got me into it. Said I'd have to push the drugs to pay my debt for bringin' my family from Mexico. Then they offered the dust to me, for free. Said it'd make me strong, to sell more drugs and pay off the debt. That was a lie. I couldn't get away . . . just kept sellin' the drugs and sniffin' the dust. It burned me, like fire. I could feel myself burnin'. Couldn't put out the fire. I wanted someone to put out the fire. But no one ever came. I smelled my skin burnin'. Till . . . ."

She asked, "Till what?"

He slumped lifelessly in the wooden chair, and his face went blank.

Mary Blair stared at him for a few moments, then she rose and pushed the red button on the wall. A uniformed guard opened the steel door to the small room. She walked through the doorway, stopped to study the condemned man once more, and left the visitors section of Huntsville Prison, walking along the white-tiled hallway toward an exit guarded by heavy steel bars. Her mind was a cacophony of thoughts: was this all a waste; wouldn't it be best to leave the work of the court alone; surely the jury was right, wasn't it? The bars slid open, and, when she cleared the threshold, Mary Blair felt a refreshing wind against her face, as though she had just gone outside on a fall day. She breathed deeply to enjoy the moment.

"Mrs. Blair?"

She turned to face Doctor Paul Lindman, the staff psychologist she had met at the start of her investigation into the case of Marquez Cabillo. He was tall and thin, almost sickly looking, like someone with a wasting disease. His black eyes stood out against a full head of silver hair and pale skin, and heavy lids hung at half-mast over the pupils. A long white coat gave the man a professional appearance, starkly different from most of the others in this windowless, concrete and steel world.

He gazed at her over glasses hanging low on a long, narrow nose. "Well, was he like I said? Totally confused?"

Mary looked at her legal pad before answering. "I'm afraid so. He said he couldn't remember anything about those children, or their murders. I wonder if he's telling the truth or if he's the greatest actor I've ever seen."

Doctor Lindman shook his head. "No actor there. I've interviewed him more than a dozen times. There's just no memory left. His brain has been gutted by chemicals. Drug induced psychosis, we call it. The brain cells are actually changed, damaged so they don't work normally. I really think he doesn't remember, and never will. You'll have to get the truth from others, if you can."

She shrugged. "I'm prepared to do that. The magazine wants a thorough investigation into his case, and they have funded the project with an investigator. We'll find something, and who knows, maybe the truth is out there waiting for us to turn over the right rock."

Doctor Lindman smiled and extended a bony hand. "Call me if I can be of further help."

Mary shook his hand. "Thanks. I might ask for some psychological information about the effects of drugs on the minds of these inmates."

He lowered his head and peered at her over black-rimmed glasses. "In a nutshell, the hard drugs, like cocaine, heroine, LSD, and meth, fry the brain, just like you were cooking it, killing the cells. The only question is how much brain is left. Hopefully, enough to walk and talk and remember. But many times there isn't enough for normal activity."

She wrinkled her brow. "That's odd. The way you described the effect of drugs on the brain is exactly how Cabillo described his experience. He said it was like burning, being on fire."

A chill ran through Mary as she envisioned her brain cooking, slowly rendering her helpless. She turned and hurried out of the prison, as though her flight could change the nightmarish mental images. Her car was a welcome sight, a comfortable home-away-from-home. She unlocked the door and settled into the supple leather seat, closing her eyes for a moment of peace. She wondered if it was wise to have taken this assignment. It was leading her into an alien world of frightening things she did not understand, a place she did not want to be. Though her stories always included some hard reality, this story was different. It seemed to point to dangers in her own world, ones that could adversely affect Matthew and her.

CHAPTER THIRTY-EIGHT

Mary drove in the heavy Houston traffic, not paying much attention to the SUVs, cars, pickups, or eighteen-wheelers surrounding her. Suddenly, a red car crossed into her lane, almost hitting her vehicle. The driver slammed on his brakes, and she swerved into the other lane to avoid a collision. The other driver glared at her, his eyes wide and threatening. He made an obscene gesture. She thought about yelling at the young man but did not, something telling her it would be dangerous to get into a confrontation. The other car fell behind, and she breathed more easily, until she noticed it on her bumper.

Mary wanted to get away from him, and she took the next exit off the freeway. Her heart began to race when he followed. She turned at the next light, and the red car turned the same way. Mary accelerated but the car stayed on her bumper. She became frightened, looking for a safe place to pull in, a gas station or store. Her vehicle lurched when the pursuer bumped her, and Mary's fright quickly turned into sweat on her face. She went faster, around other cars, praying for somewhere to stop. Her reason told Mary that the pursuer would not be deterred by regular citizens, who probably would not want to get involved.

Her vehicle lurched again, this time harder, and Mary's face was heavy with moisture. She realized she was crying. "God, please help me. This guy is crazy. Probably has a gun."

Mary noticed flashing lights ahead, and she saw a Houston police car on the shoulder, the officer writing a ticket. She accelerated to get to the officer as fast as she could and pulled onto the shoulder behind the cruiser. The sight of the policeman caused her heart to slow. Mary stayed in the car as her pursuer passed slowly, its driver making another obscene gesture, before he sped away.

The officer walked up and said through the window, "Is there a problem, ma'am?"

She found it hard to talk. "I . . . don't think so. There was a car following me. Thank God you were here."

He looked down the street. "Don't see anybody. But you still need to be careful. There are lots of crazies out there."

Mary said, "Yeah, road rage types."

"Not road rage so much as druggies. We stop lots of them. Kids high on something, looking for a mark, some with weapons. Drive defensively so you don't call attention to yourself, especially in this expensive car. The druggies are known to be looking for people to rob, especially if they seem to have money."

Mary shuddered. "Guess the cell phone won't help much."

The policeman shook his head. "Lots of times it won't. The bad guys are real good at shooting drivers and getting away fast. You want me to call another officer to escort you home?"

She looked around. "No. My house is nearby. I should be okay."

Mary pulled into traffic, still feeling weak from the ordeal. The officer's words played in her mind, and she shuddered again.

Her three-storey white brick townhouse came into view, and Mary breathed deeply and began to relax. She was home, safe from the predators.

Mary's thoughts returned to Marquez Cabillo, and she felt a chill. Her townhouse did not seem as safe as it had before.

CHAPTER THIRTY-NINE

Once inside the townhouse, Mary shook off her shoes, enjoying the cool feel of the polished wood floors. She looked in the family room. "Matt, Matthew. Are you home?"

Rock music vibrated through the ceiling, answering her question. Mary walked to the elevator and pushed the button for the third floor. As the car rose, the music grew louder. Distinct lyrics met Mary when the elevator door opened. She peered at Matthew and three other young men wailing at the end of a large room. Matthew had closed his eyes, fingers moving rapidly along the lead guitar. She knew the other members of his band, Tomorrow: Layne played the drums; Steve handled keyboard; and Ben strummed base guitar.

The song was new to her, but reminded Mary of Promise's work. She felt herself sway to the beat as she listened:

> *Don't lose all hope tonight,*
> *Make your heart be strong.*
> *I'm comin' for you now,*
> *It won't be too long.*
>
> *On and on through the night,*
> *Ridin' the race of the wind,*
> *I'll be there at first light,*
> *My brother and my friend.*
>
> *Keep on holdin' on,*
> *In a place of evil men,*
> *I won't stop till I'm there,*
> *Ridin' the race of the wind.*

Mary walked down a short hall, through an open door, into the large room serving as Tomorrow's studio. She noticed a stranger seated on a coach along one wall. He wore jeans, a colorful shirt with pearl buttons, black leather blazer, and a black cowboy hat. He was smiling, stroking his salt-and-pepper moustache, and one of his alligator cowboy boots bounced with the beat of the music. He was focused on the band and did not seem to notice Mary when she entered the room.

The song ended with Matthew bringing the lyrics to an abrupt conclusion, "Let's all live free!"

The visitor sprang from the couch. "Terrific! What a song. We're going to rock their socks with that tune, baby."

Mary approached her son. "Matthew?"

"Mom, when'd you get home? Didn't hear you."

"No wonder, loud as you were playing. Good thing for our neighbors we soundproofed the walls of this room."

The stranger quickly extended a hand, a diamond-encrusted watch hanging loosely on the wrist. "Yes ma'am, Scooter Rockman, of Austin Music. I hope it's okay for me to be here listening to our newest, and best group."

Mary looked at her son. "Your . . . group?"

Matthew averted his gaze, and Scooter Rockman came to his rescue. "Well, yes ma'am. Lots of music houses wanted them, but we were the lucky ones. Austin Music has big plans for Tomorrow—concerts, albums, tours, the works. Why, in a couple of years they will be the hottest band in the country, heck, the world."

Mary's tone was not friendly. "Matthew, I thought we were going to talk about this before you made any decisions. Didn't you agree to discuss your future plans with me first?"

"Mom . . . yes. You're right. But Mr. Rockman made us a terrific offer, accelerated exposure through all the media. We'll be on top in no time. Then, we can control our own schedule. Won't that be great?"

Scooter Rockman tried again. "Mrs. Blair, these boys have real talent, and they perform so well together, real harmony that touches the heart . . . like some of the really great bands. It's funny, but they remind me of the great Promise, rest their souls."

She looked at the visitor. "Promise was the greatest band of all time. You can't mention any other group with them."

Rockman swallowed. "Right, of course. I was only trying to show you our enthusiasm for Tomorrow's talent. But you're right. Promise was special.

Nobody can be compared with them. Too bad they didn't have any children to carry on their legacy. Their early deaths, a real tragedy. Sure was."

Mary and Matthew locked glances for a moment, before she said, "Yes, a tragedy. But I have to look out for my son, and I'm not sure a musical career is best for him. He graduated valedictorian and made a perfect score on his college aptitude test. He's making all As at Poly. It may be best for him to be a doctor or other professional. He and I had planned to discuss his future before he commits to anything."

Rockman was persistent. "That's impressive, but Matthew could do great things with his music too."

Mary ended the conversation. "Everybody, go home, and let Matthew and me discuss the matter. He will do the right thing."

The others left, and Mary shot Matthew a hard look, the kind intended to freeze you in your tracks.

"Mom, please, don't be mad at me, or Mr. Rockman."

Mary motioned for them to sit. "I'm not mad, just concerned. You have incredible talents, Matthew, and only limited time to use them. You can't go off in all different directions. Choose the best course and follow it. Maybe that's not music. Medicine holds great challenges and rewards. Wouldn't it be wonderful to discover a cure for cancer, for example? With your mind, you could do that."

"It's Dad, isn't it? You are afraid I'll end up like him."

She looked squarely at Matthew. "Maybe, and so what? Don't you think I have a right to be afraid of that? You are my family, my life, my heart. I won't lose you like I did your father."

Matthew looked at her with endless blue eyes, smiling sweetly, his boyish face radiating wisdom beyond nineteen years. "Mom, you can't live in fear. It will paralyze you, hold you back. I want to do what my heart says. Maybe Dad is talking to me, giving the right answer. Besides . . . ."

Mary began to envision her husband explaining his plans after high school, his "job," which had made no sense to her then. She could feel her resolve being tested.

CHAPTER FORTY

Mary was hard at work on the Marquez Cabillo article. She scanned the investigator's preliminary report:

"Cabillo worked as a construction laborer, moving from job to job in the Houston area over a three-year period. He made minimum wage, bringing home about $200 per week, including overtime. He reported a job-related back injury and went on worker compensation benefits of $100 per week.

"He refused to return to work after treatment. His mother states his back could not lift the heavy loads any longer. However, his sister said he began to suffer blackouts and bouts of anger. She did not know the reason and said he sought no medical treatment because he had no insurance. His sister became upset at Cabillo's increasingly harsh discipline of her son (eight years old), leading to his leaving the family in anger. The child was the first victim discovered. He was brutally beaten and decapitated. This discovery led authorities to Cabillo. While no direct evidence of the murder was proven, circumstantial evidence caused the jury to convict. He was sentenced to death. Subsequently, authorities connected him to twelve similar murders. He was not tried for any of those killings.

"We have traced Cabillo's steps to Laredo, Texas, and I plan to travel there to continue the investigation. It is likely we can discover relevant friends or personal contacts there. I will keep you advised. George McDow, Investigator."

Mary stopped reading the report and muttered to herself, "Decapitated. And Cabillo can't remember whether he killed that child? Nonsense."

Her thoughts were interrupted by the telephone. "Lizzie. What's up?"

"Oh, Mary, I'm about to go crazy."

"About what?"

"Brittany. She is threatening to leave home. We're fighting all the time. She wants independence, to come and go as she pleases. I don't think she's mature enough. Mary, she is hanging around with some wild kids. I think they are drinking too much, and maybe, using drugs. Brittany denies doing anything wrong. She says I don't trust her."

"Do you?"

"Her, yes. She's a good kid. Her friends, I don't know. Probably not."

"I can sympathize. Matthew is giving me fits right now. Same thing, freedom to do what he wants, even though he's just a kid."

"Matthew? He's always been such a great boy. So talented. Like his father. Tam was so incredible. I can't see Matthew giving you any trouble."

"Lizzie, let's be careful talking about Tam. Remember, I committed to never disclose his identity. Of course, you knew because you helped me so much after his death. You got me through, Liz. You really did. Still, at times, I feel like I betrayed him by telling our son. But Tam wasn't aware we were going to have a child, and I felt he would want his son to know." Mary stopped talking, and the two remained connected in silence. "Do you remember his father being determined to do the East Jerusalem concert? He wouldn't consider college or even a normal music career. I couldn't change his mind, even after we married. Matthew is the same way, pulled in some direction away from our family, to who knows where, and I can't seem to change his mind. It scares me, Liz."

There was more silence. "I hadn't thought about that in a long time, Mary. I can see how Matthew's wanting to follow his father would scare you to death."

"The thought of losing Matthew keeps flashing in my mind. I don't think I could live through that. I'm determined not to let it happen. He's going to do something nice and normal, like be a doctor or lawyer."

"Oh, please don't mention lawyers. None of them are normal. The one who handled my divorce was a flake who kept telling me everything was going to be fine, until he got eaten up by that shark representing my husband. How can an adulterer get away with most of the property, Mary? Tell me that."

"Okay, okay, Liz. No lawyer. Just a plain, ordinary, regular brain surgeon."

"Who will develop an ego the size of Texas and treat everybody like slime, just like my former husband, the good Doctor LeBlanc, did to me and Brittany."

"Lizzie, you're hopeless. Just because your ex is a doctor who ran off with his nurse doesn't mean all doctors are like that. Another call is coming in. Got to go. Call you later."

Mary touched a button on the phone and answered, "Hello."

A man's voice responded, "Yes, Mrs. Blair, this is Scooter Rockman of Austin Music. Just wanted to touch base and see if you had made a decision on your son's career."

"Yes, I have. It's probably good that you called. I have decided that Matthew is going to pursue a professional career. He has the brains to be a great doctor or medical researcher."

"I'm sure sorry to hear that, Mrs. Blair. Sure am. He's such a talented composer and musician. Matthew could be one of the great ones, I mean at the very top. I've been in this business a long time, and you don't see his kind of talent come along every day. That CD his band did a while ago is at the top of the charts, and it shows no signs of going down. Demand is way beyond supply right now, and the European markets want it too. Screamin' for it. I sure wish you would reconsider, ma'am."

"Afraid not. I'm looking out for his future, not profits. He's going to be a doctor, period."

Scooter Rockman almost whined. "Golly, I'm sorry to hear that. Sure is a waste."

"Goodbye, Mr. Rockman."

"Goodbye, ma'am."

CHAPTER FORTY-ONE

Matthew Blair sat in his room with the other members of Tomorrow. The drummer, Layne Newton, looked at him and shook his head. "Man, what a bummer. I can't believe your mother is being so hard. I mean, what parent would shut down a *can't miss* music career. Most parents would do anything to help their kid become successful. But not your mom. It sucks, man. It really does."

"Don't blame my mom. There are just the two of us, and she worries that a music career will hurt our family."

The base guitar player, Ben Rose, said, "Hurt? Dude, you ain't going to croak. What's she afraid of?"

Matthew looked at the floor. "I . . . don't know. Probably afraid that music will pull us apart. With all the drugs in the business, maybe she's right."

Steve Zamora, the keyboard player, laughed. "Come on. A little stimulation never hurt anybody. Heck, the adults do it all the time with their caffeine. And they criticize us?" He took a packet of white powder from his pocket and held it to his nose. "Here's to feelin' good. Anybody want some?"

Matthew reacted quickly. "Not here, Steve. We don't do that stuff, and I won't have it in my house."

Steve sealed the packet and returned it to his pocket. "Picky, picky. All right. I won't do it here."

Matthew pointed at him. "You shouldn't do it at all. It can't help you. Probably will mess up your brain. You should stop."

Steve folded his arms. "I'm just tryin' to make things seem a little better, that's all. It makes me relax, feel mellow."

Matthew got up. "Look, you guys go home, and I'll talk with my mom. Maybe I can change her mind. I'll call you."

He led the others to the front door. "Later."

Matthew returned to his room and took a magazine from his desk drawer. It was worn with age and use, but the cover was still glossy and colorful, showing Promise in concert. Tam was wailing on a gold guitar; the other band members were hard at work on their instruments; and countless fans jammed the concert venue, some of them reaching out across the front of the stage as though they were trying to touch Tam. "Dad, I'm sorry. I can feel you calling to me. But Mom is so tough. She won't let me do it. I don't think I can change her mind."

The afternoon wore on with Matthew reading the magazine and listening to Promise songs on his stereo. He accompanied the music with his guitar and joined Tam in the lyrics.

"Matthew. Are you here?" came Mary's voice from downstairs.

He looked at the clock and called to her, "Up here."

She walked into his room, obviously in a good mood. "I just got some great news. The people at the medical school called and said you can get in without graduating from college, with just ninety hours. You have almost half of that right now, with those AP hours. Isn't that terrific?"

He looked up from the magazine. "Yeah. Mom, could we talk a minute?"

Mary took the magazine from him. "Be careful what you say about this. Remember, your father wanted his identity to remain a secret. Don't let it slip that he's your dad."

"I know. You have explained. I just like seeing him in concert. Sure wish I had known him."

Mary softened her enthusiasm. "You know a lot about him, and I'm sure he would be very proud of his son."

"That's just it, Mom. I don't think medical school is right for me. I have this feeling . . . that Dad is calling to me, about something else, a different direction for my life."

Her tone became forceful. "Matthew, we discussed this, and I thought we had agreed. You are going to be a doctor. Why are you bringing it up again?"

"Because it isn't settled in my mind."

"It's settled in mine. Let's get on with life."

He snapped at her. "What if I move out and do my own thing? Then my life will be my own. I'm a grown man."

"And leave me? Break up our family? You don't mean that, Matthew."

The doorbell rang. Matthew got up from his bed. "I'll get it. We need a break."

He went to the first floor and opened the door. Layne Newton stood on the porch, looking confused.

Matthew asked, "What's up?"

Layne answered slowly, "It's Steve. We were driving to my place, and he took a snort. I didn't like him doing the stuff, but he did it anyway. Then he went crazy for a minute. I tried to calm him down. He blacked out. We got scared. Ben headed for the hospital. They took him in the emergency room."

"What hospital? I'll get over there right now."

Layne looked at him, tears brimming in his eyes. "No use. They couldn't do anything for him. He's gone. Overdose."

Matthew swallowed. "I can't believe it. We were just talking."

Layne turned and walked away. Matthew closed the door, Mary standing next to him.

"I told him not to do it. But he wouldn't listen. Thought the drugs would make him feel good. God, what a nightmare."

Mary gripped her son's shoulders. "You see, Matthew. This is why I have been so insistent about you not pursuing a music career. It's not good for you, no matter what your father did. Music is infected with drugs and foolishness, and I don't want you being a part of it."

Matthew looked at her. "Okay. I'll listen to you. But I've got to go see Steve's parents. They had a lot of hope for him. That his success would help their family. And now, it's all gone. I can't believe how fast everything fell apart."

CHAPTER FORTY-TWO

Matthew Blair stopped in front of the Zamora family house. It was a one-storey wooden structure, needing a coat of white paint. The porch railing leaned, much the same as the wooden steps. Some people were on the front porch, while others talked in the overgrown yard. The door was open, revealing people inside, probably too many for the size of the house. All of the other houses appeared about the same, consistent with the potholed asphalt streets and broken sidewalks of the neighborhood.

He got out of the car, wondering what he would say to Steve's parents.

"Hey, Matthew, lookin' for mom and dad?"

He turned to see a young girl. "Yeah, Orie. Are they here?"

"Inside, with the other family. I came outside 'cause I couldn't stand the cryin'."

"Orie, I'm so sorry about your brother. It was a shock, a real tragedy."

She cocked her head and looked at him. "I hate that he killed himself, but I told him. We all did. Lots of times. He knew the drugs might kill him, but kept doin' them. Guess he couldn't get away from the pushers. They're all over this neighborhood."

Matthew put a hand on her shoulder. "You stay away from those criminals. Don't listen to them."

She looked up at him through one squinting eye. "I'll try. But it's hard. They keep after you. Tell you all kinds of crazy things, like the drugs will make you feel good, make you stronger, take you away from all this. I don't know if I can keep away from the pushers."

He reacted quickly. "Orie, you're just a kid. How old are you, ten, eleven maybe?"

"Eleven next month. I can't wait till I'm old enough to leave. Sixteen, I think it is. Then I don't have to go to school anymore. I can get a job, and have my own place, get out of this neighborhood, away from the pushers."

Matthew tried to think of something helpful but knew he lacked the experience to solve her problems. "You have to keep trying to do the right thing. Your life will change. Everything will work out if you keep trying. Stay in school, away from the bad people. Someday, you can get a good job and live in a safe place."

She looked away. "Steve hoped for that. Said your band would take us out of this place, to a nice part of town. That we could get good doctors for my father, to make him better after the fire burned him in that accident. But it all changed—didn't look like the band was going to work out. We got scared nothing would ever change. My uncle said he could help, but they sent him back to Mexico. My parents gave up. Everyone just gave up. Steve took it hard. Thought he let us down. The drugs made it better for him. It scares me."

Matthew asked, "What scares you, Orie?"

"That I won't get out of here and the drugs will kill me too."

CHAPTER FORTY-THREE

A gravely voice came across the telephone, "This is George McDow calling from Mexico. Is Mrs. Blair in?"

The secretary said, "Just a minute, please." She pressed the intercom button. "Mrs. Blair, George McDow is calling. Shall I transfer him?"

"Yes, I've been waiting for his call." Mary Blair picked up the receiver. "George, where are you?"

"In Nuevo Laredo. Mrs. Blair, I've turned up some leads, and I wanted to tell you right away. Cabillo came here. It looks like he got involved with a drug cartel running cocaine across the border. I don't have a lot of details right now, but these are real bad people. Everybody is scared to talk. I got a little information from a local priest. One thing is for sure, Cabillo went completely crazy. Probably the drugs. The priest said even his family was scared of his violent temper. He started beating the neighborhood kids if they didn't do what he said. Looks like he got them involved in the drug running. I'm going to keep looking, but I think we're on the right track."

"Good work, George, but you need to be careful. The news has some pretty scary stories about those drug lords. If you sense any danger, get out of there fast."

"Don't worry, Mrs. Blair. I grew up in Brooklyn, and nothing gets rougher than that."

"I'm sure. But still be careful."

"Will do. I'll call soon."

George McDow ended the call. It was suppertime and he was hungry. A restaurant on the town square appeared through his hotel window, and George decided to try it. He walked through the terracotta-floored lobby, into the hot night air. The square was active, as people walked in and out of cantinas and shops around its edge, while others sat on benches and talked in Spanish.

He entered the restaurant, the smell of roasting meat beckoning him. The investigator sat at a wooden table near a window and looked at the town square, illuminated by electric pole lanterns casting an orange glow.

A waiter came to the table. "*Sí señor. ¿Qué quisiera usted?*"

"I don't speak Spanish very well. Do you speak English?"

The waiter answered, "Yes, sir. What would you like?"

George did not hesitate. "A cold beer and some of that roasted meat that smells so good."

The waiter put two fingers together and kissed them. "Roasted, marinated flank steak. 'Fajitas' you Americans call it. To us, it is a cheap cut of meat our people can afford. In the States, the restaurants get *mucho dinero* for it."

"Can I get some tortillas, corn?" George asked.

"Yes, sir, and some onions and peppers and salsa *también*."

Their attention was drawn to a commotion in the square directly in front of the window. George peered at several young men surrounding two other men. One of the captives talked loudly in Spanish and gestured wildly. Another young man pushed through the ring of captors. He was about twenty and handsome, his long, curly black hair shimmering in the light. He seemed to be the leader, quickly taking charge. The gesturing man stopped talking and bowed. The other captive stood silently.

The leader had a distinct square jaw and high cheekbones, making him look different from the others. George noticed a scar running from right eye to chin, but the mark only seemed to enhance his manly and rugged appearance. George could hear him through the glass. He talked slowly but purposefully in Spanish.

The leader took a handgun from his belt and pointed it directly at one of the men. A loud blast startled George, and a second blast immediately followed. Both captives slumped to the cobbled square.

George cried out, "My God, did you see that? Call the police!"

The waiter put a hand on his shoulder. "They will do nothing. Do not look at them, amigo. Those *hombres* will come in here and kill us all. Look at me, only at me."

George was frozen, not able to move or talk, his eyes fixed on the tabletop.

The waiter left, and George continued to look at the wooden table, one long scrape reminding him of the murderer's scar. The waiter soon returned and placed the meal of sizzling meat, onions and peppers before him. A few bites brought no pleasure; the food seemed tasteless. George wanted to flee the restaurant for his hotel room. He forced a glance out the window. The gang was gone, and the square was empty. He put a twenty-dollar bill on the table and walked quickly from the restaurant, across the square, and into the hotel. The sliding door lock made him begin to relax. Finally, he felt safe.

George fumbled with his notes, trying to divert nervous thoughts from the murders he had witnessed. Even the worst thugs of Brooklyn were not that brazen. A knock caused him to jump. Should he pretend not to be there? The knock persisted, and he cautiously rose. He stood at the door for a few moments, but another knock caused him to turn the lock and crack the door. A short Hispanic man smiled. "Señor McDow?"

George slowly responded, "Yes?"

Suddenly, the door slammed fully open, forcing George into the center of the room. Several Hispanic men entered, followed by the square-jawed murderer he had seen earlier. The scar moved upward as the man said, "You will come with us."

George protested. "I haven't done anything."

The scar moved downward. "The boss wants to see you, now."

George asked, "Who?"

"Jorge Galinda, our boss, the boss of everyone in this town. We go now," came the leader's harsh reply.

The group surrounded George and led him to a waiting SUV. The others sat tightly around him, and soon they were speeding along dark, rough-paved streets. The lights of Nuevo Laredo faded as the vehicle rumbled into the dark countryside. It turned sharply and began to climb a slight incline. George could make out a large structure ahead, a high wall hiding the first storey while bright lights illuminated the stucco second storey.

Thick iron gates opened for the vehicle, and it stopped under a portico. The captors got out. The square-jawed man motioned for George to follow him. They walked through carved wooden doors and into a marble entry.

The leader stopped. "Wait here." He disappeared through a tall door at the end of the chamber.

George looked at the gilded furnishings and tapestries, thinking that the decorations looked out of place against the beige plaster walls.

The tall door opened, and the leader stood in the opening and ordered George to enter the room. Thick cigar smoke hung in the air, puffs coming from a man sitting at a large wooden desk. His face was pocked and dark-skinned, and a full moustache matched his full head of black hair.

The man pointed his cigar at George. "Señor McDow, come and sit here at my desk."

George obeyed the order, the smell of leather distracting his senses from the pungent smoke.

The cigar smoker leaned back in his massive chair. "You came here to learn about Marquez Cabillo. You have been told that he was a drug mule. The informer said that he was an angry man. What else?"

George swallowed. "Nothing more. I don't know anything else. In fact, I was planning to return tomorrow, without any real information about him . . . or his job here."

Jorge Galinda smiled, smoke pouring from the corners of his mouth. "I see. We cannot let you leave without more information. That is why I brought you here. My friend, Agapito, will show you everything so that you can make a full report. Is that not true, Agapito?"

"The scar moved. "Sí señor."

Jorge Galinda motioned with the cigar. "Why don't you take our visitor to see the operation. Give him a tour. Treat him like a king."

The scar moved again. "It will be my pleasure, *mi jefe*."

Agapito grasped George's arm and pulled the man from the chair. "Come with me, *amigo*."

George McDow tried to resist. "But that isn't really necessary. I'll leave now, tonight."

Agapito placed a strong arm around his shoulders. "We will not hear of it. The boss wants us to show you around. Let us go."

Agapito led George McDow from the room, and the others surrounded him. They entered the SUV, and it swiftly left, bouncing over another dark road. After about twenty minutes, it stopped at a long, dimly lit building. Men with rifles or shotguns stood at the front door, and Agapito pushed George McDow inside a metal structure; a strong odor caused him to cough.

The leader stood in back and applied pressure to George's spine. "That way."

The group moved along wooden tables laden with bags of white powder. Workers weighed sealed plastic bags, while other men carefully filled open bags. The visitors continued down the tables, stopping near a series of large caldrons, their brew producing the odor George McDow had sensed upon entering the building.

Agapito said, "This is where Marquez Cabillo worked, picking up the product to take to America. He was very good at his work. Fearless. Followed orders. No question of his loyalty to the cartel."

George McDow focused on Agapito's scar. "But why show me this? I don't really need to know anything about your business."

Agapito quickly answered, "Nonsense. The boss wants you to see everything, so you can make a full report."

"Look, why don't you let me go." George McDow looked at the other captors for some sign of support. He turned to Agapito to renew his plea for freedom, only to be paralyzed at the sight of the leader's handgun pointed at his head.

George began to whine, "Please, don't do this. I have a wife and child. They need me. I won't say anything. I swear."

The scar turned upward. "Of course you will, amigo. But you can give your report to the angels.

CHAPTER FORTY-FOUR

Mary dialed the cell phone number, heard the voice message, and frowned. "Where are you, George McDow? We're running out of time. Cabillo is scheduled to be executed in a couple of months, and I need your report."

The intercom interrupted her thoughts. "Mrs. Blair, it's Lizzie LeBlanc. Can you take her call?"

"Sure, put her through."

Mary picked up the receiver. "Hey, gal. What's up?"

Lizzie seemed frightened and confused. "Mary, I need you to come to the hospital, right away! Texas General Hospital, ICU."

"What happened? Are you all right?" Mary questioned.

"It's Brittany. Something terrible has happened. Mary, please come now! I don't think I can handle this alone."

"On my way."

Mary sped through Houston's morning rush hour traffic, weaving in and out of cars, pickups, and delivery trucks. She zoomed into the parking garage, thanking God for an empty space. Mary ran across the street, through the hospital entrance, to the information desk.

"Could you direct me to the ICU?"

An older woman looked up. "Third floor, center pavilion. The elevators are straight ahead."

Mary closed her eyes in the elevator, until it stopped. She walked cautiously into the hall. She looked through the windows of the waiting room. Lizzie was sitting in a chair, her head buried in both hands.

"Lizzie? What's wrong?" Mary said, kneeling at her friend's side.

She extended trembling arms. "Mary. Thank God. It's Brittany. They called me from the hospital and said she was in the emergency room."

"What happened to her?"

"I don't know, Mary. Only that she collapsed at that beach house. They called the ambulance. She's unconscious. You don't think she had a heart attack, or a stroke, at her age?"

Mary tried to be calm. "No. It can't be anything like that. Have you talked to the doctor?"

"No. Only the ER nurse. They worked on her for a while, then transferred her to ICU. I've been waiting for the doctor. Seems like a long time, too long."

"Liz, you have to be strong. We'll be strong together," Mary said, hugging Lizzie gently. Remember, when Matthew died we were together then.

"Mrs. LeBlanc?" came from the door. Mary and Lizzie turned toward a tall man in a white coat. A stethoscope hung around his neck. They slowly walked toward him.

"Is one of you Mrs. LeBlanc?" the man asked.

Lizzie nodded, as Mary held her more firmly.

The man said, "I am Doctor Crutchfield, head of neurology. Let's step over to the corner for some privacy."

The little group moved a short distance, before Doctor Crutchfield cleared his throat. "The ER staff called me this morning to attend your daughter. She is in a drug-induced coma. We have her on life support right now."

Lizzie cried out, "Drug-induced coma. But how? She doesn't do drugs. I know for sure."

Doctor Crutchfield answered, "She probably didn't knowingly take the drug."

Lizzie asked, "How did it get into her system?"

He explained. "Her blood contains a toxic level of Rohypnol."

Lizzie sputtered, "Ro . . . Rohypnol? What is that? How did she . . . . ?"

"It is commonly referred to as a date rape drug. Most likely, someone slipped it into her drink," the doctor explained

"One of her good friends did this to her. I warned Brittany. I told her they were too wild." Lizzie stopped talking, seemingly focused on something else. "How long before she wakes up, before her body breaks down the drug?"

Doctor Crutchfield looked at her for a long moment, until he carefully said, "Mrs. LeBlanc, her EEG is flat. We see no brain activity. There is virtually no chance that will change. The brain cannot regenerate destroyed cells. I'm afraid you are going to be faced with a hard decision."

Lizzie seemed unable to respond, and Mary asked, "What decision?"

He looked squarely at Lizzie. "When to disconnect the life support."

CHAPTER FORTY-FIVE

Matthew slouched in the hard desk chair, drawing stick figures of musicians playing different instruments. He barely heard his Organic Chemistry professor. "I have your graded tests. Some of you need to reread the prior chapter. You can't go on to the next chapter without an understanding of that material."

Professor Orenson passed out the tests, some students responding with smiles while others grimaced. Matthew Blair was expressionless.

"Class dismissed."

Most of the students quickly left, but Matthew continued to draw.

"Mr. Blair, you don't look pleased. That surprises me, since you made a hundred on the test, highest grade in the class. Is there a problem?"

He looked at the professor. "No real problem. Just a little bored, I guess."

Professor Orenson sighed. "I understand."

Matthew responded, "I'm not sure anyone can really understand my situation. It's, well, kind of unique."

"I see. You know, I was bored too during college. Wanted to do something other than chemistry. My heart wasn't always in my college work."

Matthew looked up from his drawing. "What else did you want to do?"

Professor Orenson looked around, before saying, "Folk singer."

"Folk singer? What's that?" Matthew asked.

"They were musicians in the sixties. Sang in coffee shops and at peace rallies. Some of the groups became famous social icons. They harmonized well, primarily with acoustic guitar. Some used bongo drums, but no big amps or electronic keyboards or high-tech stuff."

Matthew was interested. "What made them special?"

"They touched our social conscience with songs about young men dying in war, the evils of racial hatred, a world yearning for peace, the loss of childhood innocence."

"Why didn't you follow your dream?"

Professor Orenson did not answer, his eyes glassy and far away.

Matthew tried again. "Professor, why didn't you become a folk singer?"

The elder man was back in the present. He pointed to his stomach.

Matthew laughed. "What?"

Professor Orenson said, "No guts. Afraid I wasn't good enough for anyone to like my music."

Matthew leaned forward. "What if you had found those guts?"

Professor Orenson smiled. "I would have traded that periodic table for a sweet acoustic guitar."

CHAPTER FORTY-SIX

Matthew looked at the other members of Tomorrow. "I've decided to keep the band together."

Ben Rose shrugged. "What for, man? The band can't play professionally. We don't need any more practice."

Layne Newton said, "He's right. It'd probably be better for us to break up and join other bands."

Matthew raised his voice, "You guys are just going to give up? We have gotten off to a great start. And who knows, maybe things will change."

Layne asked, "How? When?"

"I don't know. But you've seen lots of bands try for years, then hang it up. Let's keep Tomorrow together and see what happens. At least we have a major music producer convinced." Matthew stopped and glanced at the others for their reactions.

Ben said, "That doesn't solve our board problem. With Steve gone, who's going to bang the keys?"

"That guy from New Orleans is pretty good. He did fine when he jammed with us," Matthew offered.

"Wimpy. Too much blues and jazz influence." Ben stopped talking, seeming to consider the matter. "But Jake Hudson might do it, and he can rock."

Layne and Ben looked at Matthew, who asked, "But doesn't he do drugs? Marijuana?"

Layne answered, "Yeah. But so what? Lots of the professional musicians do something. Everybody knows that. If you are going to eliminate all those guys, we won't find anybody good."

Matthew was firm. "Don't you guys remember what happened to Steve? You want to go through that again?"

Ben said, "Look, man. Weed is not like the hard stuff. It won't kill you."

Matthew shot back, "It will get you arrested, and it leads to the hard drugs. I don't want Tomorrow known for that. We need to have the reputation as a bunch of clean guys. The kids will follow our examples. If we do drugs, they will think it's okay. Look at our music. It's about hope and courage and people coming together to overcome problems. That means lives without drugs. You guys don't want to send some other message."

Ben and Layne looked at each other, before Layne said, "Okay, we'll stay with you, at least for a while, and we can give the New Orleans guy a try. Maybe he'll get up to speed with us."

Ben seemed enthusiastic. "Yeah, it's like you said, Matt, things might change. I hope so. You're right about the drugs; we need to run a clean group. I don't want to tell the kids it's cool to take that poison. Too many kids are going down from the stuff. No more guys like Steve. No more."

Chapter Forty-seven

It was a sea of puppy dog tails: long ones and stubs, curlys and shaggys, short hairs and longs, sharps and blunts, brown tails and black tails, whites and combos. All of them were proudly displayed like the flags of countries held high at some international sporting event.

"How am I going to pick the ones for today? You all want to go so bad." The short, round-faced man with oriental features stopped and looked once again across the puzzlement of wagging tails. "Okay, I'm just gonna close my eyes and pick. Nobody get mad. No peein' on my shoes."

"These guys giving you a problem, Eric?"

Eric Rohmer opened his eyes. "Mr. Matthew. Happy to see you. Man, they all want to go today, but we got only one driver to take them. I'm scared somebody's gonna get mad."

"Don't worry. I'll drive the other van. We can split them up."

"That's great, Mr. Matthew. Can I ride with you? You're fun to go with. Don't make fun of me like some of the others. I can't help it that I'm retarded, honest."

Matthew stroked his thick hair. "Nobody is going to make fun of you. We'll punch 'em in the nose."

"That would be great! I bet you could punch 'em real good. You're so strong, and fast, the number one runnin' back in the country in high school and at Poly. Yeah, real good."

"Eric, go split them up. I'll meet you out back in a few minutes. I've got to get the schedule."

"Okay, Mr. Matthew. Boy, this is gonna be great. Come on guys."

Matthew walked along the corridor of empty cages, stopping at one where a light brown dog lay quietly, its head resting on front paws. He opened the cage. "Hey, old boy. How you feeling today? Not so good. I'm sorry."

He gently lifted the dog's head and stroked it, and the animal whimpered ever so slightly. Matthew Blair scratched the shaggy ears, and the whimper turned to a sigh.

"Why do you insist on driving these dogs around?"

Matthew turned to see a short, heavy-browed man, his hands resting on his hips. "Your mother runs this foundation, and you want to be a driver. Wouldn't you rather work in the main office in some executive job?"

Matthew slowly lowered the dog's head and closed the cage. "I like working with the animals and the old folks and patients, Mr. Huggins. It's great to watch them with each other, the love that develops."

The man shook his head. "I don't think I would call it love. These animals can't love."

Matthew looked straight at him. "I think they can feel deep emotions. That's what I like, watching the dogs get excited when they see a familiar face. They sure miss someone who dies. They look all around, kind of lost for a while. It seems to me they love."

The man shrugged. "Whatever you want. But don't tell your mother I assigned you to drive a van. She might not like it."

Matthew smiled as he walked away. "Everything is okay. No problem with the boss."

Matthew walked through a door at the end of the hall, into a small office. "Hello, Alice. Got a schedule for van two today?"

A red-haired girl looked up from her desk. "Oh, hi, Matthew. Yep, got the schedule right here: Elder Care, Texas Pediatric, Texas Cancer Center. Think you can do it all today?"

"No big deal. I've got a good helper, Eric."

"Don't let Huggins know you are taking Eric. He thinks the boy is good only for shoveling poop," she said with a frown.

"Eric is great on these runs. He's gentle with the dogs and pays attention to the people. I think they enjoy him."

Matthew took the schedule to the parking area and got into a white van, met by barks from his excited passengers.

"Ready to blast off, Mr. Matthew. I'm all buckled up," Eric said with a beaming smile.

Soon they were driving to Elder Care Nursing Home. Eric hummed. Matthew laughed. "Say, I didn't know you could hum so good."

"It makes me zippy to go with you. Kind of like I'm doing a special thing. This is different from the home, where they call me moron and stupid and freak and stuff like that. I don't like it. Makes me sad."

"Eric, you are special. I couldn't do this job without you. The puppies know it. Look how good they are for you, and the people brighten up when they see you. Think how much happiness you bring them."

Eric hummed a few more notes, stopping to ask, "You really mean it?" He resumed humming softly.

"I sure do. Cross my heart."

Eric stopped humming, his eyes sparkling as he gazed at Matthew. "It's great to have a friend like you, Mr. Matthew. Will you always be my pal?"

Matthew looked at him. "Always."

Eric leaned across the console and rested his head against Matthew's side. "Funny."

"What's funny, Eric?"

"How stuff changes. Right now, I can't remember anyone makin' fun of me. Maybe the people at the home aren't all that mean."

CHAPTER FORTY-EIGHT

She caressed the keys of the grand piano, the cords and notes flowing without hesitation, up and down the musical scale. Yet, at times, her fingers moved sharply and powerfully, driving the music from the instrument.

Angelica Steuben closed her eyes as she played, seeming to create the music, rather than just reproduce it. Her torso swayed with each musical creation.

Matthew Blair sat in the darkened auditorium with hundreds of other attendees to the Poly Classical Series, listening intently to the pieces Angelica played in succession. All too soon, for Matthew, she was finished. The audience showed its appreciation with a standing ovation.

The concert was over, and, while the other spectators filed out, Matthew made his way to the stage. "Excuse me, but aren't you that virtuoso who just wowed a vast, adoring audience? Can I have your autograph?"

Angelica giggled. "Sure. How much money do you have?"

Matthew responded, "Not enough."

She said, "That's okay. No money is needed."

He kissed her on the cheek, and she turned so her lips met his. "Matthew, I'm so glad you came. Hoped you would."

"I told you I'd be here." He took her arm and lead her down the steps.

"I know. You're always there. But your schedule is so busy, with school, football, the puppy foundation, and the band."

"That stuff isn't so tough. Now your piano playing, that takes a lot of time."

"I missed some notes tonight."

"I didn't hear any missed notes."

"Yeah, sure. You have perfect pitch, catch every wrong note. Am I right?"

"Let's go for a latte. You game?" he asked.

They walked from the auditorium, arm in arm, toward the parking lot. Soon, they were driving to the coffee shop. Angelica became quiet.

Matthew looked at her. "A penny for your thoughts."

"I was just thinking. Do you mind . . . dating a blind girl?"

"What? Come on, don't be silly. Look, you have talents I'll never have. You can hear a bird way off. You point it out, even the type of bird. I'm thick as a brick, never even hear the bird. And if one of our friends comes walking up, you know who it is before he gets to us. I can't do that."

She smiled. "You're sweet. Still, there are lots of girls out there who can see. Any regrets?"

He stopped the car. "No, never."

They embraced and kissed.

"Okay virtuoso girl, ready for that latte?"

The cool night air on the patio felt good to Matthew. He smelled the coffee and sipped the steamed brew. "I don't know how the band can stay together. Mom is pushing me hard to let it go."

She put her drink down. "What are you going to do?"

"Wait and see what happens. Man, she's so determined for me to become a doctor. It's tough to resist her."

"Why?"

"Cause it's been just the two of us, and I feel obligated to her. If I leave, she'll be alone. I can't stand to think of her that way."

Angelica felt for his hands, grasping them in hers. "Matthew. It's your life. You have to live it the way you want, the way your heart tells you. That doesn't mean your family will fall apart. It doesn't mean you will hurt your mother."

He laughed. "There you go, being all logical. Still . . . ."

"What?"

"At times, it's like something is telling me to hang on to the music, like that's what I am destined to do. I'm afraid to ignore that feeling."

She softly said, "Then don't. You can't ignore that voice inside you. You will regret it and hate whatever keeps you from your dream. No relationship can exist on resentment. Just promise me one thing."

"What's that?"

She kissed his cheek. "That you will be the best musician you can."

CHAPTER FORTY-NINE

"Are you sure you haven't heard from George? It's been almost a week since we talked. He was going to get more information to me," Mary said, feeling her brow wrinkle.

"I'm sorry, Mrs. Blair. But I've checked with everyone in the office, and nobody has heard a word from him. We're starting to get worried. It's not like George to go several days without calling," came from the administrator at Hawk Investigations.

Mary asked, "Do you plan to send someone down there to get him?"

"Oh, I don't think so. Mr. Hawk heard about those drug killings in Nuevo Laredo, and he's concerned about safety."

"What about George's safety?" Mary quizzed the woman.

"Mr. Hawk is in communication with the local police. But . . . ."

Mary blurted, "But what?"

The administrator whispered, "They don't seem too interested in doing much. Oh, the police say they are conducting an investigation. But nothing is happening. Mr. Hawk thinks they are afraid, or on the criminals' payroll. He is going through the FBI now."

"Please let me know if you find him." Mary ended the call.

The intercom came to life, "Mrs. Blair, it's Kathleen McDow, George McDow's wife. Do you have a moment to talk with her?"

"Put her through."

Kathleen McDow seemed panicked. "Mrs. Blair, I'm sorry to bother you, but it's George."

Mary quickly asked, "Have you heard from him?"

"No, no, that's the problem. The office hasn't talked to him in days. That is very strange. You see, our daughter is graduating from college this weekend, and I was sure he would call and say he was on his way home. As of now, we've heard nothing. I was hoping he had called you."

"I'm sorry, Mrs. McDow, but I haven't talked to him recently. Have you spoken with Mr. Hawk?"

"Yes, and I'm scared to death. He brought the FBI in. They are working with the Mexican drug agents. George just vanished. Nobody can locate him. You think he's all right, don't you?"

"I hope so. George is an experienced investigator."

"And a former Marine."

Mary continued. "Exactly. I'm sure he can handle himself. He will probably call with some ordinary explanation, like his cell phone not working."

"I'm praying he will call today. Our daughter is worried sick. Says she won't go to graduation unless he's there."

Mary tried to reassure her. "Tell you what. I'll call you right after I hear from him."

"Thank you, Mrs. Blair."

"Goodbye." Mary returned the receiver to its cradle and sat in silence. She ignored the pile of notes on her desk.

"Mrs. Blair, Alexander Hawk is calling for you," came from the intercom.

"Put him through."

"Mary, I just heard from the FBI. It's bad news, very bad," Hawk said.

She had a hard time forming the words. "What did they say?"

"They found George in Laredo, in a car trunk."

"A car trunk, but . . . . ?"

Hawk spoke slowly, "Dead, shot full of holes, and decapitated. I'm sick. Can't think what to tell his wife, how to put it to her. They were planning a trip to Hawaii to celebrate their wedding anniversary. She was so excited about it. I just don't know what I'm going to say." Hawk ended the call without any pleasantries.

Mary dropped the receiver, and a dial tone came from the phone. She looked out the window and wondered if any story was worth such a tragedy.

CHAPTER FIFTY

"You guys are on the threshold of something rare, an opportunity most people never get in their lifetimes. Last year, we went undefeated and won the bowl game. A lot of fans thought we should have been awarded the national championship, especially after our schedule. What a tough road that was, and you responded with convincing victories." Coach Masterson stopped and surveyed his Poly football team.

One of the players quipped, "Yeah, and it didn't hurt to have the best running back in the country, thirty-six hundred yards and forty touchdowns."

Unanimous approval swept through the players, as teammates patted Matthew Blair's shoulder, slapped his back or tussled his hair.

Coach Masterson raised his hand. "Matt did great. But remember, one player didn't win all those games. This team did, fifty guys working hard day after day, following the game plan. It's no shame to be ranked second. This year, we have the opportunity to show the entire country that we deserve to be the champion. Tomorrow, Santa Mansion visits us to start the season. It's ranked number one in all the polls. No one could have predicted the number one and number two teams would meet in the regular season, but things worked out that way. This is your opportunity to prove that you are number one, that the polls are wrong, that you can rise to incredible heights, and carry Poly with you. This is your moment in time, gentlemen. Be the best team you can be."

One of the players jumped up and shouted, "Poly, number one!"

The others joined in a pulsating sea of humanity, "Poly, number one; Poly, number one!"

The coach held up both hands. "Let's have a good practice today. Keep that enthusiasm burning through the game. Hit the field."

The players streamed through the door, screaming and chanting.

Calisthenics went crisply, followed by agility drills and short sprints. Coach Masterson divided the team into offense and defense, instructing the coaches to run through sets, formations, and plays. He walked among the activities, making notes and speaking to his assistants.

Suddenly, a fight broke out between the star linebacker, Stan Winslow, and a lineman. Winslow held his teammate's face mask and slapped the helmet. Coach Masterson moved between them. "Break it up! What's the problem?"

Winslow pointed to the lineman. "He didn't move laterally and let me blitz. I'll run over him next time!"

Masterson took charge. "Winslow, why don't you save that energy for the game. I don't want any animosity among our players. You always seem to be in the middle of fights. Stop it and use your head. Any more of that stuff and I'll bench you. Understand?"

Winslow nodded.

The coach instructed the first team offense to run plays against the starting defense. "All right, run at half speed, and no hard contact. We don't want any injuries before the game."

The offense executed several running plays, followed by passes to the ends and running backs coming out of the backfield. Matthew Blair snagged a pass over the middle, and Winslow plowed him into the field. The linebacker slapped Matthew's helmet. "What do you think of that, pretty boy? I can take you anytime. I'll show them who's best."

Coach Masterson grabbed Winslow's shoulder pads. "Go to the showers. You're through for the day."

Practice ended with wind sprints, Matthew easily leading his group. As the players walked from the filed, the head coach called out, "Matt. Hold up. Hey, you all right? That was a pretty hard hit."

Matthew shook his head. "I'm fine. Just some dirt in the mouth."

"Matt, don't let Winslow rattle you. He's jealous, came here as a star out of high school. Don't let him get in your head. The team needs your leadership."

Matthew smiled. "No problem. It's the other guys I worry about. He likes to bully them. I hope they stay focused on Santa Mansion."

"Matt, Winslow has a serious problem. He's on steroids, not from us. He's getting them from someone else, and we can't catch him at it. The tests don't pick up the type of steroid he's using, but we recognize the symptoms.

My hands are tied right now. I'm afraid his health is at risk. Sure, he is strong and fast with all those artificial muscles. After football, he may develop some disease from the steroids, maybe cancer. We're trying to deal with the situation, but the team looks up to you. Stay calm and keep the others on the right track. A lot depends on that."

Chapter Fifty-one

Matthew could hear the fans through the dressing room walls. Their chants and songs filled the room. Coach Masterson looked at his team, clad in their silver and blue uniforms. "Gentlemen, the game is at hand. You are about to meet one of the greatest teams in college history. That's good for us, because they are a worthy opponent. No one will be able to say that our championship is undeserved. Take the contest to them. Deliver your energy into the opponent, on every play. Remember, this is your opportunity to rise to heights few people will ever experience. Coach Reynolds will now go over special team assignments."

Paul Reynolds walked to the blackboard and drew the receiving team, explaining special techniques for the game.

Matthew glanced at Stan Winslow, who was popping one of the many pimples on his face. He wiped the pus on his jersey and popped another. Matthew looked away.

Paul Reynolds went over the receiving team and finished his comments.

Coach Masterson walked to the front of the room. "Let's take this one, for our fans, our school, our community, and ourselves. To the field!"

Mary Blair and Angelica sat together on the forty-five yard line, ten rows up from the Poly bench. The stadium was rocking, as thousands of silver-clad fans sang the school fight song, while others reacted wildly to the tumbles of the cheerleaders. Thousands of other fans wore red for the visitors, erupting in cheers and chants when their band struck up the school's fight song as their heroes ran onto the field.

Santa Mansion, two-time national champion, clad in red pants, white jerseys, and red helmets with their famous "SM" symbol on the sides, carried themselves as champions.

A man sitting next to Angelica held a portable television showing three sports announcers, while a woman in front of them listened to a radio. Mary could hear the radio announcer above the roar of the crowd, "Ladies and gentlemen, the Poly-Technical Radio Network is on the air, bringing this football contest to fans across the globe and our armed forces defending the nation. This afternoon's game promises to be a titanic struggle between the country's premier teams, one the ruler of the air and the other an unstoppable ground force. National Champion Santa Mansion is led by six-foot-five-inch Sonny Lenz, holder of every collegiate passing record on the books. And with his cadre of fleet receivers, most notable among whom is six-foot-six-inch Barron Washington, Mansion can score on every possession. Poly counters with the most prolific running back in the game, college, or professional, six-foot-four-inch Matthew Blair, the record holder for rushing yards and touchdowns in a single season, and that in his freshman year. Stay tuned for the game of the decade."

Mary watched the captains come to the center of the field. An official tossed a coin. Santa Mansion won the toss and elected to receive. The visitors sprinted to their bench and huddled around the coaches. The Poly players extended arms around teammates' shoulders.

Thousands of Poly fans stood and erupted with applause, yells, and chants as their warriors took the field and lined up for kickoff. Mary could hear the radio announcer's falsetto voice, "A long, high kick, taken by a Mansion player at the goal line; and he's up the sideline, and drilled to the turf in a vicious tackle by Poly's Stan Winslow."

Mary winced. "That had to hurt. I hope things don't get out of hand down there. I don't want them to take it out on Matt."

Angelica patted her arm. "He'll be fine. Don't worry."

Santa Mansion spread the defense with a wide formation, two receivers to the left and one to the right. The center snapped the ball, and Lenz dropped back quickly, throwing a bomb to a streaking receiver. He snagged the bullet in stride, running untouched across the goal line to a deafening roar from a sea of red-adorned fans. The Poly faithfully stood in silence, and Mary could hear the radio announcer, "And just like that, it is six to nothing. Santa Mansion has easily lived up to their billing as an incredible offensive team. But now, it Poly's turn on offense."

The home team lined up for the kickoff, and a back fielded a high ball, running up the middle to the thirty where he ran into a wall of defenders. Poly huddled and quickly ran to the line. Matthew Blair was behind the fullback in an I formation. A snap on three put the play in motion. The quarterback faked to the fullback and placed the ball in Matthew's hands. He powered through the line, ran left, weaved through two defenders, stiff-armed another, and broke free into the secondary. It was a foot race to the goal line, Matthew easily outdistancing the Mansion back. Mary and Angelica jumped up and down and screamed. Matthew had answered the Mansion touchdown, and the game soon was tied.

The radio announcer could barely be heard, "Incredible run by the Poly rocket, Matthew Blair, seventy yards through a bewildered defense. Ladies and gentlemen, what a run. Even the Santa Mansion coaches are shaking their heads in disbelief."

Mary watched the game seesaw back and forth, Mansion scoring on almost every possession, filling the air with tight spirals, and Poly matching them touchdown for touchdown. Mary could feel the tension rise to some incredible level as the clock wound down, wondering which team would falter and lose the game.

She held Angelica tightly. "I hope we don't fumble. Lord, please no fumble or injury."

Angelica hugged back. "Don't worry, Mrs. Blair. I have confidence in Matthew. He'll come through; just watch."

The man with the television said, "I don't know. The clock might get us."

Mary turned to him. "What do you mean?"

He pointed to the television screen, and Mary heard one of the television commentators say, "The clock is all important now. With the game tied at sixty-four, the team with the last possession will likely win, and that appears to be Santa Mansion. We have only thirty seconds left, and Poly is kicking off. Lenz could complete a couple of intermediate passes to run the clock near zero. Then Mansion would have two good choices to win the game, a field goal or a pass to the end zone. Either way, the visitors look good to keep their number one ranking."

Mary looked at the man. "I hope not, but he seems to know what he's talking about. Poor Poly. Poor Matthew."

Angelica turned sightless eyes toward Mary. "Have faith, Mrs. Blair. Matthew will do it. I know he will."

Mansion ran the kickoff to its twenty-six yard line and quickly lined up without a huddle. Poly called a time-out before Mansion could snap the ball.

The television announcer exclaimed, "Interesting move by the home team. They are planning something special, perhaps a new defensive set. The game is on the line. Let's see what Coach Masterson does."

Poly took the field, and the man with the television said to Mary, "They're sending your son in as a defensive back. What a gutsy move. Put your best athlete on the field and go for broke."

Mary could hear fans around her questioning the move, "What? That won't work. What's Masterson doing? Matthew Blair doesn't play defense. He'll be lost out there, especially against this Mansion offense."

The teams lined up, Matt deep in the secondary. Lenz took a long time for the snap, and the television-holding fan muttered, "Audible."

The center hiked the ball and Lenz completed a pass across the middle for a twenty yard gain. The television fan almost threw the set to the concrete floor. Mansion lined up without a huddle. Fifteen seconds remained.

Mary noticed Matthew moving up from deep safety to just behind the linebackers. The television holder fumed, "What is he doing? Just like somebody said, he doesn't know defense. That receiver will blow past him for an easy score."

Suddenly, Matt dropped back fast as the ball was snapped, and Lenz threw a long spiral to a streaking receiver. Stan Winslow was with him for several steps but collapsed to the turf, leaving the receiver alone at the goal line. The ball sailed perfectly toward his outstretched hands. The game seemed over.

Out of nowhere a sliver blur flashed in front of the receiver, and the television announcer went crazy. "Interception! Matthew Blair has the ball. He's at the ten, twenty, thirty, cuts to the center of the field, the forty, back to the sideline, fifty, forty; now only Lenz has a shot at him; oh, Blair leveled him; he's at the forty, thirty, twenty, ten, touchdown! Poly wins! Ladies and gentlemen, we have just witnessed one of the most spectacular displays of strategy and athletic ability in sports history. The brainy Poly athletes from Houston have just showed the world that they are number one!"

Mary was numb, and Angelica was screaming. Mary barely felt the hugs and pats from the fans around them, searching for her son on the field. She watched the goal posts come down, the Poly team inundate Matthew, a sea of Poly fans stream onto the field, the band mob the team, and camera-carrying reporters try to find a way to her hero. She sighed and said, "I'm worried."

Angelica stopped screaming. "Why?"

"I hope they don't crush him. Football is such a brutal sport!"

Chapter Fifty-Two

Jorge Galinda puffed on his long cigar and let thick smoke swirl out of his mouth. He pressed a button on the intercom and barked into the machine, "Send Agapito to me at once!"

In a few seconds, the young man with the scar on his cheek stood before the jefe, stone-faced and attentive.

"Agapito, my son. Sit here, near me. You know, it is good to have a man like you in the cartel. I never worry. You do everything I command. I have a special request, amigo."

The young man's eyes squinted. "Anything, mi jefe. What may I do for you?"

Galinda spoke slowly, "You know that bookie, Felipe Gonzalez, in Laredo. I placed a bet with him on the football game today. I can just see him now, laughing that my team lost. I do not like people laughing at me, Agapito."

The young man made a fist. "I will stop his laughing, forever."

Galinda rose, walked to Agapito, and patted his cheek. "That is my good son. Please do it slowly and painfully. I want him to know why he is dying."

Agapito left the room, and Galinda pressed the intercom button once again. "Is everyone here for the meeting?"

A female voice answered, "Sí señor. They are in the large conference room."

Galinda left his study, walked down a long, marble-floored hall adorned with oil paintings, and opened a heavy wooden door at the end. He smiled. "Gentlemen, so good of you to come all this way. It looks like everyone is here from the United States—Los Angeles, Seattle, Houston, Chicago, New York, Miami, and of course, Honolulu. All of my best customers. Welcome. I trust your needs have been attended to."

Most of the group of men nodded, while others said, "Yes."

Galinda sat in a large red leather chair at the head of a marble table. "Excellent. Gentlemen, we have done much business over the years. Made a great deal of money. But tonight, I have a plan that will make everything else we have done seem like nothing."

He stopped to gauge his guests' reactions, their keen attention and wide eyes telling him all he wanted to know. "Our business is divided between marijuana, which is the least profitable product, and the more expensive drugs, such as cocaine and heroine. We have been successful in adding other profitable products, such as meth." He lit a long, black cigar, holding a lighter to the end until it glowed orange. "Now, my chemists have devised a way to lace chocolate with a new drug, which we call 'Fire.' It is a heroine derivative. The chocolate hides its taste. It has the power to make a person more inclined to use hard drugs. In a matter of weeks, he will crave our cocaine. Profits will double, perhaps even triple."

One of the guests asked, "You mean a guy who never used cocaine and eats your chocolate will want the hard stuff?"

Galinda smiled. "Yes, cocaine, heroine, opium."

The guest continued. "But how can most people afford the hard drugs? Many of them have only enough money for a bag of grass."

Galinda blew smoke in his direction. "They will steal to get the money, just as they steal now. I do not care. Do you?"

The man said, "No. I just want to make sure our investment is covered."

Galinda leaned back in his chair and puffed the cigar. He studied the rising smoke, before saying, "It will be covered, and you will all be very rich men, capable of buying anything and anyone you want. I will be your exclusive supplier of Fire, cocaine, opium, and heroine, and you will have steady supplies from my new factories. What do you say, my good friends?"

Clapping and whistling, the guests stood. Galinda raised his cigar. "Let us dispense with business now and enjoy the pleasures of the evening. I have a wonderful dinner for you, followed by old brandy and Cuban cigars, and then . . . ."

CHAPTER FIFTY-THREE

Jorge Galinda studied a map of the northern Mexico mountains, wondering where he could build new drug factories to fill the demand he expected for hard drugs. The intercom interrupted his thoughts, "Señor, Governor Heminez is on the line. Do you wish to speak to him?"

"Yes." Galinda picked up the receiver. "Governor, so nice to hear from a dear friend. What can a poor peasant do for a high government official?"

"Jorge, Mexico City is asking many questions. I fear they will send more troops here, ones not on our payroll. Are you sure the operation is safe?"

Galinda spoke calmly, "Absolutely safe, amigo. Do not worry. Everything is under control. You see, the new secretary is, how shall I say, a close family friend. The troops are under his personal command. No harm will come to us. Nothing for you to fear, my dear Governor."

"That is a relief. But I worry about that newspaper editor in Tijuana. He says too many things in his paper. I think he is upsetting Mexico City and the Americans."

Galinda chuckled. "Did you not hear, amigo? He died in a tragic fire last night. Everything burned to the ground, and they found his skeleton in the ashes. My son, Agapito, was there and called me the instant it happened."

"You don't say. What a tragedy. Well then, this is a fine day. Until we meet again."

"Until then, amigo. *Vaya con Dios.*" The jefe placed the receiver on its cradle and shook his head before muttering, "Until . . . I kill you someday, amigo."

He turned to the map again, humming as he circled several points and said to himself, "But today there will be no killing. Today is a fine day, indeed. One for business and profits."

CHAPTER FIFTY-FOUR

Matthew Blair walked on the uneven sidewalk under ancient oaks. He had a hard time making much progress as Poly students stopped him for congratulations along the way. He looked at his watch. "Got to hurry. Angelica's waiting."

He began to run, only briefly slowing to acknowledge the continuous flow of well-wishers. A black sedan slowed, and a man called out, "Matthew, got a minute?"

He stopped to see who was calling him. "Yes?"

The man leaned out the window and smiled. "I'm Herb Hines. Pro scout. Get in."

"I can't. Late for an appointment."

Hines spoke calmly, "Come on, get in, just for a minute. I'll drive you. Where are you going?"

"The coffee shop down the street."

"Piece of cake," Hines said.

Matthew got into the passenger seat. "Yes sir?"

Hines wasted no time. "That was a great game. I had no idea you could play defense like that. Real smart. You foxed old Lenz right out of the win. Without you, Poly would have lost."

Matthew protested, "It was a team win. Everybody played hard."

Hines chuckled. "Your linebacker, Winslow, he came apart on the final play. You saved the game. They say he's in the hospital, real sick. Too bad."

Matthew's head fell. "Yeah, some liver ailment. Everyone's real worried about him."

Hines changed the subject. "Listen, have you thought about your professional career? I know it's early but . . . ."

Matthew interrupted, "It's not just early. Pro scouts aren't supposed to talk to college players during the season."

"Stupid legal stuff. The early bird gets the worm, as they say. If you will sign with me, I'll keep it a secret until after the season. Then you can have any team you want. Thought about that?"

"No. I . . . I'm not going to play pro ball. My mom wants me to go to medical school."

Hines raised his voice. "Bull! You can make more money as a pro back."

Matthew got out of the car. "The money isn't important to me. I just want to do the right thing for my family." He began walking.

Hines called out, "I'm talking about your future. That's important."

Matthew stopped and replied, "Exactly."

CHAPTER FIFTY-FIVE

"Before we start practice today, I have some bad news to tell you. I just got word from the hospital. Stan Winslow died this afternoon." Coach Masterson stopped to look across the obviously stunned football players. "His father said it was some rare form of liver failure. The funeral is Sunday afternoon. Stan's parents want all of you to be honorary pallbearers. His father said Stan thought of each of you as a close friend."

The team's silence gave way to scattered sniffles and sighs, as players cleared their throats, wiped moist noses and eyes, and hung their heads.

Coach Masterson said, "I wish I had something uplifting to say. But I'm just as much in shock as everyone else. Wish someone would lift my spirits. Let's dedicate this season to Stan. If we bring home the national championship trophy, we'll include his name on it, just like he was with us every game."

"He is with us, Coach." Matthew Blair stood. "Can't you guys feel his intensity? I can, just like he's here right now. He'll always be with us, a part of the university, a member of this team."

The head coach nodded. "Well said. All right, let's get on with practice. Remember, we have State on Saturday."

The players filed quietly through the door leading to the practice field.

Before everyone had left, Coach Masterson called out, "Matt, wait just a second."

Matthew stopped and faced the coach, who said, "Mrs. Winslow asked a special favor. She would like you to sing at the funeral. It seems Stan had your CD and knew every song by heart. She said he sang them in the shower, during the summer when he was home. Would you mind doing that favor for her?"

Matthew hesitated. "Me? I'm not really a gospel singer." He looked down, then at the coach. "Sure, I will be glad to do it. Tell her I'll sing something new, just for Stan."

Coach Masterson patted him on the shoulder. "That's great, Matt. Your song will probably do some good for his family."

Matthew Blair walked hand-in-hand with Angelica into the Memorial Funeral Home on Sunday afternoon. She hugged his arm. "You okay?"

"Fine."

She whispered, "What is it like?"

He asked, "You mean this place?"

"Yes."

Matthew spoke slowly, "Most of the team seems to be here. Everybody is in dark suits. Coach Masterson and his wife are with some of the other coaches. People are talking in the anteroom. Let's go inside and pay our respects to Stan's family."

Angelica asked, "Do you know his parents?"

"I met them last year, at a team party. Nice people, from Los Angeles. Dad is an accountant. Stocky, quiet guy, as I remember."

They walked a little farther, until Matthew stopped. "We're at the casket." Angelica bowed her head for a few moments. Matthew led her away, walked a few steps, and stopped again.

"Matthew, thank you for coming and for agreeing to do a song for Stan. He respected you so much," came a woman's trembling voice.

"Glad to do it for your family and for Stan. This is Angelica Steuben from the school."

"Thank you for coming, Angelica. I would introduce you to Mr. Winslow, but he can't take this too long. He's probably outside. I have to be the strong one."

Matthew led Angelica to a seat. "I'm going to join the team in the front. Looks like almost everyone's seated."

Matthew sat in the end seat on the front row. The minister walked to the lectern and smiled. He was a round man of perhaps sixty, with a full head of gray hair. The service began with a hymn, followed by prayers, the Twenty-third Psalm, and a message of Stan's virtues and his life after death. Matthew looked at the family section and swallowed at the sight of Mrs.

Winslow holding her husband. The minister motioned for Matthew to join him. "Will you need accompaniment?"

"No."

Matthew glanced at Mr. and Mrs. Winslow. "This is a song dedicated to Stan."

Angelica felt music-filled words lift her spirits:

> *Run the world with me, before the sailing wind,*
> *Brothers finding joy, past this earthly end,*
> *Through the darkest night, no matter storms or cold,*
> *Together we are friends, our souls strong and bold.*
> *Seeking out a light that leads us on our way,*
> *To a peaceful place, a bright and warming day.*
> *Over harsh lands, across the endless sea,*
> *I am not afraid; you are beside me.*
> *There, up ahead; we are not alone,*
> *The place for us to rest, forever we are home.*
> *Can you feel our victory, coming to the light,*
> *We have won the game, it is no longer night.*

Matthew hummed the melody, preparing to repeat the words he hoped would honor his fallen teammate. He looked at the family section. The Winslows were holding hands, their eyes bright and tearless. Matthew smiled and filled the chamber once again with Stan's song.

CHAPTER FIFTY-SIX

Matthew walked down the long hall at the kennel, stopping to talk to the puppies and dogs, straining to push their noses through the wire-mesh gates. He saw an employee. "Have you seen Eric?"

"No, sir. Can't say as I have. Hey, that was a great win over State. Forty-two to fourteen is sure a whuppin'. They tried to key on you all right, but you showed them—five touchdowns and three hundred yards. Sure was a beautiful win for old Poly. Sure was."

"Thanks, but it was a team win."

The man winked and shuffled off.

Matthew walked a little farther and went through a door at the end of the hall. "Eric, I've been looking for you."

"Mr. Matthew! Wow, you showed 'em, ran over the whole State team. Made *manburger* out of 'em. Get it, *manburger*?" Eric stopped talking and laughed so hard his baseball cap fell off.

Matthew laughed too, picking up the cap and placing it on Eric's head. "Say, I need to talk to you for a minute."

Eric looked up at him with sparkling eyes. "Sure."

"We have a special job for the puppies today."

Eric seemed excited. "What is it? A new place to take 'em. They'll love goin' there. Can I go too?"

"It's not a hospital or old folks home. But it's just as important, maybe more important right now."

Eric scratched his cap. "Not a hospital or home? What is it?"

"Do you remember that hurricane that went through Louisiana, the real bad one that flooded all those people out of their homes?"

"Uh huh. What about it?"

"A lot of those people came here to get food and medicine and . . . ."

"Yeah, and to get away from the alligators and snakes and mosquitoes and stuff."

"That's right, Eric. But you know, many of those people lost loved ones, family, and . . . pets. Those people loved their dogs very much. In fact, their puppies were like children. They loved them just like that."

"Yeah, just like I love them, my family. Right, Mr. Matthew?"

"That's right, Eric. Well, we have the chance to do something about their broken hearts. We can . . . ."

"Oh, no. Not give the puppies away. We can't do that. They're my buddies."

Matthew placed an arm around Eric's shoulders. "We can make them feel a lot better, fill their hearts with some love. Don't you want to help them? And the puppies will be loved, just like you love them."

"They won't get flooded out, will they?"

"No. They are safe here. When they go home, the puppies will go along, to new homes, nice and dry. We'll give the people money to buy food and vet care for them. Won't that be great?"

Eric looked at the floor. "I suppose. But what about us? We won't have any puppies to take to the old people and the sick children."

"We'll find new puppies that need a good home. You can take care of them, make new friends."

Eric looked up, tears streaming down his round cheeks. "I guess so, if it will make the people feel better. But, Mr. Matthew, can I give 'em away, to make sure the people are nice?"

"You bet. You can make sure each puppy likes his new owner. If some puppy doesn't seem to like any of the new people, then we will bring him back to stay with you. What do you say?"

"I always wanted someone to adopt me. But they never did. Guess nobody wants a Down's kid. If the puppies can get adopted, it will be great. I know just how they'll feel, bein' picked out special by a mom or dad. Christmas will be fun, lots of huggin' and presents in a real home."

CHAPTER FIFTY-SEVEN

Agapito peered through the thick glass at Marquez Cabillo. "*Hola*, amigo. How is the food?"

Cabillo seemed happy to see the visitor. "Agapito, *como estas?*"

"*Bien*, amigo. The jefe sent me. He has a special favor to ask."

"Anything for the jefe."

"Good. Have you talked to a reporter?"

"Cabillo leaned closer to the intercom. "Yes, but I told her nothing. Can't remember much. Everything is dark, amigo. My mind, it don't work good."

"Good, very good. But the jefe is worried that you might say too much. He would like for you to, how shall I say, protect the cartel. Will you do that?"

"Yes. What do you ask?"

Agapito's eyes squinted. "Tonight, a man will come to you at supper. He will give you a pill. Take it immediately. Everything will then be fine. The Americans will not have the satisfaction of killing you, and the cartel will be protected."

Cabillo's forehead wrinkled. "But kill myself? How will I see the Blessed Virgin if I do that?"

"Do not worry, amigo. The priest will pray for you. He will give you absolution. Your family will be provided for. The jefe has promised that. Will you do it?"

"If the jefe will do everything you say, then I have nothing to worry about. How will I know this man?"

"Do not worry about that. He will know you."

Cabillo nodded. "Will you tell my family I love them?"

Agapito smiled. "Of course. Tonight then, you will help the jefe. Everything will be wonderful after that."

CHAPTER FIFTY-EIGHT

Mary straightened Matthew's tie. "You look very handsome, just like your father on our prom night, sandy brown hair, deep blue eyes, sweet smile. Angelica is going to be jealous of the other girls."

"Angelica doesn't have anything to worry about. I see those guys eyeing her. Don't you think she's beautiful?"

"She is one of the prettiest girls I've seen, long black hair, clear complexion, fine features, always well-groomed, a statuesque build. But no one will ever be good enough for my son."

"Mom, I wanted to ask you something. Do you think it would be okay if we played a concert in a couple of weeks?"

"Who? Do you mean the band?"

"Well, yes. They asked us to perform at the New Orleans hurricane relief concert, for the displaced people. It's an honor. There will be some big names there."

"Matthew, I don't think it is a good idea. You are going to medical school. Let the band go. It's not important to you anymore."

"Let the band go? But . . . it's a part of my life. I can play no matter what I do. The guys are my friends."

"Matthew, why are we discussing this again? It's a waste of time. You are upsetting me and causing grief to us both."

"Okay, okay. I've got to go. Angelica and I will be late for the symphony. She wants to be on time."

"Call me so I'll know you are safe."

"Mom, please. I'm a grown man."

"Call me!"

"Okay. Love you."

Matthew and Angelica sat in the darkened audience. The Texas Symphony was in the middle of its program, and Angelica's head nodded gently to the chamber-filling instrumental.

"Missed note," Matthew whispered.

Angelica turned to him. "What?"

"The French horn section, somebody missed a note. Should have been a C sharp, not a C flat."

She squeezed his hand. "Shush. Let's listen."

"Another missed note. From a trombone."

She shook her head. "You're hopeless, too perfect for normal people."

"Sorry." Matthew focused on the music, closing his eyes to feel the combined effect of the instruments. His thoughts turned to his own music, and the melody of one of Tomorrow's songs pushed the symphony from his mind. He could hear a piercing lead guitar running the scale, accompanied by keyboard, drums, and base guitar. In his mind, he smiled on stage, Tomorrow never missing a note of the song.

"Matthew, did you like it? Wasn't it great?"

He snapped out of his pleasant thoughts. "Yeah, terrific." Matthew joined in the applause, but not for the symphony, as Tomorrow's music still echoed in his mind, lifting his spirits and filling his imagination with exciting possibilities.

CHAPTER FIFTY-NINE

"Mom, I'm about to leave for the concert. See you."

Mary hurried down the stairs. "Hold on a minute. What concert? You didn't mention anything about a concert. Didn't you and Angelica go to the symphony last week?"

"We did, but Angelica and I decided to go to a pop concert at the last minute. They're having some local bands at the new arena. We thought it would be fun. It's okay, isn't it?"

"Sure, but call before you leave so I'll know when to expect you home, and keep your phone on."

"Thanks, you're terrific. See you about midnight. Please don't worry. Everything will be fine."

Mary stood at the front door and watched him drive away, worrying the entire time.

She took the elevator to the third floor and exited for her home office. Sitting at her desk, Mary picked up a group of papers and scanned them. The top paper contained the heading, "Confidential Report from Alexander Hawk." She read aloud, "Now that Marquez Cabillo is dead, the investigation has reached its conclusion. This report relates all of the information we have gathered about the suspected boss who had him poisoned in prison. Jorge Galinda is the shadowy cartel leader in Nuevo Laredo suspected of ordering the murder." Mary stopped, rubbed her eyes, and continued to read silently. She shook her head and muttered, "My God, what kind of world do we live in?"

Mary felt tired, resting her head on the table, and fell asleep.

The telephone woke her, and she was confused for a moment, looking for the source of the noise. She lifted the receiver. "Yes."

A familiar voice came from the receiver, "Mary? Mary, is that you?"

"Lizzie, I'm sorry."

"Mary, are you all right?"

"Fine. I was asleep. What's up?

Lizzie said, "I wanted to talk to you."

"How are you doing? I hope you're feeling better."

"I take it one day at a time. That's all I can do. Some days are okay, and some are tough. I still can't believe Brittany is gone. But . . . her organs helped several other kids. I take some solace in that."

Mary spoke softly, "Me too."

There was a long silence before Lizzie broke it. "Mary, I thought you said Matthew had given up the band."

"That's right. What are you talking about?"

"Mary, maybe you should turn on channel sixty. The network is broadcasting that hurricane relief concert."

"Hurricane concert. Is it tonight?"

"Yes, and I think you should look at it."

"Why?"

"Just turn on the television. You'll see."

Mary hesitated. "Okay. Talk to you later."

She found the television remote control and pushed the "on" button, bringing the flat panel screen to life. Mary was clumsy with the channel buttons, realizing she unconsciously did not want to see what was on the television. She shuddered after her fingers had hit the right buttons and channel sixty flashed on the screen.

Mary leaned forward and gasped. Tomorrow was playing on a brightly lit stage, as thousands of fans clapped and moved to the music. Matthew was holding his electric guitar high as he played lead, dancing athletically with his eyes closed. The other band members wailed, and Mary recognized the others, except for the keyboard player. She fumed, "What the? Matthew, I am going to slam you for this. You lied to me!"

The song ended, and the place went wild. The band bowed and ran off the stage, but the applause intensified, accompanied by cheers, whistles, foot stomps, and chants, "More Tomorrow; more Tomorrow; more Tomorrow . . . ."

The show's hosts, whom Mary did not know, seemed excited, as one of them said, "They are your showstoppers, Tomorrow. Listen to the house; eighty thousand people are about to bring down the roof. What an incredible performance by this young group of superstars. Here they come again, for an encore!"

The crowd's applause grew louder as Matthew led the others onto the stage. The throng quickly grew quiet when Matthew held his guitar high and brought a hand to its face without looking at the strings. He gazed across the vast audience, and suddenly Tomorrow broke into song,

Allelu, allelu
Words of hope
Are comin' through,
From that Guy way up there,
The One dancin' above the air.

Allelu, allelu;
The Big Man's here,
Sure and true,
Liftin' us with hands so strong
Over things that are gone.

To everyone, its all the same
He's with us now
As we call His name;
Father, Father, please tonight
Help us hold on, to win this fight.

Allelu, allelu
Words of hope
Are comin' through.
From that Guy way up there,
The One dancin' above the air.

Mary saw thousands of people clapping and moving to the beat of the music, as though they were at one with Tomorrow. The scene reminded her of a Promise concert, with Matthew leading the band before a captivated audience, as Tam had done years before. In a moment she also was clapping and humming to the music.

CHAPTER SIXTY

Mary looked at the clock, 12:01AM. She was still humming the Tomorrow song, having a hard time getting it out of her mind but enjoying the melody. She forced other thoughts into her mind, to create the right attack attitude for her son when he arrived home. She heard the garage door open and close and counted the minutes until Matthew came into the kitchen. Mary hoped her expression matched her anger.

"Matthew Adam Blair. Would you please tell me again where you were tonight."

He swallowed. "At a rock concert."

"And what were you doing there?"

"I, I was playing, with the band. Mom, it was great! You should have heard . . . ."

She snapped, "I did hear! You lied to me."

He faced her squarely. "I did not lie. I was at a rock concert, just like I told you."

Mary was not mollified. "You did most certainly lie. You gave me the impression you were attending a rock concert as a spectator, not as a performer."

"Mom, you came to your own conclusions. I never said we had tickets. The fact is that the band was given an incredible opportunity to play with established groups, some great bands. I couldn't pass that up. It's not fair to the other guys. They are trying to make it. How can I shut them down? It's not right."

Mary changed to a logical mode. "You know, I've often said you are a lot like your father. And it's true both of you have shown incredible talents, intelligence, athletic ability, musical gifts, concern for others, and a sweetness that melts my heart. But your father had a strong character. He never lied. Talent alone is nothing. Do you believe that?"

Matthew nodded.

She felt successful and continued. "You know that story I was doing on the man convicted of murdering those children, the one on drugs. That man was a pawn of a drug lord in Mexico. Galinda is his name. They say that Galinda is a brilliant man, a PhD in chemistry, and that he was a great soccer player in Latin America. But he is an evil man, responsible for killing countless people and poisoning children. Do you see my point?"

"You aren't saying I am like him, are you?"

"No, you are a good person, but you let me believe a falsehood, and that's lying, a reflection on your character. This is the first time I have seen that in you, and it breaks my heart."

"It breaks my heart to hear you say that."

"Did you really believe I wouldn't find out? That concert was on television and it will be in all the papers. It's almost like . . . ." She stopped and blinked. "You wanted me to see you in concert."

He stared at her in silence before she asked, "But why?"

He took her hand. "So you could see how good we have gotten, how the audience goes with us. Mom, it's like Dad is inside of me, driving my desire to be a professional musician. Medicine is fine, but my heart isn't there. I want to uplift people, make them feel good, and that's healing them spiritually. My father is calling me to follow him. I can feel it deep inside and I can't ignore the feeling. It's part of me."

Mary felt her spirits sink but mustered enough strength to say, "We'll talk about it in the morning. You have class tomorrow."

Matthew walked from the room. Mary slouched in the chair and let her head rest on the back. She closed her eyes and tried to relax. The Tomorrow song came to her again, and she felt herself soaring somewhere in a blue sky, high above the earth, in a place of peace and calm.

CHAPTER SIXTY-ONE

Jorge Galinda looked at men gathered around the marble table in his study. "Gentlemen, I can not convey the depth of my displeasure. After all I have done for you, still my cartel has not penetrated the public schools of your fair city. Why?"

A pencil-necked, nervous-acting man responded, "It is not so easy. The new governor has instituted an aggressive drug program. Police with dogs are in the schools and the students must pass through detection devices before school. Penalties are harsh, especially for the parents. They are arrested and brought before a judge. You see how difficult it is."

Galinda looked at him through a rising plume of cigar smoke. "Difficult? You do not understand difficult, my friend. I can tell you something about difficult. My new factories cost more than fifty million dollars. They are state-of-the-art chemical facilities. Bribes to police chiefs, governors, prosecutors, and mayors are staggering. They are all thieves, demanding more and more. The only way I can control the costs is to kill some of them and start with cheaper replacements. The Americans drive my costs through the roof, always coming up with new ways to disrupt the shipments. I have to spend millions to trick them. That, my friends, is difficult."

The other man, stocky and thick-browed, answered, "You have a tough business. But as school administrators, we have limits too. The school boards, police, and parents are always problems, watching and criticizing. If we give a hint that we are allowing your drugs into the schools, we will be found out."

Galinda looked at the stocky man. "And what about the money I have given you? Are you prepared to return it, with interest?"

The pencil-neck said, "I have spent it. How can I return the money?"

The stocky man blinked several times.

"Gentlemen, that places me in a difficult position. You see, I know that my new program works. In New York, Philadelphia, Chicago, Houston, Dallas, Miami, Los Angeles, San Francisco, San Diego, and in every other major city in America, it is working. Except in yours, that is. My Fire chocolates are sold in the school cafeterias in all of those cities, and I now have a vast new market for drugs. Yet, you men do not help me. You are afraid of your shadows. You will not sell my candies in your schools."

The pencil-neck whined, "But we have explained to you our problems. Isn't that enough?"

Galinda leaned back in his leather executive chair and blew perfect smoke rings toward the gilded ceiling. "We are at the conclusion of our discussions." He pushed a button on the intercom. "Send Agapito in."

Within seconds, the young scar-faced man stood before his jefe. "Sí señor."

Galinda looked at him through half-closed eyes. "Agapito, these men have traveled far, and I do not wish for them to miss any of our experiences. Be their host and show them the city. Treat them as special guests."

Agapito's scar moved upward. "Of course. I will take care of everything."

The stocky man leaned away. "But that isn't necessary. We have to get home."

Galinda held up a massive hand. "Stay a while. I insist. You do not want to disrespect my people, do you?"

The two seemed thunderstruck, as Agapito grasped each man's arm, his forearm muscles bulging. The pencil-neck tried to turn toward Galinda, but Agapito yanked him hard, sending the man to the floor. He began to cry and tremble.

Agapito lifted him by the arm. "Get up! Do not be a coward. Act like a man. The adventures of the night await."

CHAPTER SIXTY-TWO

Mary sat in the living room, the mystery novel unable to capture her attention. Matthew was on her mind. She hated that he could be so logical. It made her feel unsure of decisions she had reached about him, creating confusion and uncertainty.

The doorbell chimed. "Who could that be at this hour of night?"

She looked at the security monitor and pushed a button for the front door camera. Two men in dark suits and conservative ties stood on her front porch. She pushed the intercom button. "Yes, may I help you?"

One of them responded, "Mrs. Mary Blair?"

"Yes."

"I am Agent Belmont and this is Agent Takamura from the FBI. Could we meet with you for a few minutes?"

She wondered if they were legitimate or scam artists. "How do I know you are real government agents?"

Both men held up badges and identification cards with the letters "FBI" printed in red.

"Fellows, I'm sorry, but any half-intelligent con-artist can get stuff like that. I am not going to let you in my house based on a badge and a piece of paper."

Agent Belmont responded, "Go to your phone book and look up the FBI Houston number. Call and request the duty desk. Ask them if we have been assigned to see you tonight. I assure you the duty officer will confirm that we are FBI agents here on official business."

Mary followed his suggestion, returning to the intercom in less than five minutes. "Okay, they confirmed you are legitimate. But why are you here?"

Agent Belmont answered, "On a matter of national security. Will you please see us now?"

Mary opened the door. "You may come in. Can I get you something to drink, some iced tea, perhaps?"

Each man said, "No," and Mary showed them to seats in the living room.

She looked from one to the other. "What matters of national security can I help you with?"

Agent Takamura said, "You are the mother of Matthew Blair, is that right?"

"Yes, but he has nothing to do with the government."

Takamura said, "He is presently not involved with the government. That is why we are here, to see if the government can enlist his services."

"For what? He's in college now. After that, I want him to go to medical school. He won't have time for anything else."

Agent Belmont took the lead. "Mrs. Blair, your son has been identified as a person with special talents, to help us fight the war on illegal drugs. We need him to participate in a unique project to influence our youth away from the drugs coming into the country. We are here to ask for his help."

"He isn't trained to help you. He's only a boy, one who's confused right now about his future. He doesn't know what he wants to do. I can't let him go off and fight drug people. He . . . would probably get himself killed."

Belmont persisted, "But this does not require a long term commitment. It's just one event."

Mary warily asked, "What kind of event?"

Belmont answered, "A concert, aimed at our youth, containing a powerful anti-drug message."

"You mean a concert of bands, of which his band will be one?"

Takamura said, "Not bands, just one band, Tomorrow."

"Only one band? But why Tomorrow? They are not the most famous rock musicians around. Pick someone else. Besides, it sounds dangerous."

Takamura nodded. "It is. The band members would be placing themselves in harm's way. That is one of the things we need to make clear. This could be a lethal mission."

Mary closed her eyes. "Gentlemen, I don't know who told you to come here. But there has been some huge mistake made. My son cannot help you defeat the drug lords. He's just a college sophomore. He has no power to change anything in the world, except maybe the outcome of a football game, and that can't curtail illegal drug activity."

Both men sat stone-faced.

Mary rose. "We can't help the government. It's time for you to go."

The agents walked from the room, and Belmont stopped in the doorway. "Will you reconsider if I tell you our best analysts have concluded that your son might well change some attitudes among the youth? If we can get the momentum going away from drugs, it could make a difference."

"Sir, I would not reconsider if the president herself asked me. My decision is firm. Goodnight."

Mary closed and locked the door, wondering what idiot had come up with the idea that Matthew could help the war on drugs. She shook her head and muttered, "The government, no wonder it's so screwed up. Why don't they start with fixing the streets and go from there? What nonsense will they think of next?"

CHAPTER SIXTY-THREE

The wind blew hard and rain pounded the windows, awakening Mary. She looked at the clock. It was 1:48 AM. Mary didn't remember Matthew coming home from the library, causing her to bolt from bed and go to his door. She opened it slightly, relaxing at the sight of him fast asleep.

She returned to bed and considered a steaming cup of tea. "Nope, the caffeine will keep me awake," she whispered to herself.

Mary snuggled under the warm covers, and shortly found sleep.

Puppies sniffing a green lawn, no, a green field, vast and punctuated with daisies here and there, places for some dogs to smell, and others to mark; skies blue and sunny, but not hot, from which cool breezes wafted across the field, unusual weather for Houston; children running and falling on the soft, thick grass, giggling as the puppies licked their faces, and rolling down slight hills with the puppies barking at their sides; an old man in a wheelchair smiling at the players, rising from his metal throne to join the play; small crutches on the ground, useless for a child now running without need of them; birds chirping and fluttering overhead, landing between the roiling mounds of play on the field; laughing sounds all around, from the children, and from the animals, becoming humanlike with each moment of play; and parents watching from unseen places, their smiles growing as kind thoughts rose to the heavens.

Death, lurking just beyond the green, so evil that not even the fire ants dared to approach; waiting and hoping for the children, wanting them, hating their laughs, and the laughs of the animals; death festering like a pain-filled carbuncle, pressured to explode and wishing to infect everything it could touch.

And the children moving closer, closer to death, to the place where it lay hidden; their laughs drowning out the cries of parents now panicked and screaming for them to stop; the children walking, skipping, running toward the evil just beyond, not seeing the death . . . waiting and hoping and expecting them.

Light, coming with music, floating on the cool winds across the green fields; turning the children; beckoning them to the source; pulling them to the source; music sent upward bringing more than the little ones, angels and eagles alike flying to the source.

Golden harps played on; no, not harps, but guitars held high by gods aglow with the light, making this music of Heaven beckon the children as though calling their names; and the puppies and birds coming too, led by the tones.

Tam and Matthew playing the guitars of life and death cursing with each step of the children toward them.

Parents crying tears, their voices stilled by this miracle over death, the music pulling the children farther from doom and evil; and the devil himself rising from the death and calling to them, but with a voice tiny and frail.

Then the guitars falling silent and the light fading; the children becoming still in the field, turning and moving once again toward the devil's cries, growing louder with each step; cries turning to laughs; death coming closer to these babes soon to be lost forever.

Mary awoke, her sheets wet and uncomfortable. She threw the moist covers aside and shuffled to the bathroom, rinsing her feverish face in cool water. "God, what a nightmare. Glad it was just a dream. Thank you, Lord. It really didn't happen."

She went downstairs and filled a kettle for tea, not worrying about the caffeine. Sleep was out of the question. She waited for the water to boil, but images of the dream remained in her brain, and she snuggled in her chair, hoping they would be driven away by morning's first hues.

CHAPTER SIXTY-FOUR

Mary watched the sunrise and sipped her third cup of hot tea, the warm liquid helping to uplift her mood. The horrific mental images were now only a fading memory, one she wanted gone as soon as possible. She heard a vehicle outside and expected the sound of the morning paper hitting the sidewalk. But she quickly realized something was different—no thud. Mary walked to the front window and peered through the shutters. A black SUV had parked in front of her house and two others rested silently along the curb a short distance behind. She glanced at the clock. It was 6:15 AM, and Mary wondered who was in the vehicles.

Suddenly, the back door to one of the vehicles opened and a man emerged and strode toward her front door. He looked familiar, and Mary soon recognized one of the FBI agents who had visited her, Takamura. He walked to the porch and rang the doorbell.

Mary hesitated before pushing the intercom button. "Yes?"

"Mrs. Blair. You may remember me from the other evening, Agent Takamura from the FBI."

"Yes, I remember you. Isn't it a little early for the government to call?"

He laughed. "It is, but this is an unusual visit."

"What do you want to talk about? I thought we had settled matters."

"Someone else wants to visit you, ma'am, someone very special. I really need to speak with you in person before the visit. Could you let me in? You will not be inconvenienced."

Mary walked to the door and opened it, peering at the well-groomed agent and feeling no fear, only curiosity. "Why so early? And who is this special person, the Pope?"

Agent Takamura laughed again. "Now that would be unusual. The visitor thinks an early meeting is best. I hope that's all right. Mrs. Blair, who is in the house right now, besides you and me?"

"Just Matthew. He's asleep upstairs. No classes today. He may sleep a while, since he was at the library late."

"May I look around? Sorry, it's protocol."

"Sure, but don't wake my son. He needs his sleep."

Agent Takamura glanced around the room and said, "I was once a college student too. Don't worry."

He walked throughout the house, Mary with him, looking in closets before repeating the process on the upper floors. Afterward, they walked to the front door.

Agent Takamura smiled. "Thanks. I'll let the visitor know it's okay to come in." He disappeared into the black SUV.

Mary waited, wondering who was so special the FBI had to do a search before he came into her house, maybe some senator or representative. A door of another SUV opened, and Mary saw a tall woman emerge. She walked elegantly up the walkway, like a professional dancer on stage.

Mary peered through the window and gasped. "My God, the president." She stood in the opened doorway, wondering if this was part of her dream but realizing it wasn't when the Afro-American woman extended her hand, smiled, and said, "Mrs. Blair, thank you so much for agreeing to see me, and please excuse the early hour, but it reduces the inconvenience for others."

Mary found it hard to respond but finally said, "Madame President, I . . . don't know what to say. It is an honor to receive you. Please come in."

She led the visitor to the living room and gestured toward an overstuffed chair. "May I get you something, some hot tea, perhaps?"

"I would love some, but I had coffee on the way, and I'm trying to watch the caffeine." President Winslow looked around the room. "You have a lovely home, not too much clutter. I like the understated, elegant decorating approach. They gave me a lot of grief when I wanted to redecorate the White House. All that tradition is hard to change. But I didn't come here to talk interior design so I'll get down to business."

Mary liked the president's friendly manner and began to relax.

"Mrs. Blair, I've read your articles and know you are interested in human rights and Third World progress. You seem to press the theme of eliminating suffering and human bondage. Your piece on Ethiopia was brilliant, how the president ignored the terrorists to promote his message of peace and love.

What a story that was. It presented facts I didn't know, which was unusual since my ancestors came from that country."

Mary nodded. "President Iyasu was a brave man. His people owe him a great deal. And his son has continued that legacy."

President Winslow's eyes sparkled. "Yes. But they did not accomplish Ethiopia's progress alone. They had help—from a special young man, your husband, Matthew Blair. They called him Tam, the leader of Promise. His special talents motivated President Iyasu to defy the terrorists and place Ethiopia on another course, one of peace and progress."

Mary blinked. "How do you know about Matthew? He guarded his personal life, and my son and I have been careful to keep his secret safe. Only a handful of people know Matthew's identity. How did you find out?"

President Winslow smiled and patted Mary's shoulder. "We must know what is happening in the world, even to the smallest detail. The events of 9/11 taught us that. I hope you aren't upset."

"I, I wouldn't say that I'm upset, only shocked . . . and worried. If it became known that my son had a father who defeated the terrorists, he could be in danger."

President Winslow spoke carefully, "Your secret is safe. Only our most trusted officials know the truth. But it is vitally important that you and I discuss those facts."

Mary felt herself frown. "Why?"

"Because the future of all our children depends on it."

Mary leaned back in her chair and sighed. "That sounds pretty serious. How can the future of our children be riding on what my husband did? He's been dead twenty years."

President Winslow folded her hands and settled in the easy chair, her eyes penetrating and focused. "Mrs. Blair, when I ran for office, I promised the American people that we would defeat crime, not just random criminal acts, but drug crime in general. I have tried my best to make good on that promise. We beefed up the drug enforcement organizations, strengthened the drug laws, and involved the military in keeping drugs out of the country. However, despite all of that, we have failed to stem the flow of drugs across our borders. In fact, there is a new drug that causes casual users to become hard-core addicts. It has found its way into schools across the country, in chocolate candy, with terrifying results. The use of cocaine and heroine among young teens is up sixteen percent. The truth is we can't stop the drugs from coming in."

Mary swallowed, remembering Lizzie's tragedy. "I knew the drug problem was bad, but I had no idea how awful it had gotten."

"The government doesn't want to divulge alarming facts. We want to present a confident front. But the facts will come out soon."

The two sat in silence for a short time before Mary asked, "What can we do to help the situation? Matthew and I are only ordinary citizens."

"Citizens, yes, but ordinary, not really," came the President's response.

Mary was confused. "What do you mean?"

"Mrs. Blair, have you heard the term "psychological profusion?"

"No."

"I hadn't either, until a few months ago. Our psychologists only recently discovered this phenomenon. We have known about people with the ability to persuade the masses."

"You mean like Christ or Roosevelt or . . . Hitler?" Mary asked.

"Not exactly. Those people were charismatic. They had devout followers, but they also had opponents. Psychological profusion is similar but more powerful than charisma. It involves a person with the ability to sway almost everybody. Somehow, that person exercises sweeping persuasive powers. Our experts tell us that psychological profusion involves the combination of personal talents like intonation, body language, timing, intellect, appearance, and interpersonal connection. Everyone seems to be captivated by such a person, even to the extent of changing lifestyles and attitudes. It is not unlike that rare person with a two hundred IQ or extreme musical genius. It is very, very rare."

"But who has such power?"

"Only a few people across history. Alexander the Great, perhaps, and your husband, and . . . probably your son."

Mary reflected on the explanation, before responding, "Matthew? But he hasn't swayed any mass of people. He is just a college kid. He . . . ."

"Has the gift his father passed on. The only reason his band isn't the most popular musical group in the world is because they aren't pursuing their careers. Their CD just hit the top of the music charts worldwide. Did you know that?"

"I didn't want to know about Matthew's music career. I want him to be a nice, safe doctor, not a musician."

President Winslow nodded. "I can understand your attitude, especially with your husband's death. Truth is that Matthew's musical popularity could easily eclipse all other groups around the world. Teens and adults alike would follow him just as fervently as Promise's fans supported them. There is no end to what your son could do, the good he could bring to the world. He could turn our youth away from drugs, win the drug war from within their hearts. At least, start that process. The country needs him. The world does too."

Mary became resistant. "You are asking me to place my son in harm's way, to put a bull's-eye on his chest. I lost my husband to that kind of service. I will not lose my son, no matter who asks, not even you."

"I am not asking, Mrs. Blair. I am giving you the facts. The people of the United States are begging for help, and your son is the only human being on earth capable of responding to those pleas."

Mary rose from the chair and walked to the window. She began to cry, stopping to regain control. "Do those people care about my husband, about me, about my son? They are strangers we will never know. Even if Matthew could change some of them, will those people really care that he may be killed in the process? No! They will continue with their selfish lives, just as before, wanting material things. Some other vice will control their lives, like alcohol or sex or money. Who will remember Matthew? Who will thank him?"

"God."

Mary and President Winslow turned toward the stairs. Matthew stood there, blue eyes seeming to glow in the dim light. He descended, stopped, and placed an arm around Mary's shoulders. "Isn't it enough that God will care?"

President Winslow rose and extended a hand. "Carol Winslow. Sorry we woke you."

He shook hands. "It is an honor to meet you, Madame President." Matthew turned to his mother. "Maybe that feeling inside me is God not letting go. I didn't give myself these talents. He did, and I can't ignore Him any more. Dad did his job and I need to do mine. Whatever happens, God will take care of us." He looked at President Winslow. "What do you have in mind for me?"

The president smiled—her white, straight teeth contrasting against ebony skin. She seemed energized. "We have planned an ambitious program. I think it will work. First, Tomorrow releases a new album, one containing songs about teens eschewing drugs. Second, we will distribute the album worldwide and promote it heavily. I am confident it will shoot to the top of the charts in a matter of weeks. Lastly, and this is the miracle we are counting on, you will do a concert in Nuevo Laredo, the heart of the drug lords' empire. The concert will also be publicized for what it will be, your attempt to save our young people from the lies and suffering of illegal drugs. If everything goes as we believe it will, millions of youth will stop using drugs, and that should be the beginning of the end of drug smuggling. Soon afterward, a vast army of agents and military personnel will finish the job with an offense in Latin America and the United States to destroy the drug cartels."

President Winslow stopped and studied Mary and Matthew. Mary's tears returned. "No, God, no. Matthew will be killed."

Matthew smiled. "I like it. We have some new songs, our best work, about hope and peace and love. They will probably work for the new album."

President Winslow hugged him. "Terrific. You will need to be placed in protective custody until the concert, just as a precaution."

Matthew's smile turned to a frown, and the president asked, "What's wrong?"

He slowly said, "That protective custody part, I can't agree to that."

President Winslow quickly inquired. "Why?"

He explained, "The national championship game is in three weeks at the Atlantic Bowl. I've got to play. The team and the whole school are counting on my playing in that game. Poly hasn't played for a national football championship before. I can't let them down. You understand, don't you?"

The president sat down gracefully and stared at the floor. "The security people won't like it. But I understand. You have to play, keep your promise to the team, finish the season. After that, you will whip those drug lords." She extended her hand to him. "Deal?"

He took her hand. "Deal."

Mary looked at them and felt tears streaming down her cheeks.

CHAPTER SIXTY-FIVE

The Poly football team sat silently in its locker room, every player seemingly focused on Coach Masterson. "Gentlemen, in one week we play for the national championship. Every practice is critical at this point. We must peak now. I want everyone to forget the eleven victories we achieved this season and focus on Erie Union." He stopped and deliberately looked at each player. His voice became low and purposeful. "The fact is we haven't encountered a defensive team nearly as good as they are. Nobody we have played this season can match their defensive speed or intensity. The linebackers are as fast as most running backs. They will key on Matthew every play. Their defensive linemen average three hundred and forty-five pounds, and they can fly as well. The deep backs are former sprinters, but not the short, compact type of athlete. They are specially recruited tall sprinters who go after every pass. That defense has notched six shutouts this season. No opponent has scored double digits on them. They are undefeated, as we are. Some of the sports writers say Erie is good enough to compete in the pros. I tell you these facts not to intimidate you but so you will understand that if we are going to win, we must play flawless, tough football, every down."

The Coach turned to the blackboard and wrote, "Deliver your energy into the opponent. Do not let him dictate the intensity of the contest."

He pointed to those words. "Erie Union plays smashmouth football. They will try and beat you up. This is the way to defeat that style of play: beat them off the ball; hit them harder than they hit you; surprise them with your energy, every snap of the ball. Do this and you will bring the championship trophy home. This is a special opportunity given to you. The victory will not come easily. You must take it to be yours. Will you accept this great challenge and bring glory to Poly-Technical University?"

The players rose, held their helmets high, and circled around Matthew. He looked at Coach Masterson, who nodded a silent approval. The young man's voice echoed off the walls sure and strong, "Poly, number one, now and forever!"

The team cheered, whistled and stomped as they reached toward their hero, the player who had led them to so many victories and would lead them once more in the greatest game of their lives.

CHAPTER SIXTY-SIX

Matthew drove the van while Eric Rohmer talked excitedly, "Man, this is great, taking the guys to a new place. Where did you say we were going, Mr. Matthew?"

"Green Garden Nursing Home. It should be up ahead."

Eric rocked from side to side in the seat. "I hope the guys do good, so the Green Garden people will ask us back, maybe for cookies at their Christmas party. Wouldn't that be fun, Mr. Matthew?"

"It would be terrific. I bet they do."

The van stopped in the parking lot adjacent to a one-storey building, and the puppies seemed to sense they were going to visit someone, their barking growing loud and high-pitched. Eric jumped from his seat and attached leashes to his six charges. "Now you guys be on your best behavior. We got to make a good impression."

The small group trotted into the building, and a rotund woman in a white uniform met them with extended arms and a broad smile. "You must be from the puppy foundation. Our residents are so excited. They are waiting in the recreation room. I hope the puppies are housebroken."

Matthew laughed. "They are mostly house-broken, but we may have an accident from one of the young ones. They are very excited."

The woman led them into a large, brightly lit room, its walls lined with wheelchairs bearing ancient men and women, some slumped over and others buckled in. Some of the residents sat in chairs, and Matthew saw that most of them seemed so small, as though shrunken from normal size. Yet, almost everybody was smiling at the energetic troupe. The woman held her hands high. "Here they are. These young men and I will take the puppies around. Please be patient and we'll get to everyone as fast as possible."

Matthew took two puppies; Eric led two others; and the woman tried to control two wigglers. Some residents reached out to pet them, while others made kissing sounds. Laughs and giggles soon filled the room. Matthew smiled at the happy scene as he talked with residents, obviously having a good time. He moved slowly along the wall, taking time to visit a bit while placing his puppies in laps and wrinkled arms.

The time seemed to pass quickly, and soon everyone had had an opportunity to receive licks and attention from the eager puppies. The woman addressed the group, "I want to thank the foundation for this visit. We all had a great time. Do you want them to come again?"

Claps responded to her question.

Matthew and Eric took the leashes and Matthew waved to the group as they left the room. The group walked toward the entrance, but before they left the building, Matthew heard a soft voice, "Mr. Blair."

He stopped and peered into a dimly lit patient room. "Yes."

"In here, Mr. Blair. Can you visit a little?"

Matthew handed the leashes to Eric. "Will you put them in the van? I'll be there in a minute."

He walked into the room and saw a woman in bed, covered by a flowered blanket. She was almost a skeleton and her skin looked dry and dull. He noticed she labored to breathe, and, for an instant, he found it hard to talk. "Yes ma'am?"

She smiled sweetly and said, "Don't you remember me? Professor Whiteside. Astrophysics. You were my student last year."

"Of course I remember you. That was a great class. You made it fun. I didn't know you were here. Why didn't you come to the rec room with the others?"

"Too tired. I stay in bed most of the time. I wanted to see you, though. Been following the team. What a season you're having."

"Yeah, it's been great. The guys are playing hard."

"Sit down, Matthew. Got time to talk?"

"Sure. How are you doing?"

"Not real good. The leukemia takes a lot out of me. When Mr. Whiteside died last month, that hurt more than anything. All my people are gone now, and it's very lonely. Sure glad to see a familiar face."

"It's good to see you. Would you like for me to bring one of the puppies here?"

"No. Not right now. Maybe next time. If there is one. They say it's only a matter of weeks." She stopped and studied him, her bright eyes seeming out of place in a withered body. "You know, I'm a closet football fan. Do you think the team can win the championship?"

"Erie Union is tough. But we can do it."

She sighed, seeming exhausted, but forced the words, "It's strange about college athletics."

"What do you mean?"

"How they affect a college's reputation. Poly is a great school, but people always make fun of us. Call us eggheads and geeks. Say we're boring. Even our academic standing suffers. We're ranked twelfth, but I know we are one of the very top schools."

He looked at the flowered blanket. "I see what you mean. Guess you're right. Notoriety often brings respect, even if it's not deserved."

"Matthew, before I leave this world, I would like to see something special for the school I gave my life to. That it be recognized as one of the great institutions. The national championship will help Poly so much."

"We'll give it our best. But we know how tough Erie Union is, especially on defense."

She smiled slightly. "Surprise them. Run a play they don't expect, like the flea flicker."

He asked, "The flea flicker? You know about that play?"

"I'm a closet fan, remember? Been one for years. Hated to see Poly a doormat for so long."

He chuckled. "I'm glad you like football. But a trick play? I don't know about that. The coach is pretty conservative."

"That's why it will work. Erie won't be prepared for it." She breathed deliberately, as though trying to find strength, then smiled. "What a way to go out, with Poly on top, where it belongs."

"Mr. Matthew, can we go now? The puppies are yappin'," came from the doorway.

Matthew turned to see Eric. He rose and patted his old professor's shoulder. "I'll see what I can do." He noticed the deep purple bruises covering her frail arms and hoped he had not hurt her.

She closed her eyes, and the smile faded.

CHAPTER SIXTY-SEVEN

We're all here to stay,
Everyone is going to play,
In the game for life we'll win,
God's prize, for you and your kin.

Can you see it up ahead,
Feel it with no dread,
Life's there for you and me
Who look with eyes that see.

Run along the path of light,
Far ahead of night,
Come with me that way
To the place of joy today.

Friends and family there
Dancin' in the purest air,
And God is partying there too;
He's wavin' to me and you.

We gonna win the run
Havin' a lot of fun,
Behind us and long dead
The lies and the dread.

We're all here to stay,
Everyone is going to play,
In the game for life we'll win,
God's prize, for you and your kin.

Angelica swayed to the music, humming the melody with Tomorrow. Though she could not see Matthew, Angelica knew he was holding the lead guitar high, wailing and dancing as the leader of the group. Mary had described his every move to her as they sat in the third-floor music studio. Suddenly, Matthew's guitar produced a combination of notes and chords racing along the scale to the end of the song.

Scooter Rockman jumped off the couch. "Fantastic! In-cred-i-ble! That song is going super platinum. No doubt about it."

Matthew laughed. "Okay. I think that's it. The album is finished. How long before it hits the market, Mr. Rockman?"

"Only about two weeks. Then watch out. It'll rocket to the top of the charts. I can't wait. Great work, guys. Thank you, Mrs. Blair, for changing your mind. The band is going to do unbelievable things."

Mary cleared her throat. "With God's help."

Matthew said, "It will be okay, Mom. I'm sure."

She walked from the room, and Angelica took Mathew's arm. He turned to the others. "Why don't you guys go home. Later."

Angelica let go of his arm. He protested. "I didn't mean you. Stay. I'll run you home later."

She turned toward him and smiled.

Within a short time, they were alone, sitting on the couch in the living room, listening to classical music.

"Matthew, why are you doing it?"

"What?"

"The concert in Nuevo Laredo? You mother was so opposed to your music career. And now, you and the band are going to some small town for a concert. It doesn't make sense to me. Why not New York or LA or even Austin? But Nuevo Laredo?"

"We were asked to do a special concert down there. It's a unique gig. After that, we can go to the big cities."

"But the news is full of drug killings in that area. It doesn't seem safe there. Will there be security?"

"Yes. They say we'll be safe."

"Your voice doesn't contain much confidence."

"How do you know that? I'm talking normally."

"I'm blind, remember? Sounds have special meaning to me, and you are not telling me everything. I sense it."

"I . . . can't tell you the whole story. It's a secret right now. Look, I'll be as careful as possible. We have a future together."

"Right. But, Matthew, I'm scared. Something tells me there is danger you can't see or control. I feel cold. Hold me."

He hugged her and placed his cheek next to hers. "If things don't work out, remember I love you. And I want you and Mom to be best friends."

She began to cry, tightening her grip on his arm. "I won't let you go, and that's it. That stupid concert can't be so important."

He released the hug and held her at arm's length. "It is. The lives of many kids could be affected. I promised to do the concert. Besides, all this talk of danger is melodramatic. Why are you worrying so much?"

She turned to face him. "My heart tells me what my eyes can't see, and right now it's breaking."

CHAPTER SIXTY-EIGHT

Scooter Rockman whined. "Nuevo Laredo? But, Matthew, that's crazy. Nobody does a concert there, especially an emerging star like you. Let me sign you for the major markets: New York, London, LA. The fans there are clamoring for Tomorrow. Your albums are red hot everywhere, just like I said. Let's arrange a major concert and give the world what it wants. I'll handle everything. You're ripe for greatness!"

Matthew looked away. "It sounds tempting, but I have to do the Nuevo Laredo concert."

Rockman asked, "Why?"

"The band agreed to do it, for a special purpose."

Rockman rose from the couch in Matthew's studio and paced for several seconds, before sitting down and saying, "Look, I know you have a good reason for the concert, some humanitarian purpose, and that's fine, but not now. You guys are getting started on an incredible career. This is not the time for humanitarian stuff. Get established and then go and save the world. That's the right thing to do."

Matthew looked squarely at him. "What about Promise?"

Rockman's forehead wrinkled. "Promise? What does this have to do with them? They're dead. The whole band died before you were born."

Matthew said, "They brought peace to the Middle East, when no one else could do it, saved thousands of lives, brought nations together, ended years of war. Didn't they do the right thing?"

Rockman seemed ready to argue. "Okay, let's look at Promise. That's a good example of what I'm talking about. Those guys were maybe the greatest rock band ever, and look what happened to them. Killed, every one, and at a young age. Their leader, Tam, was only nineteen, and he gets blown up by some nut. They could have done so much more, but some moron cuts their lives short in a godforsaken place they should never have been in. You don't want that to happen to you."

"But you are missing the point, Mr. Rockman. Promise did a lot of lasting good, even if it cost them their lives. Wasn't their sacrifice worth it?"

Rockman shot back. "No! It wasn't. They didn't need to sacrifice anything. They could have done good by playing their music from the States, where they would have been protected. For them to go to that hellhole was stupid. There was a better way."

"What was that?

Rockman almost shouted, "Play their music here, and let it move people around the world, even in the Middle East. That way, they would be alive today, still doing good."

Matthew was calm. "Do you think their music would have had the same power from here? Isn't it possible that the people of the Middle East were changed because Promise came to them to deliver their message of peace? One thing is for sure—Promise's strategy worked. They brought peace when others failed. I don't see how you can argue with that."

Rockman slumped on the couch. "I'm a music promoter, not a politician. Maybe you are right. I'm just looking out for you and your career. I know that a concert in Nuevo Laredo, Mexico, is not the thing to do. You are risking everything by going there. It won't help you, and it's very dangerous. There are some crazy drug criminals down there. The police can't protect you from them. Many of the cops are probably on the take, and that doesn't do you any good."

"The concert might help a lot of people, many of them kids."

Rockman sighed. "It might do that."

Matthew smiled. "That's the point. If we can do some good, we must do it, even if there's danger out there."

"You know, you're a great kid, too good really. All that talent, and you want to save the world. You could be anything—a rock star, a doctor, a scientist, even the president. And you want to go to one of the most dangerous places on earth for some benefit concert. So much talent at risk. It makes me almost cry."

"Who gave me this talent?"

The music promoter shrugged. "Your parents."

"Not them. They had nothing to do with it. They didn't create their DNA. God made me this way. I've got to do what He's telling my heart."

Rockman rose and walked heavily to the door. "You're also hard-headed. Look, after it's over, let's do the world tour, if you survive, that is. Okay?"

Matthew smiled and flashed his blue eyes. Scooter Rockman shook his head, walked to Matthew and gave him a hug. "I can't be mad at you. Like I said, you're a great kid."

CHAPTER SIXTY-NINE

"Ladies and gentlemen, welcome to the Atlantic Bowl in Atlantic City, New Jersey. What a perfect day for football. This afternoon we have the collegiate national championship, a classic struggle between the irresistible force, the Poly-Technical Eagles, and the immovable object, the Erie Union Bears. This promises to be one of the best contests in recent memory. Stay tuned for the pregame pageantry."

Mary and Angelica sat in the luxury box in the third level of the clubhouse high above the field. The large screen television showed a car commercial. The president of Poly walked up and said, "This is a red letter day for the university. I can feel the excitement. Is Matthew ready to play his usual great game?"

Mary was still focused on the large television screen, her thoughts somewhere beyond football, before she responded, "Yes. I'm sure he is ready. He knows the game means so much to Poly, and to Houston and Texas as well."

The commercials ended, and the sports broadcasters appeared again. "This is the championship game everyone expected almost all year. After Poly defeated Santa Mansion, it was ranked number one, with Erie Union just a few points behind. All of the football pundits have speculated about Poly's potent ground game against the Erie Union defense, leading the nation in all defensive categories."

Another announcer added, "Exactly, Martin. The Bears have shut out half of their opponents and have held the others to single digit scoring, producing a perfect eleven and zero season. They use speed and brute force to stifle the opposing offenses, sacking the quarterback an average of seven times per game, and limiting the rushing effort to a paltry forty yards a contest. But how will they handle Matthew Blair's amazing speed? That is the question on everyone's minds today."

The other sportscaster responded, "That is the question indeed, but not just today. People have wondered about that for almost the entire season, certainly since Santa Mansion fell from the ranks of the undefeated based on Blair's lightning speed and amazing athleticism."

Mary noticed a hand on her shoulder, turning to see the broad smile of President Winslow. "Madame President, I didn't know you would be here." She said, standing to greet the president.

"We didn't announce it, for security reasons. But I love football, and this is the place to be today. May I join you?"

"Of course. This is Matthew's friend, Angelica."

"Angelica, it's good to meet you," President Winslow said. For a moment, the president did not seem to realize Angelica was blind, quickly recovering to grasp the young woman's hand. "How do you do?"

Angelica lowered her head. "This is an honor." She smiled toward the president. "I have admired your work with the underprivileged."

The sportscasters caught Mary's attention. "Poly has won the toss and elected to receive. In a few minutes, Martin, we will see how Erie handles this potent Poly ground attack."

The other announcer nodded. "Indeed we will. Erie Union has one of the premier place kickers in the game, and he could prove the difference today. The teams are set, and the ball is kicked. It's a long one, going out of the end zone. Poly will put the ball in play on its twenty yard line."

Mary hugged Angelica as Matthew took the handoff and ran left, stopped by a host of red- and blue-clad defenders at the line of scrimmage, prompting one of the sportscasters to bellow, "What a hit! Erie had that play figured out. Both of their linebackers stopped Matthew Blair in his tracks."

Mary cringed. "I hope they don't hurt him."

Angelica whispered, "He'll be all right. Matthew's tough."

Poly lined up quickly, giving the ball to Matthew again. He broke through the line and accelerated left, picking up three yards before two defenders tackled him hard.

One of the sportscasters howled, "Ouch! You have to wonder how much punishment Blair can take. They're keying on him every play. Poly needs to give the ball to someone else to protect him as much as possible."

The Eagles snapped the ball, and the quarterback faked to Matthew in the center of the line. Erie's linebackers smothered him as the quarterback tossed a lateral to the tight end coming around. The end darted through a hole in the mass of defenders and ran across the thirty. A defensive end sailed through the air, meeting the ball carrier helmet to helmet. The ball squirted loose and bounced on the forty. Players from both teams dove for it, producing a mound topped by officials struggling to find the ball. Suddenly, an official motioned Erie's ball, producing a thunderous roar.

One of the announcers exclaimed, "That's what defense will do for you! They say great defense will control games, and we're seeing it here. The Bears' offense takes over at the Poly forty. Can they take advantage of this opportunity and score?"

The Erie Union offense came to the line of scrimmage, and the other announcer said, "That's an offensive line that can play in any league. Poly had better be ready to dig in or they will be blown back."

The center snapped the ball, and the silver-uniformed Poly defenders swarmed the ball carrier, resulting in no gain. One of the announcers responded, "Terrific defense. Poly is fast, and they pursue well. Erie Union may have trouble against their athleticism."

On second down, the quarterback threw a short pass, but a fleet Poly defender batted it away. Third down was a loss of two yards on a fullback draw play.

One of the sportscasters was quick to give his opinion. "Poly's defense seems up to the task. The Bears' big linemen can't overcome their sheer numbers swarming the ball. But the Bears have their long range place kicker, Smithson. He has won games for them before. Can he put Erie ahead and let their defense control the Poly offense to win the game? This will be a fifty-seven yard attempt. Smithson has hit several from this range. Can he do it again?"

The crowd fell almost silent as the kicker waited for the snap. The center hiked the ball, and it sailed parallel to the ground. The holder angled it slightly. Smithson used a soccer-style kick, sending the ball high and long through the uprights. The scoreboard quickly showed the score: Erie Union, three; Poly-Technical, zero. The Bear band erupted in the school fight song to deafening applause, shouts, whistles, and stomps by thousands of red-adorned fans.

The game settled into a pattern: Erie Union's defense used two and three players to key on Matthew every play, whether or not he had the ball; the Eagle offense was unable to score; and the Bears appeared to be satisfied with a three-point lead as the clock ran down. With the game nearing the end, one of the announcers said, "Well, the Eagles made a valiant effort, but that Bear defense was just too much, even for the best running back in the country. Matthew Blair was hunted on every play and couldn't get loose, like he usually does."

His partner answered, "True, though he has racked up over a hundred yards today. But Poly managed no points, mainly because the Erie defense bent a little but stiffened when it counted. Give credit to Poly, however. What a great season. This will be their first defeat in more than two years, in eleven seconds, that is."

Matthew called time-out. Rather than the offense going to the sideline, he motioned them to the center of the field. "Look guys, I want to call a special play. I know, it's not in our playbook, but that's what gives it a chance." He stopped and surveyed the wide eyes looking at him, before saying, "Let's run flea flicker right."

The quarterback moaned. "Flea flicker? We don't know that play. It's a gadget."

Matthew said, "Everyone knows the flea flicker. You linemen pass block. The left end splits out wide, and the halfback sets up in the slot to the left. The right end lines up three yards outside the tackle and runs a straight ten-yard button-hook route. I'll be coming behind him, and the end laterals the ball to me." He stopped and looked directly at the right end. "Lead me with the lateral because I'll be at full steam." Matthew placed a hand on the quarterback's shoulder. "Call the play."

The quarterback swallowed and slowly responded, "Right flea flicker, on three."

Mary hugged Angelica. "They have won so many games. It's no shame to lose this one."

Angelica said, "I still have confidence in Matthew."

President Winslow stood, looking at the television. "I agree. It's not over yet. Let's see what they can do on this last play. I've learned to keep trying to the end. My first job was a waitress at a diner."

Mary reached for the president's hand.

One of the television sportscasters described the scene on the field, "The Bears are celebrating on the sidelines, and their fans are going crazy in the stands. And why not? Poly is left with one last chance at its own thirty. The Erie victory is all but sealed, and with it comes the national championship. One snap to go, and Erie Union will have produced yet another shutout. The Eagles come to the line in what appears to be a passing formation. The ball is snapped. It's a completed pass to the right end, only a short completion, not long enough. But he laterals to Blair! Sweet sister, it's the flea flicker to

Matthew Blair coming from nowhere! He's at the forty-five, the fifty, the forty, pursued by two safeties, but they won't catch him. He's chewing up the real estate. Touchdown! Poly wins the national championship! What an incredible turn of events. Erie was not prepared for that play. What a brilliant call!"

Mary, Angelica, and President Winslow hugged and gyrated like schoolgirls. The president stopped, pointed to the television screen, and said, "Look at that!"

Tens of thousands of fans created a pulsating sea of silver flowing out of the stands onto the field, consuming the green turf. The Eagle band was in the center of the great mass of humanity, its bright instruments shining in the afternoon sun. The cries and chants gave way to the Poly fight song, something about a great eagle in the sky. Mary hummed the melody, and Angelica joined the singing.

Far away, at Green Garden Nursing Home in Houston, Professor Whiteside listened to the radio next to her bed. She smiled and whispered to herself, "He did it. Finally, we're on the map. Thank you, Matthew."

The radio announcer continued his falsetto analysis of Poly's victory. Professor Whiteside did not hear him finish, closing her eyes for the last time, the smile still on her face.

CHAPTER SEVENTY

"Agapito, my son. Come and sit with me. I have a special task for you."

The young man obeyed, sitting in a leather chair beside the desk of Jorge Galinda. "It is a great comfort for a father to have such a dutiful son who does what he is told, without questioning his orders."

"Your slightest wish will be done completely. What would you like me to do, my jefe?"

Galinda leaned back in his massive leather chair and stared at the ceiling before answering. "My sources have told me the Americans are planning to destroy the cartel. Their pitiful plan involves sending a singer to Nuevo Laredo for a concert. They believe he will turn the young people from drugs. Do you believe that, Agapito? The fools actually believe some singer can defeat me."

Agapito's eyes became slits. "Tell me his name, jefe, and I will cut his head off and bring it to you, a prize for your trophy room. You can hang it on the wall next to the pig's head."

Galinda roared, "Excellent! Hang the head on my wall. Yes, I shall do that. And I will send pictures of the head to the Americans so that they will tremble at my name. Those weak-willed children will fall beneath our boots. His name is Matthew Blair, and he will be in Nuevo Laredo two weeks from today."

"He is a dead man. Close your mind to him and have no worry. His head is almost on your wall."

Galinda bellowed again, laughing so hard he began to cough. "Leave me, before you split my sides." Suddenly, he stopped and became serious, saying, "Agapito, this is your most important mission. Do not fail me, or it will be your last."

"As I said, jefe, he is already dead."

Agapito left the room, closing the thick wooden door behind him. He stopped in the hall and took a switchblade from his pocket. The long blade snapped into position from the bone handle. He ran the palm of his left hand lightly across the edge of the blade, producing an ooze of blood. He sucked it and smiled, feeling anger rise, and muttered to himself, "His head will come off by my hand! It is done."

"And what manner of hell's torture are you planning, Agapito?"

He turned toward an old woman, short and round, her head covered by lace. She clutched a Rosary in both hands, fumbling with the beads as she stared at the young man.

He smiled and bowed, the anger waning. "*Señora* Galinda. A pleasure, as always. The jefe's mother is my mother. I hold you in great respect."

"Lies, all lies. *Muerte.* Killer. Only God, Himself, can save you from your sins. Pray for forgiveness, Agapito. Pray to God for your soul."

"I fear only one man, and he is not God. I fear only the jefe. He is my god."

Señora Galinda shook her head, looked at the Rosary and shuffled to the wooden door. She knocked, and a low voice beckoned her entry. "Ah, Mother, so good to see you on this fine day."

She stood silently, staring at him. "It is not a fine day. You dishonor the memory of your father by your sins."

He smiled. "What sins? I am only a businessman. Why do you say these things about your own son?"

"Because they are true. The people in the village are afraid to speak, but I will say the truth. Your sins are so great not even the Holy Virgin will listen to your prayers. Why, Jorge? Many years ago you were good, an altar boy. You even talked of becoming a priest. And now this. How did it happen?"

The smile faded, and the edges of his thick moustache moved downward. "You dare ask such things? Do you not remember, Mother? The priests. It was the priests who changed me." He stopped and his heavy fist crashed on the table. "They raped your son for years and no one helped him, no one, not you, or my father or your blessed Virgin, not even God, Himself. Until one day, I stopped it. Me, Mother. I stopped it by killing a rapist. With my bare hands, I strangled him. It felt good to kill him, to see him lifeless on the floor. He needed to be dead, and I did it for myself and the other boys. And you ask what happened to me? I vowed then to help myself, even if it meant killing others. No other person would help me. No father protected me."

"Do not blame your father. He worked hard in the Texas fields to make money for us. When he had the accident and died . . . I had to go to work for the family. I went to America and did what I could. Thank God for your older sister. She became the mother. We did the best we could, Jorge. We were poor people."

"Today you do not need to work, Mother. I can buy anything, even the church if I choose. And the priests in Nuevo Laredo, they are all good, very good. They know I will kill them if they touch a single child. I have made them good. Is that not a blessing? Why do you not praise me for that?"

She began to tremble. "*Mi Dios.* There will always be bad men, Jorge, even priests. But you cannot go against God's law, my son. You cannot kill. Repent and save yourself. God will forgive you. It is not too late."

"I am the jefe! Everyone bows to me. Have you not seen them in the village? They stand aside when I pass. I eat where I please. No restaurant dares to charge me. No woman will deny me. I will not give up my power. If I do, we will die as *pobrecitos*, and I will not allow that to happen."

She collapsed on the marble floor. "Dios. *Maria. Por favor. No mas muerte.* Por favor."

CHAPTER SEVENTY-ONE

Matthew and Angelica sat on the Galveston beach at sunset. He spoke softly to her, "The sun is almost hidden by the horizon. The sky is filled with purple, orange, and red. I wish you could see it."

She turned to him. "I can, Matthew. The warm is gone, and I feel cool breezes. I see the sunset in my mind. It's beautiful."

He kissed her cheek and then her lips. "I love you, Angelica. After it's all over, we are going to be together a lot."

She leaned against his chest. "Can we come here again?"

"You bet. As often as you like," he said with a hug.

Angelica pushed him away. "Matthew. If I ask you something, will you do it?"

"I'll try. What do you want?"

"Don't go to Nuevo Laredo. Please."

He was silent, looking at the fading colors on the horizon. "I've got to. I promised someone that the band would do that concert."

She wrapped her arms around her bent legs. "I knew you would say that. But . . . I hoped to change your mind."

"Why?"

"Because something bad is going to happen there."

"Bad things happen every day. We can't stop living out of fear," he said.

"This is more than fear. Remember, I can feel things you can't. I know someone is going to die in Nuevo Laredo. Don't go, Matthew. Please don't go."

They sat in silence, the sea gusts and the surf being the only sounds on the beach. Matthew heard a radio from some unseen place down the beach, "Glad you could join us for this special Promise marathon weekend.

We have all their greatest hits, and there are so many, all super-platinum. For the next forty-eight hours, we will revisit Promise's extraordinary career by playing their songs, both from CD and from some of their incredible concerts. And what a career it was, but much too short. We start with one of Promise's greatest hits. It soared to the top of the charts almost immediately and stayed there for sixteen months, the incomparable 'Freedom Road.'"

Matthew faced the sound to better hear the song:

> *When someday your eyes close, to bad things left down here,*
> *All the tremblin' and hurt be gone; your heart feelin' no fear,*
> *I'll be lookin' up, smilin' for those I know,*
> *Dear ones not with me, but ridin' that freedom road.*
> *And I'll be waitin' for the day, when my eyes close just the same,*
> *Wantin' to ride with them, to the place there is no pain;*
> *And we'll be thunderin' together, feeling no heavy load,*
> *Laughin' and singin' along that freedom road.*
> *Everyone we've loved, they will all be there,*
> *Ridin' close together on that highway in the air,*
> *God's free wind a blowin', and His sun showin' how to go,*
> *All along that highway, thunderin' down freedom road.*

Matthew closed his eyes and sung softly along. He opened his eyes, and Angelica had turned toward him, as though she were staring at this face. He asked, "Did you like the song?"

"It was wonderful. Matthew . . . he was your father, wasn't he?"

Matthew was startled. "Who?"

"Tam, the leader of Promise."

"Why do you say that? He . . . died a long time ago. Nobody really knew him."

"But he was your father. I have read a lot about Tam. His talents are the same as yours. I bet you two even look alike."

"That's crazy, Angelica. How can you say something like that?"

"Because it's true. I can feel things, and my feelings are always right. Tam's music lives in you. Just now, I could hear you singing with that song. It was like you were the singer, perfectly in time with the music." She stopped. Matthew did not answer. She grasped his face with both her hands. "Please listen to me. Someone will die in Nuevo Laredo. Don't go! Don't' leave your mother and me. Neither of us could stand that."

CHAPTER SEVENTY-TWO

Matthew scratched the ears of the little puppy, while the others tried to gain his attention with their whines, barks, and outstretched paws. "So you want to play. Man, you all are excited. I shouldn't have let you out of the cage all at once. What a herd. It's going to be tough to get this pack of wolves back in."

"Mr. Matthew, what a great game! You won it all, the championship for Poly, for Houston, for Texas. Can I shake your hand?" Eric Rhomer beamed as he ran toward the wiggling mass, extending both hands toward Matthew Blair. "I am never gonna wash these hands. It would be a sin."

"It wasn't just me, Eric. Say, can you help put them back?"

"Sure." The round-faced man gently pushed the puppies in the cage. He turned to Matthew, looking puzzled. "But you ran the touchdown. That's winning the game, right?"

"I didn't think of the play. Someone else did. The other guys also deserve a lot of credit. They played hard."

Eric squinted at Matthew, his head cocked to one side. "You . . . still did it, caught the ball and ran all the way for the touchdown."

Matthew patted him on the back. "Yes I did, Eric."

"And we're still friends, aren't we?" Eric asked, leaning against Matthew's side and looking up into his eyes.

Matthew tussled his hair. "We'll always be good friends. Eric, I have to go away for a while. One of the other drivers will take you and the puppies. Will that be okay?"

"Where you goin'? How long you gonna be away? Can I go with you, and maybe take a couple of the guys?"

"I have a special job to do, out of town. I wish you could come, but that's not possible. Don't worry, everything will be fine."

Eric's face sank, and tears began to fill his eyes. "But I got a funny feelin'. I'm scared. Like you ain't gonna come back. What if you don't? What will me and the guys do, Mr. Matthew? You'll for sure come back, won't you? Cause, you're . . . kind of like . . . well, my big brother. Watchin' after me all the time."

Matthew squeezed his shoulder. "That's true, and it's not going to change."

Eric's face was all smiles. Matthew spoke deliberately, "I will come back, and we'll keep taking the puppies to all the people who need them. We have lots of work to do, you and me, and the puppies."

Matthew placed an arm around Eric's shoulder as the short man wiped tears from his eyes and sung softly, "I just want to keep ridin', with you, all the time, all the way, down that freedom road."

CHAPTER SEVENTY-THREE

Agapito stood with two other young men on a hill overlooking the brightly lit concert venue on the outskirts of Nuevo Laredo. Thousands of people sat and stood on the ground rising slightly to a stage filled with drums, keyboard, guitars, and lights. Agapito studied the scene before saying, "This is perfect. You see, the police will not be a problem. Many of them are on our payroll. They stand there only for show. We will strike and kill this band leader."

One of the others asked, "When shall we fire the weapon?"

Agapito answered, "You shoot the mortar when they begin the third song. I will be in the crowd, at the right side of the stage. The shell will fall at the left side. When it explodes, the crowd will panic, and in the confusion, I will rush onto the stage and cut the throat of the leader. Then I will take his head for the jefe. Do you understand every detail? There must be no mistake. Have you sighted in the mortar?"

The two nodded before one asked, "But what if you cannot reach the leader before he flees?"

"There are others in the crowd who will kill him." Agapito smiled, turned, and walked down the hill toward the stage.

The two men sat beside the mortar, and one of them examined a large, bullet-like shell in a wooden box. He stroked it. "You know, Pablo, this will kill many people, bring fear of the jefe to everyone. It will be a glorious night."

"*Es verdad, Juan,* es verdad."

They continued to watch Agapito make his way down the hill, toward the crowd waiting for the concert to start.

Suddenly, Pablo looked to the dark sky and began to whimper. "Maria. Mi Dios." He fell to the ground, rubbed his eyes, and looked upward again.

This time, he held his hands in front of his face and cried out, "Maria, Madre de Dios. Forgive me, Holy Virgin."

Juan felt helpless at the sight of his friend. "Pablito, amigo, what is the matter? Did you get some bad *peyote*?" He also looked to the sky and cried out, "Dios. I am sorry for my sins, Maria. I will kill no more. Forgive me, Mother, forgive me." He fell to the ground in a fetal position, trembling.

Agapito reached a high chain-link fence running as far as he could see. A vast audience sat and stood inside, while many others milled about outside the barrier. He saw an entrance, guarded by uniformed police officers. Attendees passed through a metal detector. He approached the entrance and stroked the switchblade inside his shirt. Passing through the metal detector caused Agapito to set off the machine. One of the officers quickly reacted by pulling Agapito aside. "I will search this one."

He conducted a pat-down search of Agapito. When he finished, the officer looked at Agapito's eyes and said, "You may pass." He turned to the other officers. "It was only his belt buckle."

Agapito smiled and entered the mass of humanity, stretching to see the stage. As he walked forward, the assassin detected the unique odor of marijuana in the air. He muttered to himself, "The sweet smell of *dinero*."

The crowd was thick, and Agapito meandered through narrow gaps between young men and women talking and laughing, embracing and kissing, play-fighting and gesturing, all waiting for the start of the Tomorrow concert. Finally, he reached the stage, surrounded by police officers. He stood between two officers, one of them seeming to be unaffected by his presence, and the other looking squarely into his eyes for a moment. He waited there, barely twenty feet from the front of the stage.

Agapito felt for the knife and ran his hand along the extended handle hiding a razor-sharp blade.

A man walked onto the stage and held his hands high. "Welcome to this concert of Tomorrow. I am Hector Ochoa, organizer of this special event, the first major musical performance for Nuevo Laredo." He stopped when the crowd exploded in applause, cheers, and whistles. Hector Ochoa held his hands up again. "We are very fortunate to have this group. They are the fastest rising stars in America, perhaps the world. Their albums are at the top of the charts. And now, ladies and gentlemen, it is my honor to present to you Tomorrow!"

The audience reacted wildly as Matthew led the others onto the stage, waving and smiling, his blue eyes flashing as he walked to the front of the platform. Matthew held his electric guitar high above his head, moved his other hand to its face, nodded to the others, and Tomorrow broke into its first song,

> We're all here to stay,
> Everyone is going to play,
> In the game for life we'll win,
> God's prize, for you and your kin.
>
> Can you see it up ahead,
> Feel it with no dread,
> Life's there for you and me
> Who look with eyes that see.
>
> Run along the free clear road,
> You have no heavy load,
> Come with me on that way
> To the place of joy today.
>
> Friends and family there
> Dancin' in purest air,
> And God is partyin' too;
> He's wavin' to me and you.
>
> We gonna win the run'
> Havin' a lot of fun,
> Behind us and long dead
> The lies and all the dread.
>
> We're all here to stay,
> Everyone is going to play,
> In the game for life we'll win,
> God's prize, for you and your kin.

The audience moved with the song, dancing and waving in a vast pulsating sea of raised arms. The song ended, and the throng erupted in applause and cheers. Tomorrow followed with "Freedom Life," announced by a bright message board on the side of the stage.

Do you want a life that's free?
Then walk this way with me,
To places free of drugs,
Away from all the thugs,
Who lie and steal for gain,
And cause tears and pain
To those who do you right,
Away from the cold night.

Little ones yet to be
Need you to make them free.
Can't you hear their cries?
See the tear-filled eyes?
That feeling in your heart
Will help you make a start.
We shall have no fear.
The Big Man is walking near.

Come this way to live,
A gift to you I give.

Agapito looked around and noticed everyone focused on the band, not talking or distracted by others in the audience. As Tomorrow sang of a life free of drugs and sorrow, he began to feel a strange emotion, something replacing the dark feelings he had known, a sense of sorrow and pity. Agapito swallowed hard, wondering what was happening to him. He noticed a child trying to see over the crowd and kneeled to raise her up. The child smiled and hugged him, and he returned the smile. At that moment, he felt a special connection to the child. Someone patted his shoulder. He held the girl, wanting to protect her from the crush of the tightly packed onlookers. The song continued, and he kissed the little arm that held his neck tightly.

She cried out, "Look, an angel."

Agapito scanned the sky. "Where?"

The child giggled. "On the stage with Tomorrow."

Agapito rubbed his eyes. "I can't see the angel. Are you sure?"

The little girl reached out. "Close your eyes." She rubbed each lid.

Agapito opened his eyes. "Mi Dios. I see the angel, right next to the leader."

He looked toward the hill where he had planned death with his comrades, cold fear and dread coursing through him. Agapito waved off the attack, turned toward the stage, put the girl down, and gently pushed her to the front of the crowd.

Mary and Angelica watched Tomorrow on a series of monitors in the control trailer two miles from the concert. Mary quickly looked away. "I can't stand to watch too long."

Angelica grasped her hands. "We need to be strong, together. Matthew said he would be fine, and I'm counting on him being right."

Mary shook her head. "That's what I had hoped for Promise, but they all died. I'm scared to death Matthew will die too, and nobody can stop it." She began to sob.

Angelica tightened her grip. "Mary, something strange is happening. In my mind, I can see someone with him. It's . . . his father."

"Angelica, this is no time for nonsense," Mary sharply said.

"It's not nonsense. I'm telling you, Matthew's father is with him. I can feel it, see it clearly in my mind. They look so much alike, the same blue eyes and sweet smiles, and they are holding their guitars high, playing and dancing together in exact harmony."

Eric Rhomer sat in front of the television in the Houston State School for the Retarded, watching Tomorrow's concert. "That's my friend, the leader, Mr. Matthew," he proudly said to a group of the residents sitting on the tiled floor in the recreation room.

A girl with similar Oriental features rocked from side to side, before stopping to lean close to the television and place her hand on the screen. She grunted and smiled.

One of the staff asked, "Eric, how do you know the band leader?"

"I work for his mom's company. Met him there. But that's weird."

"What's weird? They look okay to me," the staff member said.

Eric moved close to the television screen. "That guy playing a guitar with Mr. Matthew at the front of the band. They look like twins, the same eyes and smile. I wonder who the other guy is. He sure looks strong, just like Mr. Matthew."

Agapito took the knife from under his shirt. The assassin pushed a button on the handle, and the shiny blade snapped into place. He stared at it as though seeing the blade for the first time.

The song ended. Agapito's hand trembled. He looked to the heavens, tears streaming down his cheeks. "Forgive me, Father. I have sinned much. Please take me into Heaven."

He plunged the blade into his chest, and warm blood poured from the wound but remained largely hidden by his shirt. The young man gasped and fell to his knees, soon collapsing to the ground. All around him, packets of white powder and smoldering, pungent cigarettes began to litter the earth, covering it like a blanket. His dying body lay on the ground, drug waste pelting him while the power of Tomorrow's third song, "Laughin'," held the audience tightly,

> *Can you hear the laughin'?*
> *Man it's gettin' loud;*
> *Comin' from up ahead;*
> *Looks like there's a crowd;*
> *People huggin' each other,*
> *Feelin' good today;*
> *Doin' a lot of laughin'*
> *Like children hard at play.*
>
> *But there is someone else*
> *Roarin' with special love,*
> *A low belly-laughin'*
> *Comin' from above . . . .*

With failing vision, Agapito caught sight of the band for the final time. He could make out a ghost-like figure standing next to Matthew, playing a guitar, with eyes just as blue. The two of them looked to be more than band members. Agapito sensed they were related, as they danced and played together. With his last strength, Agapito reached for Matthew and the other man, and, for an instant, he felt warmth replace the cold in his body.

Thousands of energized feet pulverized discarded drugs, grinding them into the earth, and light winds began to clear the pungent odor from the night air.

Mary embraced Angelica and focused on one of the monitors, watching Matthew dance across the stage holding his gold guitar high. He produced notes running rapidly along the scale, faster than Mary could follow, making her heart race with the rhythm of the music. She reached with both hands toward the picture of her son. "Angelica, look! It's Matthew and . . . ." Mary stopped, held tightly by the vision before her. "And Tam, together. They look so much alike."

All the fear was gone from her, and Mary knew no harm would come to her son that night. She could feel a new day fast approaching, filled with life and hope, a day based on a promise made and kept, a promise of a good tomorrow.